COURTING IN THE PARK

Sadie headed across the street to the park. A small patch of sunlight still shone, though most of the sky had turned a shade somewhere between dark purple and dark blue. She sat down in a swing, fully expecting Ezra to sit in the one next to her. Instead he walked around behind her and started to push. How long had it been since someone had actually pushed Sadie in a swing?

"That's too much, Ezra!" She felt like she could reach out her toes and touch the setting sun. "Slow me down now, please."

"Baby," Ezra teased. But still he moved around in front of her and caught her swing, easing it back slowly again and again until she was barely moving. He moved his hands up the chains as Sadie stood, trapped somewhere between his arms and the swing.

A heartbeat passed between them and then another. And another, until Sadie wasn't sure how long they had stood there, just staring at each other.

"Ezra," she said, her voice shaking and unsure. What was happening between them? Was this the beginning of true love? Whatever it was, she never wanted it to end. . . .

Books by Amy Lillard

CAROLINE'S SECRET

COURTING EMILY

LORIE'S HEART

JUST PLAIN SADIE

Published by Kensington Publishing Corporation

JUST PLAIN SADIE

AMY LILLARD

ZEBRA BOOKS
KENSINGTON PUBLISHING CORP.
http://www.kensingtonbooks.com

ZEBRA BOOKS are published by

Kensington Publishing Corp.
119 West 40th Street
New York, NY 10018

All Kensington titles, imprints, and distributed lines are available at special quantity discounts for bulk purchases for sales promotion, premiums, fund-raising, educational, or institutional use.

Special book excerpts or customized printings can also be created to fit specific needs. For details, write or phone the office of the Kensington Sales Manager: Attn.: Sales Department. Kensington Publishing Corp., 119 West 40th Street, New York, NY 10018. Phone: 1-800-221-2647.

Zebra and the Z logo Reg. U.S. Pat. & TM Off.

First Printing: April 2016
ISBN-13: 978-1-4201-3973-0
ISBN-10: 1-4201-3973-8

eISBN-13: 978-1-4201-3974-7
eISBN-10: 1-4201-3974-6

10 9 8 7 6 5 4 3 2 1

Printed in the United States of America

Chapter One

"I have something I need to talk to you about."

At Chris's words, Sadie's heart pounded in her chest. Was this it? She had been waiting on this moment for a long, long time. Now it was about to happen on this cold but bright January day on his father's farm. She had known something was up when he'd asked her to take a walk, but she hadn't dreamed that today could be the day. Yet from the sound of his voice, Chris had something very important to say. As important as a marriage proposal? She could only hope.

Sure, she and Chris were nothing more than best friends who had been paired off in their buddy bunch like a true couple instead of just good pals. But what better person to marry than a best friend? She knew all his little habits, all his quirks and shortcomings. So she didn't love him with that breathless wonder that the *Englisch* novelists talked about. There was more to a marriage—more to life—than that.

"*Jah?*" The one word was a mere whisper upon her lips. She had wanted to come across as strong and true, yet all she sounded was anxious and fretful. But she *was* anxious and fretful.

More than anything in the world, she wanted to get married. That wasn't so much to ask, was it? Especially when everyone around them thought they were just being secretive when they claimed to be only friends.

A couple of years ago Sadie gave up defending their friendship and let people believe what they wanted. They were doing that anyway. But somewhere along the road, she had started to think about marriage. Not in a silly romantic way, but in a strong, steady kind of way. And she knew that one day Chris would be her husband. She just knew it.

Was today that day?

He took her hand into his, turning it over and tracing the creases on her palm. "This is kinda hard to say." He glanced up at the sky, across the field where they sat next to a half-frozen pond. He looked at his lap, then back at their hands once again. "It's no secret that you're my best friend, right?"

"Of course." She did her best to sound confident, but she feared she had failed miserably.

"Best friends should be able to say anything to each other, right?" He seemed to be asking himself rather than her, so Sadie kept quiet and waited for him to continue. "It's just that . . ."

Her heart pounded even harder in her chest, so hard that she thought it might fly away on its own.

"What I'm about to tell you is between the two of us, okay?"

She nodded, breathless as she waited for him to continue.

"I'm going to Europe."

Suddenly the world was swept out from underneath her. She took her hand from Chris's, using it to steady herself though she was still sitting in the same place she had been before. Everything seemed tilted now, a little askew, not quite right. He was going to Europe?

Europe?

"Sadie? Are you okay?"

She cleared her throat and managed to nod. "*Jah*, of course." Her voice didn't sound like her own, and a sudden chill ran through her bones. She pulled her coat a little tighter around her. "I think my ears are playing tricks on me. I thought you said you were going to Europe. That can't be right." He was supposed to be proposing, stating his intentions of joining the church and making her his wife. Wasn't that what everyone thought would happen?

"That's what I said." His voice seemed small, as if it was coming to her from down a long tunnel.

"Europe?" Thousands of thoughts flew through her head at once. Europe was so far away; was he asking her to go too? No, wait. He hadn't said anything about getting married, about joining the church, about the future they would have. Just Europe.

Sadie pushed to her feet, though the world still seemed to be spinning, her emotions a strange mixture of disappointment and relief.

"I told you how I wanted to travel." From behind her, Chris's voice held a damaged edge, as if somehow her reaction had wounded him.

"*Jah*, you did." She stifled a laugh and whirled back to face him. "A lot of us talk about the things that we want to do. But they're not things that we are really *going* to do."

"You thought I was just talking?"

He had talked for hours and hours about seeing the world and what it would be like and traveling and how it would feel to be on a boat, to be on a plane, to be in a car in the remote places he'd read about on the computer at the library. But that was all she thought it was—talk. Reluctantly, she nodded and wondered how the day had turned so wrong.

Chris stood and came to stand by her side. He reached out as if he were going to touch her, then he seemed to change his mind and dropped his hands back to his sides once again. "I thought you would understand."

"I do." She wanted to. But how did she explain to him that searching for his dreams was killing hers? Was it so much to ask to want to be married? It was all she wanted from life. To work her job at the restaurant, get married to a nice man, have children, and live out her days in Wells Landing. They seemed like attainable dreams, but now they were as far away as the moon.

He expelled a heavy breath. "I'm not going yet," he said. "This summer. I talked to a travel agent, and he can get me a good deal for June. Flights and all that."

Travel agent? "You're going to get on an airplane?" Of all the questions she had to ask, that one was perhaps the least important, but the one that jumped from her lips first. She turned to him then, searching his features for some sort of explanation as to what made him want to fly half the world away when as far as she could see, everything she needed was right there in Wells Landing.

"That part makes me a little nervous." He chuckled. "But I'm looking forward to it. It's an adventure out there, Sadie. Don't you see?"

All she could see were her dreams slipping away, her best friend not joining the church, not staying in Wells Landing, and not being a part of her life for much longer.

"You're not coming back."

"Oh, Sadie, don't be like that. Of course I'm coming back. Airplanes are safe now. It's not like what you think."

Sadie shook her head. "I'm not worried about the plane, *it's you.*" Chris wasn't the only Amish man who wanted to see the world, who wanted to taste the pleasures that lay beyond the boundaries of their district. And all too often the people who left never came back. Luke Lambright, her sister Lorie, to name a few. But Sadie had never understood the call of the *Englisch* world. She was happy being Amish. She was happy right where she was. That might be simplistic or naïve, but that's just the way she was.

Chris was leaving; she was staying. It was as simple as that.

"I haven't told anyone else," he said.

"You told me."

"That's different. I knew you would understand."

Do I?

"You can't tell anyone," Chris continued. "No one. Not even Ruthie, Hannah, or Melanie. Not until I tell my parents."

"Okay," she agreed, albeit reluctantly. The one person she would want to talk to was gone. Her sister Lorie had left Wells Landing three months ago to move to Tulsa. That had been a hard time for Sadie. Their father had just passed away, and Lorie had discovered he had a tattoo that no one else knew about. That made her search for more things. She uncovered a grandmother living in a nursing home in Tulsa and a whole secret life that her father had lived without anyone in Wells Landing knowing about it. Even worse, Henry Kauffman hadn't been Amish, nor had his last name been Kauffman. Sadie had managed to keep all that to herself. What was one more secret?

Though she missed Lorie terribly, she knew her sister was happy now. She wasn't having to hide her paintings or wonder about what her life would have been like had her father not made the choice to hide her out in the Amish community, pretending to be Amish himself as he raised her Plain.

It had been three months since Lorie had left. Three long months of waiting for her visits, waiting for phone calls at the restaurant, and envying the happiness that she had found. For not only was she living out her dream getting to know her grandmother and teaching painting to the senior citizens at the Sundale Assisted Living Center, she had met the handsome *Englischer*, Zach Calhoun. They were planning their wedding for some time this June. And now this.

June was going to be a very busy month.

"Chris, you should tell them." She had been walking around with so many secrets inside, but this was different. It was one thing to hold her own secret from the community in order to not damage her father's memory within the district and quite another to keep someone else's secret from the people who loved him.

He nodded. "I know, I know. But I'm not ready to tell them yet. I don't think they'll handle it well."

"What would give you such an idea?"

"Sadie, really?"

"I'm merely saying that their youngest son decides to travel off to Europe and not join the church. Why would they find any fault in that?" She wasn't about to apologize for her sarcasm. Maybe it would shake some sense into Chris, make him see how his choices were going to affect everyone around him.

"I never said anything about not joining the church. I can go to Europe. I'm still in my *rumspringa*. I can travel, come back, and take baptism classes next year. Bishop Treger let Lorie take his classes."

Sadie didn't point out that hadn't gone over very well, and she didn't think the bishop would allow that to happen again considering the fact that Lorie had dropped out of the classes and moved away. Besides, if Chris really wanted to join the church, he would only have to wait one more year. Bishop Ebersol might not be thrilled with him waiting until he was twenty-four, but she doubted Chris would be the oldest Amish man ever to join. If he joined.

"And my parents have Johnny," Chris continued. "He's taken over the farm. He's going to run everything. They don't need me for that. Why should I not live my life? Do the things I want to do?"

"Can you hear yourself? How selfish you sound? Does that not bother you?"

Chris shoved his fingers through his hair, knocking his hat to the cold ground. "This isn't about being selfish or not. It's about an opportunity. I've saved my money. I've worked hard. I don't see why I shouldn't be allowed to spend that money as I want. I can't get this out of my system any other way, Sadie—" He growled in frustration. "I thought you would understand."

Sadie blinked back tears. This was not how this conversation was supposed to turn out. Even if it hadn't been a marriage proposal, the last thing she wanted to do was fight with Chris.

"I'm trying to. Really I am. But with *Dat* and Lorie . . ." She shook her head. "I'm sorry, Chris. I know you have to do what's right for you." Even if it meant giving up her dreams. He hadn't tagged her for marriage, which was common for men who hadn't joined the church to do for young ladies who had. It was like a promise, so to speak, that when he joined the church they would be officially engaged.

Even though Chris hadn't made that promise to her, everyone assumed that Sadie was Chris's girl, and no one came around courtin'. And so with Chris, all her dreams of marriage were flying off to Europe.

"Will you be happy for me?"

She nodded, her throat clogged with emotion. "I am."

"Will you wait for me?"

Of course she would. He might not love her like *that*, but if they were to marry, they would make a fine couple. Even though crazy love would never be a big part of it, they would make a fine pair.

"You really are coming back?" She didn't want him to promise to return, to promise to marry her, or to promise not to turn *Englisch*. If something happened and he couldn't keep that promise . . . she would be even more heartbroken than she was right now.

"Of course I am." He took her hands into his.

Despite his arguments otherwise, she knew that once he left, he'd never return.

She could only enjoy him for the time he would remain in Wells Landing, and after that . . . ? Well, she was glad that she had her job at the restaurant and her family. If nothing else, those two things gave meaning to her life.

And that was more than some people had.

"I think it's over this way." Chris pointed down the long aisle of booths set up for the weekly farmers' market in Pryor.

Sadie looked down the walkway of vendors, shading her eyes against the noonday sun. "Are you sure?" Rows and rows of booths were set up, all looking so much alike that Sadie was quickly turned around. They had passed the stand a bit ago, but Sadie wanted to wait until it was time for them to leave before she made her purchase.

"Why do you need buffalo meat again?" Will asked.

They had all come out together, her little group of coupled-off friends: she and Chris, Will and Hannah, Mark and Ruthie.

"It's bison meat," Sadie corrected. "And it's for Cora Ann." She shook her head. "*Mamm* said she could pick out some new recipes for the restaurant, and she chose something with bison meat."

Chris laughed. "What is she doing? Reading *Food and Wine* magazine again?"

Sadie returned his chuckle with one of her own. "What do you mean again? She never stopped."

Of all her siblings, Cora Ann was the most like their father. She had a love of food and restaurant work that made Sadie a little envious. Oh, to know what you wanted out of life and to be able to get it.

Sadie loved her work at the restaurant, she really did. But not like Cora Ann. At thirteen, her youngest sister was constantly poring over food magazines and recipes. Sadie even caught her on the Internet checking out different recipes on the restaurant's computer. *Jah*, Sadie was certain that one day Kauffman's Family Restaurant would be in Cora Ann's capable hands.

Mark took a couple of more steps in the direction that Chris had indicated. "I think I see it." Then he grabbed Ruthie's hand and together they started in the opposite direction.

Sadie whirled around. "Where are you going?"

Mark turned and walked backward, not bothering to let go of Ruthie's hand as they continued. "Just because you want to buy buffalo meat doesn't mean we do." He gave them a grin. "We'll meet you at the van."

"Bison meat," she corrected once again, then turned around just in time to see Will and Hannah head off down another aisle. She didn't even bother to ask them where they were going. It was like that these days. Since she and Chris were the only couple in their bunch who hadn't gotten married, she felt like a third wheel, even when they were together.

That wasn't exactly true. Lorie and Jonah had been a part of their group once upon a time, and they hadn't gotten married. And she and Chris weren't a couple. Just best friends, sidekicks. Even with all his promises to marry her once he returned from his trip to Europe.

"I guess it's just me and you." Sadie sighed. The six of them had hired a driver to come to the market so they could shop and spend time together. So much for that.

Chris smiled. "Just the way I like it."

Last week, those words would have made her heart pound in her chest, but today they only made her sad. Her time with Chris was growing smaller each day.

Together they made their way through the milling shoppers. The market was a great place to find fresh produce and other ingredients for the restaurant. Normally, Sadie loved coming and wandering through the stalls and stands, learning of new foods and tools. A little of anything and everything could be found at the market.

"Are you serious about Europe?" She hadn't meant to ask the question, but it had been building inside her for days. Ever since Chris had told her about his plans.

"*Jah*. Of course."

She nodded.

"You haven't told anyone, have you?"

"No." And she wouldn't. Not until he broke the news to his parents.

Chris pointed up ahead. "There it is."

Sadie recognized the sign. "Hein Ranch," it read. "Exotic Meats and Animals." But the man standing at the booth was not the one who had been there earlier.

This man was . . .

She stumbled as he turned to face her.

The most handsome man she had ever seen.

A Mennonite.

"Can I help you?" he asked. His voice was smooth, not too deep. Just right. In fact, everything about him was just right, from his sun-streaked blond hair to his dark brown eyes.

He wore faded blue jeans like she had seen Zach Calhoun wear, an orange and white checkered shirt, and black suspenders. Suddenly she felt more than plain in her mourning black. Not that it mattered.

"*Jah*, I was here earlier talking to a guy about some bison meat."

"That was my cousin. He was watching the booth for me. Ezra Hein," he said with a nod.

"Sadie Kauffman. Nice to meet you," she returned. "He gave me some quotes when we stopped by earlier. I have them here." She reached into her bag and pulled out the piece of paper with the price per pound that the cousin had written down for her. Her hands were trembling as she handed it to Ezra.

"That's a lot of meat," he said.

"My family owns a restaurant in Wells Landing."

He nodded.

Was it her or was this conversation awkward? Probably because instead of talking about meat and restaurants, she'd rather be talking about anything else with him.

He had to be the most intriguing man she had ever seen. Attractive, polite . . .

She pushed those thoughts away. He was a Mennonite, and she was Amish. He was handsome, and she was plain. What would a guy like him want with a girl like her?

"Do you get the meat locally?" she asked, trying to remember all the things *Mamm* had wanted her to ask.

"You could say that. We raise them ourselves, then send them to a butcher in Tulsa. He packages everything there and we pick it up when it's ready."

"Really?"

He smiled. "Yes. We also have ostriches and deer, if you're interested. All of our stock is organically fed. Even the camels."

"Camels? You don't eat them, do you?" She tried to not make a face. But camel meat?

Ezra laughed. "No, we keep them for brush control."

"Camels, ostriches, bison, and deer? That sounds like quite a farm."

"It's a ranch, really. You should come out and see it sometime."

She would like nothing more. And suddenly Chris going to Europe didn't seem like the end of her world. "I would like that." She smiled. "So can you supply us with that much bison?"

He nodded. "Of course. When would you like delivery?"

She waited as he worked out the details of the order. Then she signed the papers, handed him a business card for the restaurant, and shook his hand, loving the feel of his strong grip and his warm, calloused fingers.

What was wrong with her? She must have been out

in the heat too long, though it was the prettiest day in January that she could ever remember. Seventy degrees couldn't really be described as hot.

"Well, Sadie Kauffman. I'll be seeing you."

She smiled at his words. Was that promise she heard in his voice, or merely wishful thinking on her part?

"He's flirty," Chris commented as they turned to go. He wore a frown on his face, his brow wrinkled with disapproval.

Sadie had almost forgotten he was with her. "He's just nice," she said.

"If you say so."

"I do." As they walked back down the aisle to find their friends, Sadie looked back at the stand.

Ezra was looking after them, her business card in one hand and a smile on his face. He caught her gaze and gave her a little wave.

Sadie returned it, then faced front, trying not to count down the days until she would see Ezra again.

Chapter Two

Ezra packed up the last of his stand and closed the tailgate of his ranch truck. The card that Sadie Kauffman gave him burned in his pocket somewhere over his chest. How a tiny piece of paper could feel so heavy and warm was a mystery he was sure to never uncover. But he was intrigued. It was that simple.

He went around to the driver side and slid onto the bench seat. His cousin, Logan, slipped into the passenger side as Ezra started the engine.

"It was a pretty good day, don't you think?" Logan asked as they pulled the truck from the parking lot.

"Yeah," Ezra said as he eased onto the street that would take them to the highway and back to the Mennonite community of Taylor Creek.

"Did that girl come back?"

"Which girl?" Ezra asked, though he knew. Logan was talking about the Amish girl, Sadie. The one Ezra couldn't get out of his head.

"The Amish girl looking for bison meat. Kinda plain. A little on the quiet side."

Quiet Ezra could agree with, but plain? Not a word he would use to describe her. He supposed if a person took all of her features and examined them, she might be considered on the ordinary side. Her smile maybe. Or it could be her eyes. Though they were merely hazel and not anything traditionally unusual. Still, there was something about Sadie Kauffman. An energy that hummed around her like electricity during a thunderstorm.

"Yeah," Ezra finally managed. "She came back." He turned on his blinker and changed lanes. "She said her family owns a restaurant in Wells Landing."

"That one on Main Street?" Logan asked.

Ezra shrugged. "I guess so." Unlike his friends and cousins, Ezra rarely made it out of Taylor Creek. He had work to do. And a lot of it. His mother depended on him. He couldn't be running all over the county. That was why he hired others to deliver his exotic meats. That was one thing he could trust others with. But his animals . . . they were like family members. He didn't trust them with anyone. He couldn't walk down the street and randomly pick out people who could take care of his exotics. That responsibility was his and his alone.

"You, cousin, need to get out more." Logan smiled at him in that rascally way that he had. Ezra knew the look well. A few years back he would have returned the grin with one of his own, equally mischievous. But that was before . . .

"Yeah, yeah," he said, hoping his cousin would drop the matter. He was tired of defending himself. Tired of having to explain why he worked so hard. None of them seemed to understand. Of course, none of them had come home to find their father gone and their mother weeping on the floor.

He shook his head, releasing those thoughts. They

led nowhere good. No sense looking back. Only to remember and know what *not* to do.

"So are you in?" Logan tapped his hand against the seat between them, shaking Ezra from his thoughts.

"In?"

Logan sighed. "The volleyball game tonight. Michael got the rec center and everything."

"I don't—"

"Before you finish that, remember, you promised to play tonight."

He had, but somehow his heart wasn't in it. He sighed. "Right. Volleyball."

Logan nodded. "You'll be there?"

"I'll be there," he replied. In body. But he had a feeling his mind would be someplace else.

"Ezra, is that you?"

"Yeah, Mom." He tossed his truck keys onto the table by the front door and ran a hand over the back of his neck. He felt antsy and strange, like he was waiting for something to happen but he didn't know what.

"Did you have a good day at the market?" she called again, most likely from the kitchen. It seemed she spent a lot of time these days looking out the back window over the small table just off from the breakfast nook. She said she liked to watch the animals play and walk about in the bright winter sun, but he had a feeling it was more than that. From her favorite perch she could see half the ranch and the road that ran in front of it. Was she expecting someone to come?

He shook his head as she rolled her wheelchair into the living room. She caught sight of him and he stopped. "What?" she asked.

"Nothing." He bent to kiss her cheek. He never went

a day without showing his affection. She was everything to him. All he had left in this world.

Sort of.

"Michael called," she said. "He wanted to remind you about the volleyball game tonight."

He was going to get no peace in the matter. Like it or not, he had to go. Well, that wasn't exactly right. It wasn't that he didn't like it. There was so much that needed to be done at the ranch that he hated taking time out for games.

"Are you going?" Mom asked. It was as if she knew his thoughts.

Ever since his dad had left, his mother had been a little more wrapped up in herself. It was understandable, really, but that didn't mean Ezra had to like it. But when it came to him, she seemed to have a sixth sense, some sort of direct line to his thoughts and emotions. She didn't always use it, but he knew it was there.

"Of course." What else could he say?

Mom smiled. "Good. You don't get out enough."

He might not get out enough, but she didn't get out at all. Where was the justice in that?

Saturday morning dawned much like Friday had, bright and sunny and chilly. Such was to be expected of January in Oklahoma.

Ezra started out to the barn for his morning chores, not at all surprised when he saw his cousin pull into the drive.

"Good morning." He waved to Logan, who pulled his older-model Ford F-150 onto the side yard and cut the engine.

"Hey," he called in return. "What brings you out on

this fine Saturday morning?" He asked the question, but he knew. It was sort of a game they played. Every three or four days, Logan would come out to the ranch and offer his help. Ezra would insist that he didn't need it and would send Logan on his way.

"I thought I might come by this morning and give you a hand." Logan shut his truck door and pulled a pair of work gloves from his back pocket.

That was a new part of their dance. Ezra had never known him to bring gloves.

"No need. I've got it all under control."

"Huh-uh. That's what I thought you'd say." But instead of getting back into his truck, Logan continued toward the barn.

Ezra hustled to catch up. "You aren't staying. There's no need."

"That's exactly what I thought you would say."

"Then I'll see you later." Help was the last thing he wanted. He had everything under control. He didn't need outside assistance. He didn't want it.

Like a calf trailing behind its mother, Ezra followed his cousin into the barn.

"See?" he said once their eyes had adjusted to the dim interior. The barn was immaculate. Exactly the way he always kept it. He worked hard and diligently to keep up his ranch. He was proud of the work he did. And he did it alone. Always.

"It's perfect. Which only means one thing."

"That it's time for you to go home?"

"That you need a girlfriend."

Ezra propped his hands on his hips. "Says who?"

Logan hooked a thumb toward his chest. "Says me."

"And why is that?" Unable to take much more of the banter, Ezra snagged a shovel off the wall and started toward one of the stalls.

"Just being a good cousin," Logan said.

Ezra wasn't buying it. "Why are you really here?"

"I want to help you so you can have more free time."

"I've got plenty of free time."

Last night, volleyball had been fun if not frivolous. But he had taken a spill and had a goose egg on his knee that ached like the dickens. He was going to have to be more careful if he was going to be able to complete his work and please his friends and his mother.

He had to put up with a lot of good-natured teasing from his friends, but he was determined to make something of his ranch, provide for his mother, and live the best life possible for God. Couldn't find a lot of fault with that, he supposed. But he knew that everyone thought he didn't take enough time to have fun.

"Sure you do," Logan countered.

"I do," Ezra shot back. Maybe he should have ignored his cousin and set about his work, but Ezra felt as if he constantly had to defend his choices.

"Seriously, though," Logan said. "You work way too hard."

It was the same old argument, time and time again. But no one understood. How could they? They didn't walk in his shoes. He did what needed to be done, in the time that he had to do it, in the life that he was given. There was no more to it than that. He had responsibilities, a ranch to run, a mother to take care of. And quite frankly, he'd grown tired of defending his very existence.

"Uh-huh," Ezra murmured, totally shutting out anything else Logan said. It wasn't like he really needed to hear it again. It was the same argument from yesterday, and the day before that, and the day before that.

Instead, he made a mental note to call his butcher in Tulsa and talk to him about the bison meat. Normally his customers tended to be families looking for low-fat organic alternatives to grocery store beef. He hadn't sold anything to a restaurant before, and he was excited at the opportunity. Maybe this was what he needed to get Hein's Exotic Meats on the map.

He finished up the stalls while Logan fed all the animals. Ezra hated to admit it, but the work did go much quicker with another set of strong, capable hands there to help. But he knew that assistance wouldn't come without a price.

"So," Logan started. He pulled off his gloves, slapped them against one thigh, then tucked them into the back pocket of his jeans. "About tonight."

And so it begins. Ezra narrowed his gaze at his cousin. "What about tonight?"

"Well, there's a singing . . ."

Of course there was. It was Saturday night. What else were Mennonite boys and girls supposed to do but get together and sing?

"And I thought maybe you might want to go with me."

"You and me?" Ezra asked. "Like in a date?"

"No, no, no, no, no, that's not what I mean."

Ezra loved watching his cousin squirm. "Then what do you mean?"

"Mindy and I are going, of course."

"And?"

"Well, Mom and Dad said that Jennifer could go with us. And I thought it might be fun if you joined too."

"Jennifer, as in your sister Jennifer? Are you trying to set me up with my own cousin?"

Logan said something under his breath, then he ran his hands through his dark brown hair. "That's not it either. Jennifer likes Dustin."

No big secret there. Ezra nodded. "Go on."

"Well, word about town is that Dustin is going to the

singing tonight with Annie K. So we thought that if you came with Jennifer . . ."

"You thought that if I went to the singing with Jennifer, then Dustin would get jealous, drop Annie K for Jennifer, and then I could escort Annie K home. Is that right?"

Logan ran a hand over the back of his neck as a sheepish grin spread across his face. "When you say it like that, it sounds a little—"

"Crazy?" Ezra raised one brow to show this to be his thoughts on the matter as well. "It's beyond crazy." Which could only mean one thing. Only half of it was true. It seemed to him that Logan was doing everything in his power to set him up with somebody, most likely Annie K.

It wasn't that he didn't like Annie K. He just had lots and lots to do. Too much to go running about, courting and finding a wife, and all the other little details that went along with having a girlfriend.

"Thanks, but no thanks," Ezra said.

"Don't be like that," Logan argued.

Be like what? was on the tip of Ezra's tongue, but he bit back the words. Arguing with Logan was somewhat like beating his head against a brick wall. It wasn't fun and it served no purpose. He wasn't going to win.

"Thanks for helping out today, man." Ezra nodded in his direction, then spun on his heel and headed out of the barn.

"Wait!" He heard Logan move behind him, hustling to catch up. "It's only one night. Surely you can spare that."

They didn't get it, and Ezra had grown weary of explaining. One night tonight, another night tomorrow, two more days later and he was so behind he couldn't see the light of day.

"Do this for me. This one time," Logan begged. "And I won't ask anything from you again."

"Why is it so important to you for me to go to this singing?"

"Mindy and I are setting a date." Logan's words were quiet in the cool January air.

Ezra swallowed back the lump that rose into his throat and reached his hand out to his cousin. "Congratulations, man."

Logan shook it with a sappy grin. "We're so happy."

"And I'm happy for you," Ezra said.

Truly he was.

But he didn't see what that had to do with him.

Logan caught his gaze. His blue eyes filled with sincerity and love as they met his. "I don't want you to be alone."

Ezra smiled. "I'm not alone. I have Mom."

To Logan's credit, he didn't point out the obvious. With his mother's illness, she was not likely to live for another ten years. But in ten years a lot of things could happen, medical advances could be made; people changed, health issues could improve. Who knew? Maybe she could learn to let go of the past, and with it, some of the bitterness that turned her mouth down at the corners. And if she could do that . . . Well, maybe she could get a little better. Live a little longer. Stay with him a little while more.

Until then, he had vowed to take care of her. Make sure that she had everything she needed and more. It was a vow he intended to keep.

No, there was only room for one woman in his life right now. And that was his mother.

So why did those hazel eyes of Sadie Kauffman's rise to his thoughts at that exact moment? He pushed them away and concentrated on his cousin. "I've got everything under control."

Logan looked at him with sympathy on his face. "You keep saying that, buddy. And maybe if you keep it up, we'll all start to believe it."

Logan left without the promise he wanted. He wasn't happy about it, but Ezra could be as stubborn as Logan when he chose to be.

Ezra finished up the morning chores, then called the truck driver. If he had someone else take the animal into the slaughterhouse, then that was one less thing he would have to do. His driver assured him he could be there first thing Monday to pick up the beast. That left only a couple of days to decide which one he was sending. One, really, seeing as how the next day was Sunday.

But he had a nine-hundred-pound young bull that would fit the order nicely. Now he just had to cut him from the herd and put him in the holding pasture to await the truck driver.

The next call he made was to the slaughterhouse to let them know the bull would be arriving on Monday; then he called his butcher. He was as excited about the order as Ezra himself. They made arrangements for him to pick up the meat next Monday afternoon.

That was nine days away. Nine days until he got to see Sadie Kauffman again. He wasn't sure why, but the thought sent his heart tripping in his chest.

Chapter Three

"Lorie's here!" Sadie nearly squealed as the familiar orange car pulled up in front of the restaurant. It'd been over two weeks since she had seen Lorie, and she missed her terribly. But she knew that Lorie was happy, and that mattered most of all.

Impatient to wait on her sister to come into the restaurant, Sadie hurried outside without her coat.

"What a fantastic surprise," she gushed as she rushed toward her sister. Lorie had barely made it out of the car before Sadie wrapped her in a warm hug. "I'm so glad you're here."

Lorie chuckled as Sadie pulled away. Then she tucked a strand of her long blond hair behind one ear. "I'm glad to be here too. Here." She handed Sadie a sack, the kind that came from the grocery store.

"What's in here?"

Lorie looped one arm through Sadie's and led them back toward the restaurant doors. "Some stuff for Daniel." Lorie knew as well as anyone that Daniel loved coloring almost as much as he loved Lorie herself. And every time she came to visit, she brought him different pictures to color, different coloring books, and different types of crayons that she bought in Tulsa. Bigger cities had so much more to offer than small Wells Landing.

"I didn't know you were coming down today," Sadie said as they hurried back inside.

"It was an unexpected day off. Zach is off doing his 'war' thing again. It wasn't quite time for him to go yet, but he seems to like that so much that he volunteered for this exercise."

Sadie stopped before they could reach the booth the family usually sat in. It was in the back, close to the office door. "You don't think he's going to completely join the army, do you?"

Lorie shook her head, and the lights glinted off her pale locks. "No, but he gets some kind of extra-credit pay if he goes. Since we're having the wedding and everything, he took the opportunity to make an extra dollar or two."

Sadie exhaled in relief. "Oh, good." Not that she understood anything of what her sister just said. Only the part that Zach wasn't going to be gone forever and get killed overseas in this war. And that was the most important part, as far as she was concerned.

The restaurant bustled with people. A tourist bus had come in earlier, though most everyone had been in and gone. Only a few slow eaters were left. Or maybe they were people who merely wanted to sit and drink coffee while everyone else went from shop to shop in the January air.

Sadie slid into one side of the booth and Lorie the other. She set the grocery sack for Daniel on the seat next to her. She'd give it to him as soon as he got home from school.

"Do you want some coffee?" Lorie asked.

"That'd be good." Sadie shook her head. "You don't work here anymore. I'll get it." Some habits died hard.

"I don't mind," Lorie said. But Sadie would hear nothing of it. She jumped up from the booth and made her way to the waitress station to pour them both a cup of coffee. How long had it been since she had sat with her sister and talked about nothing and everything all at the same time? She had missed Lorie so much in the months that she had been gone. And so much seemed to have happened. She couldn't wait to tell her sister all about it.

She took the coffee back over to where Lorie waited and set the cups down in front of them. Lorie immediately added three packages of artificial sweetener to hers. But Sadie preferred vanilla creamer and nothing else. As stepsisters they shared a lot of qualities, but they were as different as two people could probably be. Lorie was adventuresome, fun-loving, outgoing, or was that just because now she'd found where she'd truly belonged in life? She had grown up thinking she was Amish, only to find out later that she was truly *Englisch* hiding out from her mother's wealthy family, who wanted to take her from her father. All those relationships had been repaired. And her grandmother had ended up leaving Lorie a great deal of money.

"Wait, why do you need money for the wedding again?"

Lorie smiled. "Zach invested most of what Ellie left me. We have a small nest egg in the bank and then the rest of it's in an IRA. We don't want to spend any of that for the wedding, so this was his solution."

Sadie nodded and took a sip of her coffee. "Chris is going to Europe." The words seemed to jump from her brain out her mouth without any permission from her. She had been walking around with the secret for so long, it had been eating a hole in her. Now that she had her sister here, someone that she could trust and could talk to, she couldn't keep the words contained.

Lorie stopped stirring her coffee. Spoon still in hand, she stared at Sadie. "He what?"

"He's going to Europe." There, she said it again.

Lorie seemed to recover from her shock and set her spoon to the side. "And what about the two of you?"

"Oh, you know." Sadie couldn't quite meet her sister's dark brown eyes.

"No," Lorie said. "I don't know."

"Well, it's just that . . . He wants to travel and see Europe and he's been saving his money and he's going in June." Even to her own ears the words sounded like nothing more than a flimsy excuse.

"And the two of you?"

"Oh," she started brightly. "We're going to get married when he comes back."

"He's joining the church?"

Sadie shook her head. "Next year. He's leaving in June and asked me to wait on him to get back. Then we'll get married." And everything would be fine, she silently added.

But Lorie shook her head. "He said that? That he was coming back to marry you? And that you should wait for him to return?"

"Well, he didn't say it exactly like that. He told me he was going and then he asked me if I would wait for him to get back."

"That's exactly that." Lorie blew out a breath, stirring the hair that fluttered around her face. After years of wearing her hair put up in a bob and hidden under a prayer *kapp*, Lorie now wore it long and straight, framing her face and making her eyes look all the larger. "And you told him yes?"

"Of course I did." What had she expected her to do? "Chris and I have been together forever. He's the one I'm going to marry. What else would I do but wait for him to return?"

"Find somebody else and get married?"

Lorie made it sound so easy, but it was anything but simple. "I can't do that."

She could almost feel the frustration rolling off her sister.

"But you can." Lorie sat back in her seat, then leaned forward and grabbed Sadie's hands. Lorie's hands were warm against Sadie's ice-cold fingers. Dread filled her.

"Sadie, you can't let him lead you on this way."

"He's coming back. He's only going to be gone a couple months."

Lorie shook her head. "Do you really think he's going to spend two months in the *Englisch* world and then just come back?"

Sadie nodded numbly, even though she knew in the deepest part of her heart that Chris wasn't coming back. Not ever. As much as she wanted to believe he'd marry her, Lorie was right.

"What do I do?" Tears rose in her eyes. For years it had been her and Chris. Once he went to Europe it'd just be her.

"Tell him no. That you won't wait." Lorie's words were quiet but held the force of a tornado, sending her thoughts whirling in her head. Tell him no? How could she tell him no when he was her best friend? How could her life be the same if Chris wasn't in it? But then how was her life going to be the same when he went off to Europe seeing whatever sights?

"Trust me on this," Lorie said. "The *Englisch* world . . ." She shook her head. "It's not easy out there.

And there are temptations. If he wants to go to the *Englisch* world so bad that he's willing to fly to another continent . . . I got caught up simply going to Tulsa. Do you understand what I'm saying?"

Unfortunately she did. It was time she faced the fact Chris was going to Europe. And despite his promises otherwise and her desire to believe that they were true, he would never come home.

"So what do I do?" Sadie asked, though Lorie had already given her the answer. She wanted her sister to say the words again. Maybe this time she could listen with her head instead of her heart.

"Tell him you aren't going to wait. I can't say it'll be easy, but it's necessary. Unless you want your heart broken in two."

That was the problem, she thought. Since Chris's revelation, her heart was already broken.

Sunday was an off Sunday. Sadie's favorite. She loved going to church and she loved seeing everybody, but there was something to be said about taking time out to visit friends and family. And the only time the Kauffmans really had an opportunity to do that was on off-church Sundays.

She and Cora Ann made everyone breakfast that morning. Lorie had gone back to Tulsa, leaving her advice hanging around Sadie like a yoke around the neck of an ox. It seemed too heavy a burden, and she wasn't sure she could carry through. But what choice did she have? Lorie was right. It wasn't fair of Chris to live out his dream while she waited on him to return. If he didn't return, where was her dream then? She had been taught her whole life to put others before herself. But in this case it was time to put herself in front of everyone else. As it was now, her broken heart could be mended, but much more of this and the breaks would be so severe she would never get it back together again.

After breakfast everyone cleaned up. Daniel sat down at the table to color some of the new pictures Lorie had brought for him, and Sadie made up her mind. She grabbed her coat and her scarf and her gloves, pulling each on with the force that none of the articles of clothing deserved.

"Going somewhere?" *Mamm* asked. She had settled down in the rocking chair and leaned her head back. It was one of her favorite things to do these days, sit and allow herself time to truly rest, maybe even think about their father and everything that had happened since he died last year.

"I need to . . . go over and talk to Chris." That was an understatement, but she didn't want to tell her mother that she was going over to tell Chris that she wouldn't wait for him to marry her when he returned from Europe. She had promised not to tell his story, and she would keep that promise.

"Be careful," *Mamm* said, then sat back in her chair and closed her eyes once more.

Cora Ann jumped up from the table where she was coaching Daniel on his coloring and ran to the door. "I'll get the horse for you." Next to restaurant work, Cora Ann loved animals most. Sometimes Sadie wondered if she knew where all the meat she cooked actually came from. But she wasn't going to remind her.

"Thank you, Cora Ann." Her sister ran out the door and Sadie went back up to her room to get something that Chris had given her long ago. If they weren't going to be a couple, then she felt like she should give it back.

Under her bed in the shoebox she kept there with all her little mementos was a paperback copy of a book called *Gulliver's Travels*. It was a silly book really but Chris had wanted her to read it, wanted her to keep it. Maybe he wanted her to understand his love of travel in the adventure that could be found there. But Sadie wasn't the adventuresome one in the family. That was Lorie, and though Sadie kept the book because Chris had wanted her to, it was time to give it back.

She tucked it under one arm and made her way back down the stairs.

"I'm going now," she said.

Mamm didn't move, so Sadie didn't disturb her. Cora Ann would tell her later if she needed to know.

The buggy was ready to go when Sadie set foot on the porch.

Cora Ann smiled. "Be careful now." She sounded so much like their mother that Sadie almost laughed.

"I will." Tears rose in the back of her throat. This was going to be so hard. And she wasn't sure she was up for it. But when would she ever be ready to tell her best friend in the world that she didn't support his dreams? She might not be saying those exact words, but the meaning was still the same.

Her thoughts tumbled and jumbled around inside her head as she drove over to the Flaud residence. She passed the many fallow fields and ones planted with winter wheat as she drove, but nothing kept her attention more than her mission. She could do this. Right? And it was the only way. Right? And it had to be done. Right?

She pulled her buggy to a stop toward the side of

Chris's parents' house. It was a typical Amish farm, at least for these parts. Two or three pieces of heavy farm equipment stood off to one side, their green and yellow color a splash against the bare winter trees. Chickens pecked in the yard, white domestic geese strutted around, and every so often she could hear their milk cows low from the barn.

She hadn't even made it out of the buggy when Johnny, Chris's younger brother, tripped down the porch steps. As usual, he had a bright smile on his face and a twinkle in his eye. For two brothers so very alike in looks, they were miles apart in personality. Chris was more introspective and quiet, some might even say stern, whereas Johnny was full of life and something of a jokester.

"Sadie! What brings you out today?"

Like she could actually answer that. "I came by to say hi." That might possibly be the dumbest thing she had ever said. "I mean, is Chris here?"

Johnny scratched his head as if to say where else would Chris be, then nodded toward the front porch. "He's in the house. You want me to take care of your horse?"

Sadie had no idea how long she would be there. It could take minutes or hours. She still had to gather her courage to actually tell Chris, so it might be better if the horse was turned out to pasture. Just in case.

"That would be *gut*. Thanks."

Johnny smiled and took up the reins before unhitching the mare.

Sadie headed toward the front door. The journey seemed to take forever, yet went by in an instant.

"Go on in." Johnny had that perplexed note in his voice again, but Sadie couldn't say anything. She opened the door and went inside.

The Flauds' house was so different than her own. Maybe because at twenty, Johnny Flaud was the youngest member of their household. The two boys had one older brother, Joshua, who had long since married and moved across town.

For their small community he was more like city Amish. He worked for an *Englisch* company, had a driver take him to work every day, and had no farm to speak of. Not even his own animals to get milk and eggs from. As far as Sadie was concerned he was as close to being *Englisch* as a person could get and still remain Amish.

"Sadie." Chris's mother came out of the kitchen. In a flash she had wrapped her in a hug and squeezed her tight. Guilt swamped Sadie. This woman had never been anything but kind to her, and yet she was holding secrets for her son. Secrets that a caring mother would want to know.

"I brought some cookies." Sadie held up a small container of cookies that she'd packed that very morning. Oatmeal raisin. Chris's favorite.

"*Danki.* Would you come in and have some with us?"

Sadie shook her head. She felt so guilty keeping Chris's plans a secret that she didn't think she could sit down at the table with his mother and not spill the truth. "I've come to talk to Chris."

His mother made her way to the stairs, calling up, "Chris? You have a visitor."

Before she could even sit down, Chris appeared from the upstairs bedrooms. He wore a scowl on his face that remained firmly in place until he caught sight of her. Then it burst into the best and sweetest smile she had ever seen. It was that smile that kept her hanging on. And that smile that would be her downfall if she didn't fortify her heart right now.

"Can you come talk to me for a little bit?" she asked.

Confidence turned to confusion on his face. "If you want me to."

"I want you to," Sadie said. *I need you to.*

"In here?" He motioned toward the living room to the left of where they stood.

"Not exactly. Can we walk?" She needed to get him out of the house and away from all the ears that could listen in on a conversation that was best not heard by anyone save the two people who had the most at stake.

"I'll get my coat."

In no time at all, she and Chris were walking across the field behind his father's house, the one with the little pond that she loved to come to so much. It seemed to be their special place, this little pond, but today they hadn't brought a quilt for a picnic or even food to share. Today was about something wholly different.

"Why do I have the feeling that something is terribly wrong?" Chris asked as they walked.

The lump in her throat prevented her from responding. She needed to get herself together, and quick, or she would never be able to do this.

He took her gloved hand into his as they walked, and Sadie heaved a big sigh. She stopped. "Oh, Chris."

"What is wrong, Sadie?"

The concern in his voice was her undoing. She pulled her hand from his and wiped the back of her gloves against her cheeks. "I've been thinking about this, and I . . . I have decided that I cannot wait for you to return from Europe."

His eyes grew wide. "What? Why?"

"I love you, and I can't continue to do this. I can't pretend that you're coming back from Europe when we both know that you're not."

A wrinkle of confusion creased his brow. "I promised that I would."

"It's a promise that you cannot keep. I've seen what the *Englisch* world does to people. Look at Lorie and Luke. How many others have left and never come back?" Over the years they had lost several friends, mostly ones older than them who hit the end of their *rumspringa* and decided that the *Englisch* world was the place to be. She couldn't say it happened a great deal, but it happened often enough that it scared her to her core. "Lorie only went to Tulsa. You're going to Europe."

"But you said you would wait for me."

Sadie shook her head. "I can't promise that any longer. You're living out your dreams. You're going to Europe to see whatever is there that you think you need to see. All I want to do is get married and have children. That's what every Amish girl wants. It's what we are raised to want—to get married and have children, start a family and bake cookies and churn butter."

"I know for a fact that you've never churned butter in your life."

"Will you be serious?"

"I don't want to. I don't want to hear any of what you're saying."

Sadie took a deep breath. "You're asking me to put off everything I want in life while you live your dreams. And I can't do that."

Chris propped his hands on his hips and breathed out his nose. His nostrils flared, and she knew he was upset. Perhaps she had hit on the truth of the matter.

"So you're throwing away everything that we've built these years," he said.

"I'm the one throwing it away? You're the one going

half the world away. And for what? To see a bunch of ruins and a big metal thing in the middle of France?"

Chris dropped his chin to his chest. The action prevented her from seeing his face, but she could tell by the tense line of his shoulders that her words had struck home. Slowly he raised his head, his gaze searching for her. "I love you."

"Enough to cancel your trip?" Her eyes fluttered closed, and she shook her head. "Don't answer that. That wasn't fair. We both know the truth."

"And what is that?"

"That this means more to you than I do."

He opened his mouth to protest, but she cut him off with a wave of her hand. "You don't have to defend yourself. You don't have to lie to me and tell me that that's not true. Because I know that it is. We've been through too much together for you to start that now."

Chris only nodded. She wasn't sure if that or the haunted look in his eyes was worse. She blinked back tears, determined to see this through without shedding another one. "I love you too. Always have. You have been my best friend for years, the one person I always knew I could count on."

"But not anymore?"

"We have different goals now."

"But you love me."

Sadie shook her head. "I do. But sometimes love isn't enough."

Chapter Four

"He said he was coming in today, right?" Cora Ann asked for what had to be the fifteenth time since she had arrived at the restaurant after school let out.

"That's what he said." Sadie bit back a sigh. Not because Cora Ann was pestering, but because she was as anxious for Ezra Hein to arrive with the bison meat as Cora Ann was. Albeit for entirely different reasons.

She thrust those thoughts to the tiniest corner of her mind. Just because he was handsome to a fault didn't mean she could go all loopy. Or maybe Chris's surprise revelation about traveling to Europe had her not looking at things clearly.

Surely that's what it was.

"He's here," Cora Ann whispered, her excitement apparent even with her soft tone.

Despite Sadie's assurances to herself that she had no reason to be excited at the prospect of seeing Ezra Hein again, her heart tripped over itself.

Mouth dry as ash, she looked toward the door of the restaurant.

A hefty truck driver pushed through the door of the restaurant, invoice in hand. "I got two hundred and fifty pounds of bison meat here. I need someone to sign for it." He waved the papers toward Sadie.

She managed to get her feet into motion and stepped from behind the waitress station. She hoped her disappointment didn't show on her face. Not that she cared what the driver thought, but she didn't want Cora Ann to pick up on the fact that she was anticipating seeing someone else this afternoon.

Quit being stupid.

But Cora Ann was too wrapped up in asking questions about the meat to notice Sadie.

She signed the form and passed it back to the driver.

"You can see for yourself when I wheel it in," he told her, effectively dodging all of Cora Ann's questions about marbleization and the ratio of fat to lean meat in the ground product.

"You can bring it through the back," Sadie instructed the driver.

He gave her a nod, then tipped his hat toward Cora Ann.

The teen smiled, then spun on one heel to head through the kitchen to the delivery door.

"Cora Ann." *Mamm* called from her place in the restaurant's cramped office. "I need you to clean the restrooms. Now."

Her sister stopped in her tracks, her shoulders drooped. "Can it wait until after they deliver the meat?"

"Cora Ann." *Mamm*'s voice held a beat of warning. She did not like being questioned. If Sadie had to guess, she would say that it was her greatest shortcoming. But Sadie figured her rigid attitude came from years of trying to produce the best food in three counties.

"I wanted to see the meat when they bring it in."

"Cora Ann, leave the men alone and let them

unload. The meat will still be here after the bathrooms are cleaned."

"Yes, *Mamm*."

They didn't normally clean the bathrooms at this time of day. Sadie figured that *Mamm* was trying to keep the anxious thirteen-year-old out from underfoot.

She shot Cora Ann a sympathetic smile and went to let the men in the back.

She knew Cora Ann was excited about starting the recipes with bison meat, but the actual shipment of meat was a little on the disappointing side. And not just because Ezra was nowhere to be seen.

The driver brought the meat in large, wax-coated cardboard boxes, stacked four high on a dolly and stamped with the name of Ezra's ranch. Sadie lifted the lid off one box, peering inside to see individually wrapped parcels.

"That's the ground meat."

Sadie let the box top drop, then turned toward that familiar voice. "Ezra!"

"I was wondering if you would be here."

He was?

She wanted to say something clever and charming like "where else would I be?" but the words stuck in her throat. "*Jah*."

Great. Very clever. Very charming. He probably thought she was just a dumb Amish girl. And right now he wouldn't be far from the truth.

"Yeah." His brown eyes sparkled. "So? Does it pass the test?"

Sadie nodded, though she had no idea what bison meat was supposed to look like and it was still wrapped in white butcher paper and completely hidden from view.

Ezra gestured toward the stack of boxes behind her.

"That's the boneless round. These are the packages of ground. Each parcel is two pounds. Or thereabout."

"Terrific." Sadie nodded, realizing that any time she had with Ezra was slipping through her fingers. "I, uh . . ." She had nothing to say to keep him close for a while longer. She wanted to know him a bit better, find out about his ranch. His ranch! "So you have ostriches?"

Ezra nodded. If he thought the question strange, he didn't say. "We have five now. Four hens and a cock."

"Oh." Maybe not the best question to ask to spark up a conversation. Sadie shifted from one foot to the other, searching for something more to say.

Ezra smiled. "Would you like to come out and see them sometime?"

"Yes! I mean, that would be interesting. It doesn't sound like a typical ranch."

"It's definitely not typical." He scooted the bottom of the dolly out from under the stack of boxes. It scraped against the floor as he moved.

What now? Should she give him a business card so he would have her phone number? But she had already done that. Maybe a new one in case he lost the other one? That seemed a little desperate, and no matter how badly she wanted to spend a little more time with Ezra, she couldn't bring herself to be that bold.

"How about this weekend?" Ezra asked.

Sadie straightened her shoulders so she didn't deflate with relief. "That would be *gut, jah.*"

"Saturday morning?"

She made a face. "I have to work until three."

"Saturday afternoon it is, then." He smiled and his whole face lit up.

Sadie ducked her head, hoping her blush wasn't as

obvious as it felt. "Saturday afternoon." She would have to get a driver to go all the way out to Taylor Creek, but she had a feeling it would be completely worth it.

"Should I pick you up at three?"

She shook her head. "I can find a way out there. As long as you give me directions."

"I can come get you."

"I don't want to be a bother," she said.

Ezra smiled. "It's no bother. See you Saturday."

"See you Saturday."

"He's cute." Cora Ann spoke from behind her. If Sadie hadn't been so wrapped up in watching Ezra let himself out the back door, she might've jumped in surprise. As it was she nodded.

"Hefty much, he is," she murmured.

"What?"

"I mean, I suppose. If you like guys like that."

Cora Ann stared at the door where he had disappeared. "What's not to like?"

"Well, he's Mennonite, for one." Even as she said the words they seemed silly somehow. Was that the worst thing she could think of to say about the man?

"That doesn't take away from his cuteness," Cora Ann said. "You just can't go around marrying him," she teased.

Like that was going to happen.

What followed had to have been the longest days in Sadie's life. She tried not to think about it too much, about how he was coming to pick her up like it was a real date instead of her going to visit his ranch. She couldn't think about it in terms like that. He was

Mennonite, and as silly as it sounded, there was a world of difference between Mennonite and Amish. So nothing more would come out of Saturday afternoon but a friendship. She was okay with that. There was something about Ezra that made her want to know him better. And if friendship was all they could have, she would take it. She scooped up ice out of the bin and dumped it into one of the amber-colored plastic glasses they used for tea.

"So have you told *Mamm* yet?" Melanie sidled up beside her, dropping her voice so that only the two of them could hear. It was Friday afternoon. Only one more day before she saw Ezra again.

"No." Sadie shrugged. Telling *Mamm* made it feel like she was doing something wrong. And there was nothing wrong with driving out to the ranch to see Ezra's animals.

Then again, how would *Mamm* feel about her riding out to the ranch with a man she barely knew?

"Melanie," Sadie said, shooting her sister the sweetest smile she could muster. "Would you like to go with me?"

Melanie grimaced. "I can't. Noah and I are supposed to go to his parents' for supper."

Sadie sighed. It had been like that since Melanie had gotten married and Lorie had moved off to the *Englisch.* She supposed she could call Ruthie or one of the other girls. But on a Saturday afternoon, they more than likely had plans with their boyfriends and husbands and wouldn't care to go look at ostriches in Taylor Creek.

"Hey," Melanie said. "Why don't you take Daniel with you? He would love that."

Why hadn't she thought of that? Taking Daniel was a great idea. Not only would he be able to see animals that he had never seen before, it would get him out of the restaurant for the evening.

Since Lorie had left and Melanie had gotten married, it seemed that their baby brother spent way too much time sitting in the booths coloring pictures. Sadie knew that he was happy simply being close to them, but Daniel was the sort that was happy no matter where he was. He could find joy in the smallest thing, the beat of the butterfly wings, the breeze on his face, and being alive. Some called him special needs; Sadie just thought he was special. She smiled to herself. "That's a great idea, Melanie. Thanks."

"I want to go." Cora Ann came up behind them, bouncing up on her toes with excitement. "That's the ranch where we got the bison meat, right?"

"The very same."

"Please, please, please, Sadie. Please let me go."

She couldn't have said no to that even if she had wanted to. But having Daniel and Cora Ann along for the trip to Taylor Creek would certainly deter any objections her mother might have about her going there with Ezra.

"He'll be here at three tomorrow," Sadie said. "You have to make sure you're ready to go. Okay?"

The smile that spread its way across Cora Ann's face was the biggest Sadie had ever seen. Maybe even bigger than the one she had when *Mamm* finally agreed to let them serve bison meat dishes in the restaurant. "I'll be ready."

Cora Ann danced off, humming a little under her breath.

Melanie shook her head. "That girl."

Sadie agreed. Cora Ann was at that strange age. Thirteen was hard on girls. She was half woman, half child and hadn't figured out where she fit into either world. She ran around the restaurant acting like their father, too grown up for her own good. And then there were the times like this when she danced and smiled and wanted to do nothing more than go look at ostriches with her sister and her brother. It made Sadie realize how young she still was.

"Go where?"

Sadie whirled around, one hand pressed to her beating heart. "*Mamm!* You scared me."

"Apparently. Where are you going?"

This was the moment Sadie had been dreading. Not that she had been avoiding it or anything. In fact, she had hoped to avoid the matter altogether, slip out tomorrow, get in Ezra's car and head off to Taylor Creek without her *mamm* being any the wiser. It was a foolish thought at best, and now that Daniel and Cora Ann were along for the ride, she would have to come clean and tell her mother everything.

She pressed her hands to her waist and smoothed down her black dress. "To Taylor Creek."

Mamm raised one eyebrow. "To the Mennonite community?"

"*Jah.*" Sadie knew the one word wasn't going to appease her for long. "Ezra Hein," she started, "he's the man who brought the bison meat."

Mamm nodded. "I'm aware of who he is. What I need to know is why you are talking about him now."

"His family has a ranch in Taylor Creek. All exotic animals. And he invited me to come out and look around."

"And you're doing this tomorrow?"

"*Jah.*"

Mamm's stare was steady, and Sadie was barely aware

that Melanie had slipped off sometime during the conversation.

"And who is going to be with you?"

"It's not like that. But Cora Ann and Daniel are coming too. Cora Ann wants to see where the bison meat comes from, and I thought Daniel would enjoy himself."

Mamm nodded. "I think he would enjoy that very much." She smiled, and relief filled Sadie. "Just make sure you're not out too late."

Ezra pulled his pickup truck to the front of Kauffman's Family Restaurant and cut the engine.

This was not a date. Not really. Just a girl who wanted to come look at the ranch, and he was picking her up so that she could. That's all there was to it. Two people spending the afternoon together. That wasn't really a date, was it?

He slipped his hands over his hair just in case and let himself out of his truck. Regardless of whether it was a date or not, he couldn't sit out front and wait for her to come to him. Plus, he was about fifteen minutes early. Nothing like being excited over seeing a girl again.

The smell of fried chicken and biscuits met him as he pushed into the restaurant. He scanned the room looking for Sadie, but she was nowhere to be seen.

The restaurant was practically empty. Just a few stragglers snacking on coffee and pie. A young Amish boy sat in one booth, his tongue sticking out of the corner of his mouth as he concentrated on the box of crayons and the picture on the table before him. Ezra could only assume that he was somehow kin to the

Kauffmans, though he looked nothing like Sadie. Whereas her hair was dark, this little boy was blond, as was the girl who approached.

"How many in your party?" The girl couldn't have been more than thirteen, but she spoke with the ease and maturity that said she had done this a lot.

"Actually," he started. It was on the tip of his tongue to tell her that he was Ezra, and he had come to pick up Sadie. But she turned her blue eyes to his with a small gasp.

"You're Ezra."

He nodded. What else could he do but stand there and watch politely as she hopped up and down happily in place?

"I'm Cora Ann. You got the bison meat for me."

Ezra chuckled. "It's going to take you a while to eat all that."

Cora Ann laughed, and the sound sounded so much like Sadie he knew they had to be sisters.

"No." She giggled. "I found the recipes for bison meat, and *Mamm* said that we can make them."

Ezra gave her a small bow. "I appreciate your business."

"You're welcome."

He waited there for a second and she stared at him, smiling with an excitement he couldn't name.

"Is Sadie here?"

"Oh! Of course." She turned on one heel and hustled back toward the swinging doors he could only assume led to the kitchen.

"Sadie," she called from the door. But he couldn't hear the rest of what she said after she lowered her voice.

He shifted from one foot to the other as he waited.

A few moments later Sadie bustled out of the other door, brushing off her apron as she drew nearer. She was dressed in black again, but still managed to look like a ray of sunshine as she approached.

"Ezra. You're here."

"Yes, I am." He tried not to laugh, but he had a feeling she was about as nervous as he was. The whole thing was utterly ridiculous. She was merely coming out to the ranch to visit. It wasn't a date.

She smoothed her hands down the front of her black apron and wadded up the one she had been wearing. He supposed she wore that over her clothes to keep them from getting soiled while she cooked.

"Are you ready to go?"

"I need you to meet my *mamm* first."

"Of course." Why hadn't he thought of that? He nodded. "Okay. Sure."

This was feeling more and more like a date. But it wasn't a date, he told himself again. Two people getting together to look at exotic ranch animals. It didn't matter that he picked her up from her place of work. It didn't matter that he was meeting her mother. Just two people. Not a date.

"She's in the office. I'll take you back there." She started toward the waitress station.

Ezra followed behind her, winding around the fountain drink machine to a thin wooden door on the other side. The word "office" was spelled out in gold letters across the top.

Sadie gave a gentle knock, then opened the door and stuck her head in. "*Mamm*, Ezra is here." She opened the door all the way and allowed him to step inside.

The room was a disaster. Boxes of paperwork and files were stacked in every available space. It didn't help that the room was about the size of the bathroom. A Formica-topped table took up half the wall.

The woman sitting behind it looked up as they approached. Her face was lined with wrinkles. Her mouth appeared to be turned down into a permanent frown. She was thin and had a no-nonsense air about her that made the hairs on the back of his neck stand on end.

He stepped forward and reached out a hand. "Ezra Hein," he said.

The woman looked at his hand, seemed to hesitate for half a heartbeat, then shook it. "Maddie Kauffman. So you're the bison farmer."

He had never really been called that before, but he was sure he had been called worse. "Yes, ma'am." There were worse things to be known as.

An awkward moment passed, then Sadie took his elbow and directed him out of the room. "I'll see you later," she tossed back over her shoulder as they shut the door behind them.

She seemed to breathe a sigh of relief that Maddie didn't call them back into the office.

"So are you ready to go?" Ezra asked.

Sadie opened her eyes and nodded. "There is one thing, though."

His heart gave a weird lurch. "And that is?"

"Is it time? Is it time?" The girl who had led him into the restaurant rushed toward them, her cheeks pink with excitement. "I'm so ready for this."

Ezra looked at Sadie.

She shrugged. "I asked Cora Ann and Daniel to come too. I hope that's okay."

She didn't say it, but Ezra knew. It was better for her to come with two of her family members tagging along with the man she didn't know. He had forgotten that the Amish could be so conservative about such things.

"Of course."

Cora Ann squealed and danced a little jig. She already had her coat on and her scarf tied over her prayer *kapp*. She was actually more than ready.

Ezra half expected her to drag him out to his truck without waiting for her sister. He looked over to where Sadie had gone. She slid into the booth next to the little boy who was coloring. He looked up at her, his eyes magnified through his thick glasses. He was missing a couple of teeth in the front and had a dusting of freckles across his nose. But it was apparent that he was not an average child.

Sadie spoke softly to him. He nodded, then loaded all of his coloring supplies into a string backpack sitting next to him in the booth. Sadie slid out and allowed him to come behind her. He made his way to the office, returning a few moments later wearing a thick black coat and a black hat. He slung his string backpack across his shoulders, and Ezra could see it bounce as he walked.

He scanned their faces, realizing that they were as different as siblings could possibly be. It was apparent that Cora Ann and Daniel were siblings, but Sadie with her dark hair looked so different than they did. Or maybe it was the huge span between their ages. "Are you ready to go?"

Cora Ann did her little dance again.

Dumb question.

"Do you really have camels?" Daniel asked. His words held a slight lisp. Without warning he slipped his hand into Ezra's and gazed up at him with those magnified blue eyes.

"I do," Ezra replied, touched by the young boy's trust and apparent admiration.

Sadie grabbed her coat, and together the four of

them walked out of the restaurant. Ezra was the last one out, as Daniel reluctantly released his hand to go through the door before him. But Ezra came to an abrupt halt to keep from bumping into them as they stood, staring at his truck.

"What's the—?" He had been about to ask what the matter was, but he could see it right in front of his eyes. Four people—two adults and two children—could not ride in his single cab pickup truck. Somebody was going to have to stay home.

He turned to Sadie hoping she had some sort of solution, but she was already on it.

"Cora Ann," she started.

The young girl's excited expression had melted. She knew what was coming next. "Of course." She nodded dejectedly, and Ezra had the feeling that the family did everything in their power to make Daniel's life as interesting as possible. Yet, it wasn't fair that since he drove a truck and not a car, Cora Ann had to stay at home.

He lightly touched her shoulder. "That's a real sweet thing you're doing. And I'm sure your brother appreciates it."

She nodded again.

"But that doesn't mean you can't come out and see the ranch another day."

Her face lit up once again. "You mean that?"

"Absolutely."

"Tomorrow?"

He wasn't sure how to answer, but Sadie stepped in, saving him the trouble. "Tomorrow is a church Sunday."

"*Jah.* Right," Cora Ann replied. But it didn't change the disappointment covering her face.

"How about next week?" he asked. "I could come and get you next week and take you for a tour."

Cora Ann did the little hop-step she had shown him earlier.

"As long as your mother says it's okay," he added.

The stipulation didn't quell her joy. She danced a couple more steps, then stopped and turned back to Ezra. "What about Sadie?"

"What about her?" he asked.

"Can she come too?"

He didn't think that Maddie would have it any other way. "Of course," he replied. And just like that, he had another "not date" with Sadie Kauffman.

Chapter Five

"Look, Sadie!" Daniel ran ahead of them toward the pen of ostriches. His coat flapped behind him as he climbed up the white wooden fence. "They're so big!"

Sadie smiled, and beside her, Ezra chuckled. "Is it okay for him to climb up there?" she asked, eyeing the big birds as they strutted toward her brother.

"It should be fine," Ezra said. "They're not mean birds by nature. Though they are attracted to things that are shiny. But I don't think Daniel has on anything that sparkles."

True, the Amish didn't wear a lot of shiny things. He should be safe. She crossed her arms and watched as he waited for the ostriches to come closer.

The wind held a definite chill, though the sun shone bright. Daniel turned toward them, those golden rays twinkling off the lenses of his glasses. The speed of the ostriches increased.

"Oh, no!" Sadie rushed toward Daniel, hoping to get to him before the ostriches did. She wasn't exactly sure what they would do, but she wasn't taking any chances.

Ezra's footsteps pounded behind her, rustling in

the dead grass. His stride was longer than hers and he passed her quickly, scooping Daniel into his arms and out of harm's way.

Unaware of the danger, Daniel laughed. Sadie couldn't help but follow suit. No sense in getting upset about something that didn't happen.

"That was close." Ezra sat Daniel on his feet and comically wiped his brow.

"Again!" Daniel cried, bouncing with glee.

"No way, buddy." Ezra patted his shoulder in apology.

"Maybe we should look at the camels instead," Sadie suggested.

"That might not be a bad idea," Ezra agreed. He led them toward a different pen, this one more like the traditional farms with a barn in the middle and land all around. She counted three camels, but they were milling around amid the other animals and she couldn't tell if she'd counted any more than once.

"They are bigger than I thought." Of course, she never thought about camels much. But with their long legs and lofty humps, they towered over both of them.

"They're beautiful," she added, in case he thought she didn't like the animals. She supposed they smelled like any barn animal; but with their shaggy, caramel-colored fur and long eyelashes, there was a certain charm to the camels. Or maybe she wasn't used to seeing such exotic creatures in Wells Landing.

They wandered around the edge of the pen, watching the camels and the bison and keeping a close eye on Daniel. Sadie was glad that she brought him. He was having such a wonderful time. Other than school, he didn't get out near enough, and she made a personal vow to take him to the park at least once a week.

"Well, that's it." Ezra came to a stop and turned back around.

Sadie supposed they were at the edge of his property. Or at the edge of his workspace.

"How about a cup of coffee?"

Sadie nodded pointedly toward Daniel.

"Hot chocolate?"

Sadie smiled. "Sounds perfect." She called to Daniel and together the three of them made their way to the house. Daniel looked mildly disappointed at having to go inside, but he was such an accommodating soul that he didn't protest as he walked with them.

They hadn't gone into the house when they first arrived at the ranch, mainly because Daniel was so excited he led them straight away toward the animals. They had seen the bison, camels, and the ostriches, all the creatures Ezra had told her about.

Ezra's house was different than Sadie's. The Amish normally had white houses with clapboard siding, and built a little like a box, with large wraparound porches and no shutters. This house was a sprawling brick structure that seemed to stretch forever. Orange shutters contrasted nicely with the beige-colored brick, and empty terra-cotta pots waited on the front porch for spring and flowers to come.

Ezra led them to the side door and into the house. They walked into a small room with a sink and a washer and dryer, then on into a large and airy kitchen.

Sadie glanced around, checking out the appliances on the countertops. She spent so much of her day in the kitchen, she was always interested in the instruments others used to cook.

"Ezra? Is that you?"

"Yes, Mom. It's me."

"Are your friends still here?"

"Sadie," Ezra said, lightly taking her elbow and leading her toward the doorway at the opposite side of the kitchen. "Come meet my mother, then we'll get us something warm to drink."

But they didn't have a chance to set one foot outside the kitchen before Sadie heard a metallic clink and Ezra's mother came into view. She had crutches on both arms and moved slowly through the house as if it cost her a great effort.

"Mom, where's your chair?"

The dark-haired woman shook her head. It took only a moment for Sadie to realize that Ezra must take after his father. "Sometimes it's more trouble than it's worth," she said.

Ezra shook his head, but didn't respond to her words. "Mom, this is Sadie Kauffman and Daniel."

"It's nice to meet you," Sadie said, as Daniel gave a small wave.

"Sadie, Daniel, this is my mother, Ellen Hein."

Ellen nodded in both their directions. "It's nice to meet you too." Though Sadie wasn't sure she meant it.

She pushed away that unkind thought. But it seemed as if Ellen Hein was a lot like Sadie's own *mamm.*

"We were about to have some hot chocolate. Would you like to join us?" Ezra asked.

Ellen shook her head. "No, I think I'm going to lay down and take a nap."

Her tone held a dejected note that saddened Sadie. Ezra's mom looked unhappy. Sadie didn't know another word to describe it. But the woman's mouth turned down at the corners, and her forehead was creased with wrinkles as if she was perpetually frowning. Sadie wondered what happened to put such a look on her face, for her mother wore one almost identical. Had the same thing that placed her in a wheelchair put that sadness in her eyes? Sadie knew what happened with her own *mamm,* but she might not ever know Ellen Hein's story. After all, come next week, she wouldn't have an excuse to see Ezra again.

Not until they needed more bison meat.

If *Mamm* even let them reorder.

The thought made her heart stutter. It was ridiculous really, this need she felt to get to know Ezra better. She blamed it on Chris's recent revelation. When he broke his news to her, all her hopes flew out the window. She supposed it was only natural for her to pin them to someone else. But using a Mennonite man was absurd.

Ellen gave them one last frown, then clinked her way back into the other room. Sadie and Daniel made themselves comfortable in the oak chairs surrounding the oval table set off to one side while Ezra got down coffee mugs and started filling them with water.

"Ezra," Sadie started hesitantly. "Are you making the boxed hot chocolate?" She almost hated to ask. After all, he was kind enough to offer them a drink. But powdered hot chocolate? She mentally shuddered.

"Of course." Ezra frowned as if he couldn't figure out any other form hot chocolate could come in.

Sadie shook her head and stood. "Do you have a saucepan?"

"I'm sure we do." He started opening cabinets, peering into each one until he found a copper-bottomed saucepan for her to use. "I take it you're going to make the hot chocolate."

"*Jah.*" She smiled to take any sting from her word. "I need milk, sugar, cocoa," she rattled off the ingredients quickly, "and vanilla."

Ezra turned from where he had been peering into the refrigerator to find the milk. "Vanilla?"

"Trust me on this."

A few minutes later Sadie had all the ingredients laid out on the counter, including the questionable vanilla, and the milk warming on the stove. It didn't take long before she had the rich hot chocolate poured.

Daniel had been sitting there while she worked, swinging his legs and watching the two of them with great interest. He tended to do that; either he absorbed everything around him or he blocked it out. Sadie thought it was a defense mechanism. But at least he wasn't coloring. When things became too much, he shut down and got out his crayons. Once he began, it was hard to talk him into doing anything else.

"Wait." Ezra made his way back to the refrigerator, pulled out some whipped cream in a can, and gave each one of them a squirt on top. "Perfect." He smiled, his brown eyes sparkling, and Sadie's heart did that stutter thing again.

Why did he have to be so handsome? Why couldn't he have been a normal Mennonite boy without such thick blond hair and bottomless brown eyes? It would've been a lot easier on both of them. Still, she had no regrets about bringing Daniel out. In fact, the whole situation was win-win, as the *Englisch* said.

They sat down at the table with their hot chocolate mugs in front of them.

Ezra took a sip, then closed his eyes. "Wow, that's good. Thanks for making it."

Sadie smiled. "You're welcome. I'm glad you like it." As far as compliments went, it wasn't the best she had received. So why did she feel like she had won an award?

Ezra took another drink, this time coming away with a smear of whipped cream dotting his upper lip.

"Uh, you have a little . . ." Sadie said, gesturing toward the smudge.

He smiled and tried to lick it off, but only managed to get part of it.

She laughed and grabbed up a napkin from the wire holder in the center of the table. Leaning in close, she dabbed at the spot as the air grew thick.

Ezra held his breath, and his eyes darkened until she could no longer see his pupils.

"There," she said on a rush of air, only then realizing that she had forgotten to breathe as well.

"Thanks." His voice sounded hoarse. He cleared his throat as Sadie became all too aware that she was sitting way too close.

She sat back away from him, suddenly mindful that Daniel was sitting at the table with them.

Her gaze met Ezra's, but she couldn't read his expression. Did he feel it too? That draw? That pull? Or was she merely seeing something where nothing existed? After all, they both understood that this really wasn't a date. So why did it feel like one now?

Needing something to do, she took another sip of her cocoa, trying to put things into perspective and failing.

"Sadie, I—" Ezra started, but was cut short by the sound of a car pulling up outside.

"It looks like you have more company coming," Sadie said.

Ezra didn't act surprised, but he did glance at the clock over the kitchen sink as if someone had arrived right on time.

A knock sounded at the back door, and the other man from the auction let himself in. Sadie couldn't remember his name, but Ezra quickly introduced him as his cousin, Logan.

Logan's blue eyes studied her intently, though he didn't say what was obviously on his mind: What was the Amish girl doing in this Mennonite house?

Sadie wasn't about to explain herself. Nor did Ezra have to explain himself to his cousin. It wasn't like they were doing anything wrong.

"I came to tell you that we're on tonight," Logan said.

"On?" Ezra asked.

Sadie sipped her hot chocolate and pretended not to listen intently to their conversation. Across from her, Daniel swung his legs and sipped his drink.

"Robert got us the rec center again."

"Another volleyball tournament?" Ezra asked.

That was one thing that the Mennonites and the Amish shared, a love of volleyball.

Logan smiled mischievously. "Nope. This time around we're going to play kickball."

"What happened to the singing?" Ezra shook his head. "Never mind. I don't want to know."

"Kickball." Logan waggled his eyebrows as if that would entice Ezra to come.

"I think I'll pass."

Logan looked from Sadie to Ezra then back again. "Whatever you say, cousin."

He started toward the door, but Sadie had a feeling the conversation between them wasn't over. It seemed that Logan didn't like her being at Ezra's house. But why? There wasn't anything going on between them. Couldn't an Amish girl and a Mennonite guy hang out and be friends? Were their beliefs so far apart that innocent friendliness was a stretch?

Sadie waited until Logan had gone before looking

back at Ezra. "I don't think he likes me." She wasn't
sure why she said it. It wasn't that voicing the words
would change the facts.

"He's weird like that."

That might be the case, but after experiencing his
mother's frown, Sadie had a feeling that he wasn't the
only one.

Ezra pulled his truck to a stop in front of Kauffman's
Family Restaurant. The sun had set long ago, leaving
them shrouded in darkness. He left the engine run-
ning, and Sadie knew he was headed back to Taylor
Creek, back to his world, back to the Mennonites.
"Thanks for coming to get us."

"No problem. I enjoyed myself."

"Me too." A painful heartbeat passed, then Sadie released her seat belt. "Come on, Daniel," she said, releasing his as well. Her actions felt stiff and uncomfortable
as she opened the truck door and slid to the ground,
then helped Daniel down beside her.

"I really did have a good time," Ezra said. "I'm sorry
about Logan." He shook his head, but Sadie understood. The Amish and the Mennonites had split
hundreds of years ago over the issue of shunning.
From there the changes increased. The Mennonites
were as varied as the Amish in their traditions and
beliefs, but for the most part, the Mennonites had
electricity in their homes, drove cars, and didn't dress
as plain as the Amish did. But did that really make
them so different?

"It's okay. Thanks again." She shut the door and
took Daniel's hand, leading him up onto the sidewalk.
Ezra waited a moment for them to get clear of the

vehicle before he backed it up into the street. He gave them both one last small wave. Then he was gone.

Ezra drummed his fingers against the steering wheel as he drove home. He going to get a lot of flak over Sadie. He could see it coming in the surprised gleam in his mother's eyes and the twisted smirk Logan had given him. Why couldn't two people be just friends? Why did everybody have to put romantic labels on everything if two different genders were involved? It was ridiculous, really.

The moment she had touched his lips with the napkin, something exploded inside him. He wasn't sure what. He'd never felt that way before. But he felt a little dejected when she moved away. What was he supposed to make of that?

That he was attracted to Sadie. But that didn't mean anything. Sure, she was the only girl to spark his interest in a long time. Maybe even ever. But that didn't mean he could act on it. And so what if he did? The Amish and the Mennonites alike talked about not judging, then they proceeded to judge each other to a fault. If he wanted to see Sadie again, why should he not?

Friends and family alike would have trouble with any relationship he might forge with Sadie Kauffman. He was pretty sure his mother didn't want him dating anyone. Since his father had left, she relied heavily on him to take care of things. She couldn't remarry since her husband was still alive, though as far as they knew he could be dead, remarried, or living in another country. They hadn't heard from him since he walked out seven years ago. In that aspect, Ezra couldn't blame her for being a little bitter. He himself had hard feelings toward his father. Jakob had treated them both unfairly, walking out without a word or any communication since that date.

But Ezra wasn't thinking about marrying Sadie Kauffman. He had too much on his hands at the ranch, too many things he still wanted to do. Aside from the issues of their faith, he had too many responsibilities as it was to add another. But that didn't mean he couldn't spend time with her. After all, he'd already told her he'd pick her up next Saturday and bring her sister out to the ranch. Now he had to figure out what to do with the desire to see her again until then.

"Sadie! There you are!" Chris pushed out of the restaurant and hustled to her side. He'd been waiting for a while now. Waiting on her to come back from this unplanned excursion.

"Yes, here I am." Sadie looked down at her brother. "Daniel, why don't you go on in the restaurant?"

Daniel nodded and did as she bade, leaving Chris the privacy he needed to find out exactly what was going on.

"Is that the Mennonite?" He nodded toward the blue truck rolling down the street. "The one from the market?"

"Yes." A frown worked its way across Sadie's brow.

Chris hadn't meant to get her on the defensive. She'd said that she wasn't marrying him when he returned from Europe, but what was she doing running around with a Mennonite guy on a Saturday night?

"Is that why you came here?" Sadie asked. "To find out if he was the Mennonite?"

Chris shook his head. He was making a mess of this. "No, it's Rook night." He and Sadie along with William and Hannah had started playing Rook on Saturday nights. It was a fun time to get together and enjoy each other's company, and he wasn't about to let a Mennonite come between them. They might not have plans to get married, but she was still his best friend.

"Right." She gave a quick nod, as if she had known that all along, but Chris knew that she had forgotten.

"What's gotten into you, Sadie?" He did his best to keep his tone soft and even and not filled with the frustration he felt.

"Nothing," she said, though she crossed her arms and tucked her hands under, a sure sign that she was unhappy.

"I don't believe you." Was it too much to ask to have an honest answer? He wasn't the one running around with strange Mennonites when he already had plans with her.

For a moment she looked like she was about to blow, then she deflated like a balloon with a small pinhole in one side. "Things are changing. You're leaving and . . ."

"Is that why you're hanging out with another guy? A Mennonite?"

"Why do you keep saying that? Mennonite. Like it's a disease instead of a religion."

Chris couldn't explain. And he wasn't about to. Sadie knew the differences. She knew what was at stake if she were to become further involved with this Ezra guy. "I don't want to see you get hurt." Yeah. That sounded a lot better than what he really wanted to say. But the words didn't sit well with Sadie.

Her back stiffened, and though her arms fell, it was

only to prop themselves on her hips as she glared at him. "You don't want me to get hurt? That's ironic."

At times like these he felt like he was floundering in dark waters and had forgotten how to swim. "I'm worried about you, Sadie."

She paused for a second, and at first he thought she might lose some of the blazing anger that surrounded her like waves of heat in the summertime. "Go to Europe, Chris. Have fun."

"Is that what this is all about?"

She didn't answer. Nor did she meet his gaze. A sure sign if he ever saw one.

"It is. You're mad at me because I'm going to Europe?" They had been friends forever, best friends. Why did she pick now to go all wacky on him?

"How did you expect me to feel?"

How indeed?

"Everyone thinks we're getting married now as it is. Then you're going to go traipsing off to Europe, you'll probably never come back, I'll be left behind. Spinster Sadie. At least I can take care of Daniel."

Chris shook his head, trying to get this thoughts to settle. But he only succeeded in sending them knocking around his head once more.

She'd thought they would get married. And maybe they would have. Sadie was a fine woman, hardworking, sweet as pie, even if she wasn't what most would call a beauty. She was easy enough on the eyes, he supposed. Maybe a bit plain. She would make some man a wonderful wife someday. But he never thought about her being *his* wife. Not truly.

Tears sparkled in her hazel eyes, and she bit her lip. Something funny happened to his stomach. She deserved better than what he had just handed her.

He took one of her hands into his, grabbing her fingers as if he needed to memorize every curve, bump, and knuckle. "Sadie," he gently said. "You are the best friend I've ever had. And if I were staying in Wells Landing, I would want nothing more than for you to be my wife."

Chapter Six

Somehow Sadie made it through the next few days without constantly thinking about Chris's declaration. So he didn't actually confess his love. But he cared about her. How could he not? They had been friends for so long. But as disturbing as his words were to her heart, they were calming at the same time. She might still end up a spinster, but at least she would know that someone had cared enough to want to make her his wife. That was something. Wasn't it?

Thursday afternoon came, and Sadie was waiting for Cora Ann to get in from school. She was due anytime. In fact, she was a little late, which meant she had stopped off at the library to see if any new cookbooks were delivered this week.

Sadie smiled to herself at her sister's love of all things culinary, and once again she wished she had something in her life that she could be so passionate about. Something other than Daniel.

Their young brother had not taken well to Lorie leaving the Amish. Or maybe it was because she left so soon after they lost their father. But Daniel had cried for Lorie for days, finally taking up with Sadie and barely letting her out of his sight. She didn't mind really; with Chris heading off to Europe soon, she would have plenty enough time on her hands to take care of Daniel and work her regular shifts at the restaurant.

The bell over the door jangled as Cora Ann came into the restaurant, string backpack flung across her shoulders. As usual, her eyes were bright and sparkling. Simply being at the restaurant seemed to make her happier. Sadie wished she could say the same for herself. Not that it mattered. She was headed home to meet Daniel's bus and get supper started for everyone before heading off to the bowling alley. Thursday was their usual night, and though they had lost Jonah and Lorie, the three couples still met to have fun. Sadie tried not to think about the day in the future when Chris would be gone and she would be the fifth wheel at the alley.

"Anything exciting happen today?" Cora Ann asked as she washed her hands at the waitress station sink.

Sadie shook her head. "Not unless you consider mashed potatoes interesting."

"Well, if you added a touch of rosemary and garlic . . ."

Sadie shook her head and laughed. "This restaurant's lucky to have you, you know that, Cora Ann?"

Cora Ann dimpled in return. She dried her hands on a towel and tied an industrial apron around her waist to protect her dress from her restaurant work. "You headed home?"

Sadie nodded. She had just enough time to meet the bus and get Daniel his after-school snack, then get ready for bowling. Everyone could eat when they got home.

The phone rang and Cora Ann, still tying her apron behind her, rushed toward the front desk to answer it. Sadie wadded up her apron and threw it in the dirty clothes hamper right inside the office door as Cora Ann called out to her. "It's for you. It's Chris."

Very rarely did Chris call her at the restaurant. The Flauds had a phone in their barn, but more often than not Chris was more interested in studying world maps than talking on the phone.

Sadie brushed off the front of her dress and made her way to the front where Cora Ann waited, the receiver pressed against her shoulder as if to mute the sound.

"Is everything okay?" she asked. "He sounds sort of weird."

"I have no idea." Sadie held out her hand for the receiver. There was only one way to find out. "Hello?"

"Sadie, it's Chris. Listen, I can't make it tonight. Something's come up." He did sound sort of weird, distracted, and Sadie wondered what was going on. Had his family somehow found out about his plans to go to Europe?

"You can't make bowling?" She had wanted her voice to sound even, maybe even concerned. So much for that.

"I'm really sorry." His tone backed up his sentiments, and Sadie immediately felt remorse over her harsh tone.

"It's okay. Is everything okay with you?"

"Yeah, just some family things that I have to take care of."

Sadie looked around to see if anyone was listening

in. *Mamm* was in the family booth rolling silverware. Cora Ann was filling up the ice bin and getting ready for the dinner crowd. No one was paying her any mind. "This isn't about Europe, is it?"

"No," Chris said, though his voice choked a little at the end. Something was definitely going on. "I can't make it is all."

"I understand." She didn't really, but what was she supposed to say? If they were such good friends, why couldn't he confide in her what was going on in his life? Why did he just leave her hanging?

She sighed. It seemed the more they tried to pull together, the more they ended up being pushed apart. She hated it. If they couldn't survive in Wells Landing together, how could they ever make it through him going to Europe?

After she got home, Sadie made Daniel a snack and waited for his bus to arrive. He came in, all smiles and hugs as he usually was, a bright ray of sunshine in a gray January world. Sadie shook off those thoughts. She was letting things get to her, and she shouldn't. Chris, Lorie leaving, all of it seemed to be building on her and weighing her down, making her wish things were different, when she knew better. She'd have to pray about that tonight, not trusting God to give her what she needed. But how could He know what she needed when she didn't even know herself? She almost laughed out loud at her ridiculous thought. This was God she was talking about; He knew everything. The problem was could she recognize what she needed when God provided, if she didn't know what it was now?

Daniel swung his feet under the table as he ate his cheese and crackers. "It's bowling night," he said.

Sadie smiled. He might not be able to recite the days of the week in order, but he knew Thursday was the night she and Chris went bowling. "Yes, it is. But I'm not going. Not tonight." She had called Hannah before she left, leaving a message at the phone shanty just down from her house. There would only be the two couples there tonight at the lanes, seeing as how they hadn't replaced Jonah and Lorie yet. But even two couples could have fun bowling.

"Why not?" Daniel's head bobbed again as he continued to swing his legs.

"I don't have anybody to bowl with."

"Ezra." Bob, bob, bob.

Her heart started to beat at the sound of his name. She unhitched her breath and looked at her brother. "Ezra?"

Daniel nodded, and along with the kicking of his feet the action was almost dizzying. "You like him, *jah?*"

More than I should.

"Then go bowling with him."

Daniel continued swinging his feet, eating his crackers, and otherwise looking around as if he hadn't said anything momentous. She could ask Ezra. Why not? If he liked bowling, surely he would come. And then she wouldn't have to miss. They could have a good time. And everyone would be happy. Right?

Sadie smiled at Daniel. "That's a good idea. I'll go call him now."

* * *

Ezra was pitching the alfalfa hay down from the hayloft when his phone started buzzing in his pocket. It went off periodically during the day, with most people leaving a voice mail message for him about meat that they wanted, special orders, and the other various products and services he had on his ranch. But something possessed him to look at the screen this time. He took off his leather work gloves, slapped them against one hip, then tucked them into the back pocket of his jeans. He fished out the phone and looked at the screen. It was a 918 number, but that wasn't saying anything. Most of his customers were local. He hesitated a bit longer before deciding to answer the phone.

"Hello?"

"Ezra?"

Sadie. "Yes?" He wasn't sure why he acted like he didn't recognize her voice. Despite the fact that they could only be friends, it wasn't a good idea to let her know exactly how much he liked her.

"This is Sadie Kauffman. I wanted to thank you again for giving me and Daniel a tour of your ranch."

Surely that wasn't why she had called. He hoped it wasn't. She'd thanked him four or five times on Saturday. And it was really no big deal. He enjoyed spending time with Sadie. There was a calmness about her that spread into his bones, even though an energy followed her wherever she went. It was a strange and interesting combination that he wanted to stand next to always. "You're welcome out here anytime."

"And we're still on for Saturday with Cora Ann, right?"

"Of course." He was excited at the opportunity to

see her again. Even though he knew he shouldn't be, he was looking forward to it.

"That's not why I called."

Ezra smiled. "Yeah?"

"Do you like to bowl?"

It was perhaps the last thing he expected her to ask. And that was surely why it took him a moment to answer. But just in case . . . "Like in an alley? On lanes?"

"Is there any other kind?"

Ezra shook his head. "I guess not."

"So do you?"

"Do I what?"

"Like to bowl?"

"Yes. Of course. But I'm not any good."

Sadie laughed. "You don't have to be good. Just breathing."

"I think I qualify."

Her chuckle came across the line again, and he realized that he'd do almost anything to hear that sound. "Do you want to go tonight? My normal bowling partner can't make it, and I hate to let my group down."

Ezra stood still for a second, letting the question wash over him. Had she just asked him out on a date?

"I mean, it's only bowling, right? Nothing else. Unless . . . I mean, I think it would be fun if you came, but you don't have to. Never mind, it was a dumb idea."

"No, no, no, and don't hang up, Sadie. Of course I'd like to go bowling with you. What time?"

"We usually start at seven."

"Pick you up at six thirty?"

"That's okay, I can take the buggy and—"

"And drive home after dark. I'll come get you in my truck."

"Okay," she said. "See you at six thirty?"

"I'll be there."

The moment Sadie heard his truck rumbling down the road, she grabbed her bag and rushed out the door. After she had gotten off the phone with Ezra, she called Hannah back with her change of plans. Thankfully, this was *Mamm*'s day to work the open-to-close shift at the restaurant. Sadie didn't want to hide the fact that she and Ezra were going bowling together, mainly because there was nothing to hide. But she surely didn't want to try to explain that to her mother. Not after Lorie left.

Lorie's discoveries about their father and the double life that he'd been leading had almost torn the family completely apart. Lorie had wanted to go off to Tulsa and experience the *Englisch* world like her father had known, but *Mamm* was not having any of it. She told Lorie straight out if she went to the *Englisch* world, she wasn't welcome back in their home. Never mind that Lorie hadn't joined the church and couldn't technically be shunned. *Mamm* was just like that, a little on the stern side and very much concerned with the actions of all of her children. It was a good thing to be loved as much as Maddie Kauffman loved her children, but Sadie had no doubts that their sister Melanie had gotten married so young simply to get out of the house and out from underneath *Mamm*'s thumb.

Cora Ann had come home from the restaurant to watch after Daniel while Sadie went bowling. As she had expected, Cora Ann had stopped by the library and checked out a couple of new cookbooks. Sadie caught sight of *Your Double Boiler and You: A Hundred and One Recipes You Never Thought to Make* and *All About Pies* before she hustled out the door to meet Ezra.

He turned down the drive when she cleared the porch. She raced toward him, the strings of her prayer *kapp* flying out behind her as she ran.

"Hi," he said with a smile as she came around the passenger side.

"Hi," she returned. She was staring at him like a young girl with a serious crush.

"Are you going to ride with me the rest of the way to the house?"

She shook her head. "There's no need to go back to the house."

A small frown furrowed his brow. "I don't need to meet your mother?" She had told him all about her father's death the day they were out at the ranch. He'd understood and nodded, apparently figuring out there had been a death since she was always wearing black. A few more months of that, and she could go back to wearing her favorite blue.

"She's at work." Sadie reached for the door handle, hoping he'd let the matter drop. "Besides, this isn't really a date."

The words gave him pause, then he nodded. "Right. Bowling."

She slid into the cab of his truck. "Just bowling," she repeated.

Ezra looked into his mirrors and backed the truck out into the street before starting them toward town once again. "Buckle up," he said, nodding pointedly at her seat belt.

"Of course." She wrapped the thin strap around her

and snapped it into place. With all the work they did at the restaurant, she hardly ever traveled by car. That was why she didn't remember to buckle her seat belt. It had nothing to do with those dark brown eyes that were smiling at her from across the truck cab.

"So who are we bowling with again?"

"There's William and Hannah Lapp. They got married this past October. And Ruthie and Mark Chupp."

"Let me guess, they're not brother and sister."

"No," she said. "They got married in January."

"It is January."

Sadie chuckled. "So it is."

"So we're going bowling with two sets of newlyweds?"

It sounded terrible when he said it like that. "Three. My sister Melanie and her new husband, Noah, will be here too."

"And you're not bringing your boyfriend?"

Heat rose into her cheeks, and she knew she had turned a bright shade of pink. "I don't have a boy-friend."

"So who do you normally bowl with?" Ezra pulled the truck onto the highway that would take them back into town.

"Chris is usually my partner. Chris Flaud."

"Is he the guy that was waiting for you at the restaurant Saturday night?"

Sadie turned to study him. The sun had long gone down, and darkness had settled around them. She couldn't read his expression. How had he seen Chris on Saturday night? "*Jah,* that's Chris."

"What does he say about you asking me bowling?"

"He doesn't care. We're just friends." For some reason she wanted to tell him about Chris's plans to go to Europe that summer, but she kept them to herself. She wouldn't want anything to accidentally get back to Chris's parents before he had a chance to talk to them. She had made a promise, after all.

Ezra nodded, but didn't say anything further on the matter as they continued into town.

As usual, the bowling alley was full. There wasn't a whole lot to do in tiny Wells Landing on a Thursday night in January. Once the summertime hit, hardly anybody would be indoors. There would be nighttime softball games, fishing after dark, and a ton of other activities that involved a bunch of kids being together.

Ezra found a space and parked the truck.

Sadie got out, shutting the door behind her before reaching into the truck bed and retrieving her bag.

"Is that what I think it is?" Ezra pointed to the bag she held in her hand.

"It is if you think it's a bowling ball."

Ezra nodded. "I've never known anyone Plain to have their own ball."

"Amish and Mennonite?" Sadie asked as they walked around the side of the building toward the front doors. She could already hear the music blaring from their nighttime bowl. She couldn't say she liked the music. It was loud, rock 'n' roll, they called it. But it somehow made her more anxious than she wanted to be. There were times when she found that she left the bowling alley and her heart was pounding in her chest way faster than its normal rate. Or at least it felt that way.

"Uh, neither, I guess." He held the door for her and waited for her to enter, then shook his head. "You know what? Forget I said that. That's got to be the dumbest thing I've ever said." He chuckled at himself, and Sadie found herself joining in.

"Well," she said in the small foyer. The bowling alley had two sets of double doors with a small room in between. It was the last chance to talk without screaming before they went into the actual bowling alley. "Me either."

"You either what?" Ezra's brow wrinkled with a frown.

"I don't know anyone Plain either that owns a bowling ball. Except for me."

Ezra shook his head. "Then where did you get it?"

"It belonged to my father."

The air between them got a little thicker. A little sadder. And somehow despite the rock 'n' roll blaring on the other side of that thin sheet of glass, a little quieter.

Ezra reached for the silver handle, his eyes unreadable. "Okay then, Sadie the owner of bowling balls. Show me what you got."

Chapter Seven

"What were you thinking, bringing him here?" Sadie glanced up from the scorecard as her sister Melanie flopped down in the seat beside her.

"What do you mean?" She knew what Melanie meant, and she would have to answer that question eventually, but for now she was playing dumb.

"If *Mamm* found out that you brought a Mennonite boy bowling . . ."

Sadie briefly closed her eyes and let out a heavy sigh. When she opened them again, Melanie was still staring at her intently. Her sister was not going anywhere.

"Who invited you, anyway?"

The comment was meant to be a joke, and Melanie knew it, but still she crunched up her forehead into a scowl. "He's a Mennonite."

"I wish everyone would stop saying that like it's catching. So what if he's a Mennonite. I'm not planning on marrying him."

Melanie's stare was hard and steady. "You know what *Dat* always said."

"Never date a boy you won't marry."

Now that Sadie knew that her father had truly been *Englisch* pretending to be Amish instead of Amish like everyone in the community thought, that comment had a whole new meaning. No wonder he said such things; *Englisch* boys were so different than Amish boys. But Ezra was a Mennonite. It wasn't like he had completely different values than Amish. Were they so different after all?

"That's right," Melanie said. "And you know that you could never marry a Mennonite boy."

"So because I won't marry a Mennonite boy, I can't bowl with one."

"Sadie, a date is a date."

"This is not a date."

Melanie leaned back in the molded plastic chair and gave her another one of those looks. With that expression on her face, her sister looked so much like *Mamm* that Sadie almost grabbed her shoes and headed for the door. "Did he pick you up tonight?"

"*Jah.*"

"And is he going to take you home tonight?"

"*Jah.*"

"That, my sister, is a date."

"Melanie, I need you." Hannah waved to her from the other side of the ball return.

"Think about it." Her sister's voice was so soft she almost didn't hear it, then Melanie gave Sadie one last look and went to see what Hannah wanted.

It wasn't a date, Sadie argued in her head. No matter what Melanie said, no matter what anyone said. She and Ezra had agreed this wasn't a date. It was two friends who were going bowling together with other friends. Never mind that all the other "friends" were newly married and very much in love. That didn't mean she and Ezra had to be. Look at her and Chris. They had been bowling with this group for years. And he hadn't exactly promised his undying love to her, now had he?

"How's it going?" Ezra eased down into the seat next to her, the one that Melanie had recently vacated.

Sadie pasted on a bright smile and turned to face her new friend. "Everything's great."

"Then why do you look like you could bite nails in half?"

Sadie sighed. "It's nothing. Really."

He studied her with those so-brown eyes, but after a moment, he gave a small nod. "Okay, but don't think I believe you. You can tell me when you're ready." With that, he rapped his knuckles on the Formica-topped desk, then sauntered away.

Sadie watched him go, her emotions a jumble of twisted turns and knots.

Why was everybody making such a big deal out of this? Even if everyone insisted on calling this a date, who was to say anything more would come of it than this one night? As much as she liked Ezra, and she was finally admitting that she really truly liked him, who was to say that he wanted anything more from her than merely friendship? He himself had never given her any indication that he held feelings for her outside of friendship. But everyone assumed that their one bowling date would lead to something more.

She tapped the eraser end of the pencil against the paper-thin scorecard. And even if their one date led to more, why was everyone so upset?

She knew the Mennonites and the Amish were on different sides of the fence. All over shunning eons ago. But did their views on shunning make them all that different? Most folks outside the Anabaptist had no idea the difference between Amish and Mennonites. And as much as she knew their differences, she could not wrap her mind around them. Was it such a big deal that they had electricity and the Amish didn't? The Kauffmans had electricity at the restaurant. They used a phone on a regular basis. *Mamm* used a computer to take care of all the bills. The big difference in the Amish like her family and an Amish family like the Riehls was that the technology that the Kauffmans used was solely in place to keep them on the same level with other businesses—*Englisch* businesses—of the times. Unfortunately, old-fashioned methods did not make for good twenty-first-century business practices. The Mennonites had electricity, but they didn't use it to power televisions, radios, computers, or other things that might lead to the temptations of the outside world. So were they really that different after all?

Sadie looked up as Ezra approached the ball return. He looked so different standing there in his blue jeans and patterned shirt, but that stuff was on the outside. Did it really make a difference?

No, she decided. It didn't. Ezra was a nice person, generous and handsome. He took care of his disabled mother. He raised animals on his ranch. He even cared enough to drive from Taylor Creek all the way into Wells Landing to pick up her and Daniel and take them to his ranch. And he had asked nothing of her in return.

She watched as he executed a perfect throw, but the ball had a bad spin and hit too far down the side, leaving him with a seven/ten split. She couldn't help but smile as the boys all groaned. Ezra threw his head back and sighed with the impossibility of the pickup. No, she decided, they weren't so different after all.

Of all the luck, Ezra couldn't believe his. He managed to pick up the seven pin, but missed the angle enough that it didn't ricochet and collide with the ten. He took his seat on the bench and watched as Mark took his turn.

"Tough break." Mark sat down next to him. A few inches away but still close. But Ezra had to scoot a little closer as Noah sat down on the other side. The two of them effectively pinned him in, and he knew what was coming next.

Sadie didn't have any brothers save Daniel. And he was too young by far to make sure that a guy treated his sister right. Ezra felt these two had appointed themselves as honorary brothers to Sadie Kauffman.

"So," Noah started. "You like Sadie."

That was a question that had no right answer. "She's a nice girl." There. That was good enough.

Apparently not for Noah. Perhaps he thought as Sadie's younger sister's husband, the duty of both brother and father fell to him. "She is. How did you two meet?"

Ezra had the feeling that Noah knew how he and Sadie had met, but wanted to see how Ezra himself felt about it. "She came to the market with her friend." He'd almost said boyfriend, but was that what Chris was to her, a boyfriend? And if he was, what right did Ezra have coming bowling with her tonight? She had said they were only friends. Now he was wondering if perhaps she had talked him into coming bowling in order to make Chris jealous. The thought made acid churn in his stomach. He didn't want to be used for anybody's revenge.

"And then you invited yourself bowling?"

"I think you guys have this all wrong." Ezra stood, unwilling to put up with too much of an interrogation. "Sadie wanted to bring Daniel out to my ranch and allow him to look at the animals I keep. So she did. Then she asked me to come bowling with her. As a friend. That's all."

Before he could walk away, Will finished his turn and came up next to him. "What the guys mean to say is, we all like Sadie. She's a good girl, good friend, and deserves to be treated right."

"And then there's Chris," Mark added.

If Chris and Sadie were truly just friends, then his friends evidently hadn't gotten the memo.

"Listen, guys," Ezra started, not really sure how he was going to finish. "I think Sadie is a nice girl, but I'm not looking for a girlfriend right now. She invited me to come bowling, so I did. Really. That's all there is to it."

Noah stood to stand beside him. Ezra was fairly tall, and Noah hardly reached his shoulder. But there was something fierce in his gaze, and Ezra thought he had heard Sadie mention that he was a bishop's son. That explained a lot.

"Know this," Noah said. "We're a peace-loving people, but hurt Sadie and I can't guarantee what happens from there."

Ezra gave a small nod. "Understood, and can I say that Sadie couldn't ask for a more protective bunch of guys to look out after her. She's a very lucky girl."

* * *

"I'm sorry about that." Sadie took off the rented bowling shoes and handed them to the guy behind the counter. He grabbed them and handed back her black walking shoes as Ezra stood beside her, waiting for his own lace-up boots.

"About what?"

"The interrogation." She grabbed her shoes off the counter and headed back to the bench, Ezra right behind her.

He sat down next to her as they started putting on their shoes.

"I know they mean well, but those guys . . ." She shook her head. "Well, they're good friends to have."

Ezra nodded. "I can see that. You're a very lucky girl to have friends like them. That they care about you enough to, well, care."

"I suppose it's because I don't have any brothers except Daniel. I know they mean well, but sometimes . . ." She shoved her feet into her shoes, tying them before she continued. "I thought they would understand."

"That we're friends?"

At the laughter in his voice, she whirled around to face him.

"What?" he asked innocently.

"Did you tell them that? That we're just friends?" Sadie had mixed feelings about that. It was okay for her to go around saying it, but that tiny little piece of her that wanted to get married more than she knew she deserved, hated it. Wanted more, if only once in her life.

"I believe it was tell them that or end up bleeding on the floor of the men's room."

"They threatened you?" Sadie gasped. "They really

are okay guys. I don't think any of them would actually hurt you. But they like to go around acting tough."

"Why would they want to do that?"

Sadie shot him a small smile. "We've all been friends for so long. We've all looked out for each other all these years. I'm kind of the last one out."

"What about Chris?"

She shook her head, unsure of what she should say about Chris and the things he wanted from life. "I can't speak for Chris." At least it was the truth.

She wasn't sure why she was so reluctant to tell Ezra that Chris had big plans that didn't include her. It wasn't like Ezra knew that all these years she had hoped that she and Chris would one day get married. Or maybe she didn't want him to think she was pathetic, to hang on to a guy for so long only to have him reject her for a continent.

Mentally she took that thought away. She wasn't being quite fair, but it was hard to be fair when her heart was half-broken. She had big dreams. And they hadn't been crazy dreams. So why couldn't she have them? Why did the one guy she thought could make those dreams come true want to go travel, see the world, and leave her behind?

No, she couldn't tell Ezra that. She couldn't stand to see the pity in his face.

Thankfully, he didn't press, just took her elbow and led her back to the area where her friends waited.

She said her good-byes, completely aware that while she did, Ezra hung behind her, not really part of their group, not interacting the way she did. Was that too much to ask? Maybe it was. But if nothing else, she wanted Ezra to come and have a good time. She had a feeling he worked way too hard on that ranch of

his. She saw no other signs of hands to help, just him
and his mother—who was on crutches at best, in a
wheelchair at worst—and then his cousin, Logan. But
how much could Logan truly help if he had work of
his own to do?

Ezra walked her through the parking lot back to his
truck. He opened the door for her, and she murmured her thanks as she climbed into the cab. As he
walked around to take his own seat, she watched her
friends pair up, get on their respective tractors, and
head out of the parking lot. Were tractors so different
than the truck?

It didn't bear thinking about. She wasn't going to
change the thoughts and views of others. And she might
as well not try. She should have learned that lesson long
ago, watching all the *Englischers* come in and whisper
behind their hands in the restaurant. You would think
that if people wanted to come to a restaurant and eat
they wouldn't talk about the staff where they could hear
them, but some people did. Some people would never
understand, be they Amish or *Englisch*, or maybe that
was Amish or Mennonite?

"Does this mean you're not coming out on Saturday?" Ezra kept his eyes on the road as he asked the
question. He could pretend all he wanted that it was
because it was dark, that his driving demanded all of
his attention, but he also felt he needed to allow Sadie
a bit of private time to form her answer. Frankly he
wasn't sure he wanted to see the look on her face when
she told him no, she was not coming back out to his
ranch on Saturday with Cora Ann.

The thought disappointed him for two reasons. One,
he wouldn't get to see Sadie again. And two, Cora Ann

had been so excited to come see the animals that he hated to break her heart. The whole family was in black, and he knew that their father had passed away recently. It didn't feel right to offer another blow like that to a thirteen-year-old girl. Perhaps there was another way. Perhaps he could get Cora Ann and Sadie's mom to come out to the ranch. But that didn't allow him to see Sadie, now did it?

"Are you saying you don't want me to come out to the ranch?"

He was making a mess of this. "That's not what I said at all. I got the feeling that your friends don't like us hanging out with each other. I was trying to save you the trouble of telling me yourself."

"So you do want me to come?"

A loaded question if he'd ever heard one. "I want you to do what you want to do. I'm going to be at the ranch either way come Saturday night." Mainly because he wasn't dating anybody. Never really had. Traditionally, the Mennonite guys got with their honeys on Saturday night. The boy would be invited to the girl's home, and the two young people would sit in the parlor and talk. It was as good a way to get to know each other as any, he supposed. But he would much rather walk around the ranch and show Cora Ann all the animals and Sadie the new emu he'd brought on the property this week. She was a pretty thing, a lot smaller than the ostriches. Now if he could find a male to go with her, he'd be all set. For now, anyway, until he finally got the alpacas he was always talking about.

He shook his head, trying to bring his thoughts back in line. He was tired, or not thinking right because of all the emotional baggage that came along for the ride tonight. They'd gone bowling. That sounded easy enough. But he should have known that nothing would be that simple when a Mennonite and an Amish were involved.

He pulled his truck onto the side of the road and left his lights on in case any oncoming traffic needed to see him.

"Listen, Sadie, I like you. You're fun to be around. But I understand. You have a life. So does Chris, right?"

Sadie nodded.

"I've got the ranch. It's not like we have tons of time on our hands to explore any of this."

"Can you tell me exactly what you mean? I'm confused now."

He reached down and flipped on the interior lights so he could see her expression. She was cute when she was muddled. And he had to stifle back a small laugh.

"I enjoy spending time with you."

"Me too." She appeared nervous in saying those words and rubbed her fingers down the black skirt in her lap.

"But I have a lot to do these days. And I don't have time for a girlfriend."

"I'm busy too," Sadie said. "I'm not looking for a boyfriend." He heard the words, but somehow felt she didn't mean them. Maybe it was the way she looked at her fingers instead of at him when she said that she didn't want a boyfriend. Or maybe there was something still going on with Chris.

Oh, the drama, he thought. He could do without that. "I think we would make good friends, don't you?"

She looked up at him and smiled. "*Jah.* I do."

Was that relief on her face? Was she thankful that he didn't want her as a girlfriend and that she would have another friend to lean on? He might not ever know.

"So it's official. We're friends, right?"

Sadie nodded.

"Just friends."

"Yeah," Sadie agreed. "Just friends.".

She was fairly certain that the conversation she had with Ezra at the side of the road on the way home from bowling was the most bizarre conversation she'd ever had with a man. But something he said made her feel warm inside like someone had let loose a small ray of sunshine. She did want to be his friend. The thought was kind of strange, considering she'd been friends with Chris for so long and when she finally wanted more from him, he was leaving. But it was good to know that she had Ezra. She would have a friend after Chris had gone to Europe. She didn't want to say that Ezra would take Chris's place, because that couldn't happen. But she was sure she could find room for Ezra in her life.

He pulled his truck to a stop and put it in park, though he didn't turn off the engine. "Do you need me to walk you in?"

Sadie shook her head. Her *mamm* was still at the restaurant, another of the reasons that it was okay that Ezra came to get her for this outing. Maybe with a little time, *Mamm* would to get used to the idea that her daughter had a Mennonite friend. Sadie was sure they would go through the whole boyfriend-just-friend conversation four or five more times before it finally took hold. But she was okay with that. Ezra was worth it.

"I'll be fine. Thanks for going with me tonight. And I'm sorry if my friends—"

"Say no more." Ezra shook his head and held up a hand to reinforce his words. "I had a really great time, and as strange as it may seem, I'm kind of glad that you have friends who look out for you like that. There's a lot of girls out there who need someone to watch out for them, and you've got three."

Sadie smiled. Noah, Will, and Mark were like the three older brothers she never wanted. But she was still glad to have them on her side.

"About Saturday," Ezra started. "You get off at three again?"

"*Jah.*"

"Pick you up at three fifteen?"

"That'd be good. I'll see you then."

Ezra nodded, and acted as if he want to say something else. Then he gave her a small wave and headed back down the driveway.

Sadie started toward the house, not really understanding why her footfalls seemed so heavy. She had such a good time with Ezra, if she took out the interrogation she got from her friends over the matter. Being with Ezra was a lot of fun. She was glad to have him as a friend. She was to the door of the house before she realized she had left her bowling ball in the back of his truck.

She'd have to get that later, she thought as she let herself in.

"There you are!" Her *mamm* jumped up from the rocking chair and rushed toward her. "I cannot believe what I am hearing."

A thousand questions popped into Sadie's mind all at once. Topping the list were "Why are you here?" and "What can't you believe?" But she refrained from asking either.

Instead she looked at her mother's hand wrapped

in a pristine white bandage. One finger had been splinted with some sort of metal. The bandage ran from the end of her pointer finger on her left hand all the way to the wrist. "*Mamm!* What have you done?"

"I cut myself at work. It's no big deal."

It looked like a big deal to Sadie. It was obvious her mother had gone to some kind of medical facility to seek help. Which meant she had to leave the restaurant. Which meant somebody had to take her. "How did you get to the doctor?"

"Esther took me." She shook her head as if not wanting to think about such matters at this time. Esther Fitch ran the bakery at the end of the same building that housed the restaurant. Esther was a good friend to them all. They looked out for each other, being in the same building and all. And it didn't hurt that Esther and her new husband Abe Fitch shared an apartment in the back of her shop, the same apartment she had once shared with Caroline Hostetler before Caroline married Abe's nephew, Andrew Fitch.

"Who took care of things at the restaurant?"

"Sadie! Hush up. I want to know about this Mennonite boy."

Sadie's concerns burst inside her chest, invading every part of her, or maybe it was anxiety. How many times was she going to have to defend her relationship with Ezra Hein? Or her lack of relationship. They'd decided tonight to just be friends. It was a decision they both made, they both agreed upon, and she couldn't help what anybody else thought.

"You've met him. His name is Ezra. He's a rancher. He raises the bison that we bought to serve in the restaurant. Among other things."

"*Jah*, I know all this," *Mamm* snapped. "I want to know why you saw fit to go bowling with him tonight."

How had her mother found out about that? "*Mamm,* we're just friends."

"You know what your father always said."

"*Jah,* I do. But that doesn't apply. He's a nice guy, and he wants nothing more from me other than friendship." Her heart gave a funny flip-flop when she said the words. It felt like a fish out of water, gasping for air, tossing around to find what it needed to live. Why she felt that way was anyone's guess.

Chapter Eight

Sadie wasn't the only one counting down the days till Saturday. Cora Ann was about as excited as any one girl could be. Sadie couldn't help but smile as she bustled around Saturday, humming under her breath as she waited tables, filled water glasses, and otherwise floated through the restaurant.

She half expected *Mamm* to tell them they couldn't go, but when three fifteen came and the blue pickup truck pulled up out front, she only said for them to be careful and not come home too late.

Sadie grabbed her coat while Cora Ann slipped her arms into hers, and together the two of them walked arm in arm out of the restaurant.

Ezra smiled when he caught sight of them, giving them a tiny wave as they approached.

"Hi," he said as he came around and opened the passenger side door.

"Hi," she said. It wasn't a date. They had decided that. They were friends. Nothing more. So why was she standing there acting all nervous?

Her gaze snagged Ezra's and they stood there for a moment just looking at each other while Cora Ann chatted on about all the dishes she had made with the bison meat.

Sadie rustled herself around and turned to her sister. "Cora Ann, I'm sure Ezra isn't interested in your bison-stuffed bell peppers," she admonished as gently as she could.

"He might be."

Ezra laughed. "Only if you make some for me." He waited for them to get in the truck, then shut the door behind them and went around to the driver's side again.

"Of course I will!" Cora Ann clapped her hands together in excitement. "When do you want them?"

Sadie opened her mouth to protest, to tell Cora Ann that after today she'd probably never see Ezra Hein again unless they ordered more bison meat. And who said even then they had to see him? But Ezra spoke first.

"I'm supposed to deliver some emu oil to the compounding pharmacy on Tuesday. How about then?"

"Deal." Cora Ann stuck out one hand to shake Ezra's. "Unless you'd rather have the bison steak I made. I put horseradish sauce on it. Yum."

"Either one is fine with me. They both sound delicious. You decide." He leaned forward a little as he pulled the truck back onto the road.

Sadie wanted to believe that he did that so he could see her and not necessarily to watch the traffic. But it was a dream of her own making. Hadn't they decided they could just be friends?

Ezra and Sadie rode in silence while Cora Ann chatted nonstop all the way to Taylor Creek. She didn't mind, though her thoughts went around in a circle the entire time. And she was more than glad when they pulled in front of the turnoff with its wrought iron sign declaring it "Hein's Exotic Animal Ranch" for all the world to see.

Ezra pulled his truck to a stop, and they all scrambled out, Cora Ann nearly climbing over Sadie in her haste to get out of the cab and see everything all at once.

A rusty-colored dog with long, pretty hair came sauntering up, nudging Sadie's hand as she watched Cora Ann run to the fence much like Daniel had when he first saw the exotics.

Sadie didn't fuss at her sister. Instead she patted the dog on the head and he sat down obediently. He wagged his tail and waited for her to touch him again.

"Silly dog. That's Rustyanna," Ezra said.

Sadie looked down at the dog, who merely blinked at her and continued to wag his tail. Her tail, she supposed. "That's a very interesting name."

"Yeah." Ezra laughed. "I thought we were getting a boy puppy when we got her."

Sadie raised one brow in his direction, but said nothing. "You couldn't tell?"

"Well, I was only ten. And I had my heart set on a boy dog. But she was the one that picked us, and I had already decided to name my new dog Rusty, so she became Rustyanna."

Sadie patted the dog on the head again, for the first time noticing the little gray hairs on her face. The pooch had to be at least fourteen. Sadie wasn't sure, but she thought that was very old for a dog. "I'm sorry he gave you such a silly name, sweetie."

"I've more than made up for it." Ezra reached into the pocket of his jeans and pulled out a dog treat. The dog's tail wagged fiercely as she waited for him to toss it toward her. He did, and quick as a wink, she snatched the treat from the air. Then she trotted off, back into the barn.

Sadie turned to look at her host. It was easier to think about him that way instead of a great-looking guy who had taken the time out of his day to go and get them from another town, then bring them here just so her sister could see his ranch animals. Yes, "host" was a much better word. Ezra had moved closer to Cora Ann, pointing out the different birds he had in the field. He truly was a remarkable kind of guy. This might be all they ever had, this friendship, but she was still thrilled to call him that.

After their walking tour of the ranch, Ezra returned to his guests. "Are you ready for some hot chocolate?" he asked. "Or some coffee? Logan's mom brought over some sugar cookies. We can eat some of those if you'd like."

"That sounds terrific," Cora Ann said. "Are they good cookies?"

"The best." Ezra smiled at the young girl. She really was adorable. Not so much like Sadie. Her hair was lighter and her eyes blue. But Cora Ann held the same kind of humming energy that Sadie trailed behind her like a cloud of dust.

"Will she give me the recipe?"

"Cora Ann!" Sadie cried.

"What? It's a compliment."

Sadie shook her head. "Not everyone feels that way. And not everyone wants to share the recipes."

"You never know until you ask."

Ezra watched the exchange between sisters, a smile twitching at the corners of his mouth. He kept quiet, though. He didn't want to interrupt and he surely didn't want to laugh and have them think he was making fun of them. They were so cute together. "I don't think Logan's mom will mind. But let's go in the house and taste them first before you decide."

The three of them walked to the house. Ezra's stomach sank. He hoped his mother was more understanding of him bringing Sadie out today. His mom had seemed so . . . bitter lately. It had started when his father left. And for that he couldn't blame his mother, but that had been seven years ago. Now it was time to move on, time to live, even if she couldn't start over. But he couldn't tell his mother that. He just couldn't. And he didn't think she would listen to him if he did.

He let them into the kitchen. "Hot chocolate or coffee?" he asked.

"Coffee," both girls said.

In no time at all, he had coffee brewed and the plate of cookies in the center of the table.

"Is that you, Ezra?"

"Yes, Mom." He could hear the swoosh of her wheelchair as she came closer to the kitchen. The small warning gave him just enough time to compose his expression before she came into the room.

"Oh," she said, coming to a swift halt. "You have guests."

She knew full well that he was going over to Wells Landing to get Sadie and Cora Ann. Why had she picked now to pretend like she didn't know?

"Mom, you remember Sadie. And this is her sister Cora Ann."

Cora Ann nodded politely. "It's nice to meet you."

His mother didn't respond. Well, at least not with words. Her mouth turned down a little more at the corners, and her cheeks took on that pinched expression that he knew all too well.

It was hard to overlook her sour attitude every day,

yet somehow he managed. The grace of God had no boundaries.

Unable to get a rise out of anyone, his mother tried again. "You'll ruin your supper eating cookies at this hour."

Cora Ann and Sadie seemed not to know what to say. Sadie ran a fingernail over a mar in the kitchen table and Cora Ann studied her sugar cookie as if the recipe for the lemon icing was right there on the top.

"It'll be fine." He managed to keep the exasperation and frustration out of his voice, but just barely. If only he could take her back a few years, maybe he could stop all this from happening. Maybe he could do something different so his father wouldn't leave. Not that he wanted him back on the ranch. He was fine without him, but his mother wasn't. And that broke his heart most of all.

Mom didn't speak, just gave a hard stare to the room in general, then whirled her chair around and left in a flash. She could turn that chair on a dime when she had a mind to.

"Why don't you have dinner with us?" Cora Ann asked. Her voice held that zing of excitement he had heard all day from her. He couldn't help but wonder if she was this excited about everything or if today was special. Whatever the case, her enthusiasm made him smile.

"Cora Ann," Sadie cried. She turned to Ezra, the smile of apology pulling at her lips. "I'm sorry. She gets so excited sometimes and . . ." She trailed off.

"It's okay," Ezra said. "In fact, I'd love to."

He was coming to supper with them. Tonight. At the restaurant. *Mamm* was not going to like this. But

Sadie wasn't willing to do anything about it. Ezra had been nothing but nice to them—sweet, caring, a perfect gentleman, as the *Englisch* would say. And there was no reason not to have him over for supper. He had done so much for them in the past few days, they practically owed him. Maybe if she put it to her *mamm* that way. . . .

Sadie shook her head.

"Everything okay over there?" Ezra asked, nodding in her direction as she sat opposite him at the oval table.

"*Jah,* sure," Sadie said.

"So why are you frowning?"

"You don't have to eat with us."

"Yes, he does!" Cora Ann exclaimed. "I invited him, and I want him. What's wrong with that?"

Nothing, really. How could she tell Cora Ann that it wasn't a good idea to sit down with Ezra and eat? Tonight. Where *Mamm* could see.

That was truly the problem. It wasn't eating with Ezra, or what they would talk about over supper or the hundred other things that had popped into her head since Cora Ann had issued her invitation. *Mamm* would have a fit. She was mad enough at them for coming here today, but to bring him back and blatantly sit and eat with him in front of her might possibly be her undoing.

"It's okay," he said.

But it wasn't. Sadie shook her head. "No, I'm wrong, come to dinner tonight with me. Uh, with us. At the restaurant. It'll be fun."

"If you're sure?" Ezra said.

"Yes, of course."

"Perfect." Cora Ann clapped her hands together with joy.

She wouldn't say that, Sadie thought as they all

piled back into Ezra's dusty pickup truck and headed back toward Wells Landing. It might end up being suspenseful at best. But how could she expect everyone around her to understand her growing friendship with Ezra if she allowed them to separate the two of them without good reason? To say he couldn't come eat with them because he was Mennonite was about the dumbest thing she had ever heard. Why couldn't they be friends? Not too long from now, Chris was going to head off on his trip, and she might never see him again. Over the years all of her girlfriends had gotten married, and she was continually the odd person out. Now she had this great friendship with Ezra, and she wasn't willing to let it go like it was nothing. So she would sit down with Ezra, eat a meal with him, and *Mamm* could just get used to it.

As she had on the trip to Taylor Creek, Cora Ann chatted all the way back to Wells Landing. Not that Sadie minded. She was more than willing to sit and listen to Cora Ann talk away while she herself could remain quiet, not knowing what to say.

Ezra pulled his truck to a stop in front of the restaurant, and they all piled out. Cora Ann skipped to the door, apparently more excited than she had been when she left.

Ezra took hold of Sadie's arm. "Are you sure about this?"

Sadie tossed back her head like she had seen *Englisch* girls do, hoping that she appeared as confident and collected as they always seemed. "Of course. We're only going to eat."

"Then why do I have a feeling this is some kind of challenge?"

She pressed her lips together and tried to think of a proper answer. Was she that transparent? Could he see her thoughts? "I just don't like how people—my friends—have acted since we met. They go around like we are doing something wrong."

Ezra nodded. "Regardless, I don't want to cause problems between you and your family. Or your friends."

Cora Ann stopped at the door, realizing that the two of them weren't right behind her. "Will you two come on?" She danced in place a moment or two, her impatience growing.

"Go on in," Sadie said. "We'll be right there."

Cora Ann seemed to think it over, then nodded, pulled open the door, and skipped her way inside.

"That only gives us a few minutes," Sadie said.

"Before what?"

"Before *Mamm* comes to find me."

"Is that what this is all about? Are you trying to get back at your mother or something?"

Sadie shook her head. "It has nothing to do with that. She's overprotective. My sister, Lorie, left the Amish late last year. She turned *Englisch*."

"No joke?"

Sadie closed her eyes a moment, trying to find the words to explain in the shortest way possible. "It's sort of complicated, but she never was Amish to begin with."

"That's a story I want to hear some day."

"You've got it. But for now . . ."

"Right. So what do I do? What do I say to her?"

"Just be yourself. And she'll have to love you."

"And if she doesn't?"

Sadie smiled. "She will. I'm sure of it."

Without another word, she turned on her heel and started toward the restaurant. She could hear his boots against the pavement as he walked behind her, so she knew he followed. They were just friends. And the sooner everybody got used to that idea, the better off they would all be. Hiding would not help the situation at all.

There were a few late diners in the restaurant, but most of the dinner crowd had long since cleared out. Melanie was wiping down tables while Andre, the young high school student *Mamm* had hired to help out on Saturday nights, was busing tables with a speed that made Sadie's head spin.

"Come on," she said, looping her arm through Ezra's.

He jumped, and she knew that touching him was unusual. She had no idea what got into her, touching him like that, but it felt so natural, so much a part of the two of them, that she had caved to the impulse. She was glad that she had, regardless of the look that Melanie shot her.

Sadie led Ezra to one of the newly cleaned booths on the other side of where Melanie worked.

"Are you wanting to eat dinner?" Melanie's tone held a "please say no" note that almost made Sadie smile. Maybe it would have if it hadn't been so ridiculous. Honestly, what did they expect the two of them to do in the middle of the restaurant, surrounded by her family?

"That's right. Is there any of the special left?"

"I think I can rustle up a plate or two." Melanie finished wiping down the vinyl booths and grabbed her spray bottle and extra bag before heading for the kitchen.

"You don't think she'll spit on my dinner or anything, do you?"

Sadie laughed. "Of course not. She might not understand our relationship, but she's got a great heart.

Give her some time. She'll come to realize that we're just friends."

"That's what we are, right? Friends?"

Sadie's heart gave a weird thump, and she was glad that Cora Ann had skipped on ahead. Now the thirteen-year-old was nowhere in sight, most likely in the back overseeing whatever food was left at the restaurant.

Sadie dropped her tone so only the two of them could hear. "If that's what you want."

"That's not what I asked you."

Sadie sighed. How could she explain? She really didn't know what she wanted, other than she wanted to spend time with Ezra. She'd never said anything so bold to a guy before, but somehow she knew that she needed to say it now. "I don't know how to say this."

"Just say it."

"Chris, the guy I was at the market with, we're just friends. Everybody thinks that we're going to get married, but we're not. In fact, he's going away in the summer, and I'll probably never see him again. But you can't say anything. No one here knows anything about that."

"Okay, I won't."

"All my friends are married. My sister left to be *Englisch*. My sister Melanie just got married too. And it feels like . . ."

"That you're all alone?"

"*Jah*, but more than that." She bit her lip, trying to find better words to explain her feelings. She had never been much good at this. "You're the first person I've met in a long time that I wanted to spend time with. I'm not sure why."

"Thanks a lot." Ezra chuckled.

"That's not what I meant," Sadie said, lightly smacking the top of his hand. "I don't know what it is about you, but there's something, and I guess I want to find out what it is. I enjoy your company." Wow, had she just said that?

Her words must not have been too forward, for Ezra didn't blink an eye. "I enjoy your company too."

"Is that all there is to this relationship stuff?"

"Have you never dated anyone before? Or been more than friends with a boy?"

"Just Chris."

"I'm not sure that counts."

"It's kind of hard to explain," Sadie said, "but . . . well, Chris and I have been friends for a long time. For a while I thought we would get married, and I think everyone else did as well. None of the boys considered me for anything more than a friend, even less than since everyone thought Chris had already tagged me. But then he decided to take this trip and I realized that I want to get married like everybody else. I suppose that's not going to happen now, but I really want to spend time with somebody I enjoy spending time with."

"It is hard to spend time with your newly married friends because they're always more interested in—"

"Each other more than me," they finished together.

They laughed for a moment, then the sound faded into a weird sort of silence Sadie didn't know what to think of. Ezra reached across the table where her hand lay and held it in his own.

"What if . . ." He sighed, shook his head. Then started again. "What if we were dating? What then?"

She wanted to snatch her hand away, yet at the same time she wanted to curl her fingers around his. Was he asking what she thought he was asking? "I don't know."

"You don't know what you think or you don't know how your family would feel?"

"Either one." A small laugh escaped her, followed by a hiccup. This whole ordeal was more than she had bargained for. What would she do if they were dating? Simply thinking about it sent a tingle through her.

"I know how your friends feel about us."

Us? There's an us?

"My family . . . my mother . . ." He shook his head. "Your family doesn't seem to approve. But do you think they ever will?"

This had to be the strangest conversation she'd ever had with a boy. Even stranger than the one in the truck after they went bowling. "I don't know."

"I'm willing to try if you are."

Sadie jerked her gaze to his. She searched his face for any signs that he was joking. But as sweet as Ezra was, he wasn't one to play around with people's emotions, or say things he didn't mean, or make too many jokes. No, he was serious.

"You want to date me?" The words were barely a whisper from her lips.

"I'd like to get to know you better. And I suppose that means dating. What do you think?"

It would go against friends and family. Yet before her stretched a life of spinsterhood. She could see it. Chris was the one who could keep her from that, not that he would marry her even if he stayed. Oh, he'd said he would. But she had a feeling they would remain friends until the day they died. And that would be all. He would be the eccentric bachelor, and she would be the spinster. Wrinkled as a raisin, the one no one wanted, no children. Alone.

She shook her head to release those thoughts. No, thinking about Ezra, going out on dates with him, getting to know him better, somehow the future didn't look so bleak. And she was willing to go against what her friends wanted from her, what her family thought she should do, what Ezra's mother wanted from him, if it meant the two of them being together. Was that too much to ask? To have a companion? Did it matter that he was a Mennonite? Should it matter if he was a Mennonite? No. No, it shouldn't. The Bible said they were all God's creatures. And just because their ancestors had split up over shunning and tore apart the Anabaptist church didn't mean that they had to spend their lives apart.

What was she even saying? Just because they started to see each other and maybe went on a few dates did not mean they were going to get married. But even if they did, it was nobody's business but theirs.

"Yes," she finally said. "I want to get to know you better too."

He released her hand in a hurry as her sister came up bearing a tray with two iced teas and two plates of roast beef with gravy. It wasn't Sadie's favorite item from the menu, but it was good comfort food on the January day when you might've just decided to go against the wishes of everybody in your life and date a boy from a different church.

"*Danki*," she said. Her sister only nodded in return. How much of the conversation had Melanie heard? And what of it was she willing to tell their *Mamm*?

She didn't care. She and Ezra had made the decision, and she was sticking to it. It was easy for everyone else to tell her to stay within the Amish faith and not to worry, to marry Chris, and all the other things that they continually said to try to make her feel better when they themselves had no idea what she was going through. They weren't twenty-two, all alone, with no boyfriend and no prospects. Until they walked in her shoes, they would never know how she truly felt.

But Ezra grabbed the pepper and liberally sprinkled it on his food.

Sadie watched with a smile on her face. One more thing she could chalk up that she knew about Ezra Hein. He liked black pepper. Not a bad trait in a guy.

Ezra picked up his fork and started to dig in, then stopped and looked back up at her before actually scooping up a bite. "Is this the bison?"

"No, that's beef. We'll have the bison another time."

"How about Monday?"

Sadie shook her head. "Monday's no good; bison's on the menu for Tuesday. That's when Cora Ann gets to experiment. New Food Tuesday, she calls it."

Ezra chuckled. "She's something else."

Sadie smiled in agreement. "That she is."

"So Tuesday?"

Sadie swallowed hard, her mouth suddenly dry. "Tuesday," she agreed. "It's a date."

Chapter Nine

He almost felt guilty being this excited over having dinner with someone. Almost.

Tuesday afternoon he made sure his mother had something to eat at the ready, then went to clean up.

He was standing in the bathroom, towel around his neck as he shaved, thoughts of Sadie Kauffman pinging around inside his brain. Maybe that was why he didn't hear his mother before she spoke.

"Shaving, Ezra? At this time of day?" She moved her small electric wheelchair around so she could face him as he scraped the whiskers from his chin.

"I am, uh, going out." Okay, so he should have told her long before now that he had dinner plans, but he didn't know how she would take it.

"On a workday?"

Ezra bit back a sigh. "Mom, every day is a workday." That was part of a rancher's life. "I'm not planning on staying out long." Just long enough to have dinner and see Sadie once again.

He really couldn't say why, but she pulled him in like a magnet, like a moth, like a hundred other things that couldn't resist something more powerful than them. And there was no fighting it. Not that he wanted to.

He had worked hard in the years since his father left. He had done everything he could for his mother and her advancing illness. He had been both provider and friend to her, when everyone else had turned away.

True, the Mennonites did not traditionally shun. But after his father decided he could take no more, he had walked out without looking back. It didn't take long before the good people of Taylor Creek started to wonder what his mother had done to make him leave. No one said anything outright, but he'd heard whispers when no one thought he was around, when no one thought he would hear. That was the problem with small towns and even smaller Mennonite communities. Word spread like wildfire through dry timber. Of course, it didn't help that his mother's disposition had turned sour and she stopped going out herself. These days she didn't even make it to church.

"So where are you heading off to tonight?" Her voice held an edge that he knew all too well. When he told her what he was doing, she was going to explode.

"I'm going over to Wells Landing."

His mother crossed her arms, a sure sign that a storm was brewing. "And what are you going to do there?"

Ezra wiped the last remains of the shaving cream from his face, inspected the job in the mirror, then smacked on some aftershave for good measure. "I'm going to have supper with Sadie Kauffman and her family. At the restaurant."

"The Amish girl?"

Ezra turned, for the first time facing his mother.

"Mom, she invited me to come eat at the restaurant and try out the bison meat recipes that her sister has been experimenting with. That's all." Okay, so that was a flat-out lie, but what was he supposed to do?

"And you didn't think to take me?"

"Would you have come along if I had asked?"

His mother frowned. "Well now, we'll never know, will we? Since you didn't ask."

Another sigh swallowed back and Ezra replied, "Would you like to go with me tonight and have dinner at the Kauffman Family Restaurant?"

"No." Before he could respond, she turned her chair around and headed back down the hallway.

Ezra tried not to be frustrated with his mother's attitude and bitterness. As far as he could tell, she needed to turn to God and trust Him more, but she didn't seem to be able. And frankly that broke his heart.

Simply by chance, he had found someone he wanted to spend time with. And he was going to spend time with Sadie Kauffman whether his mother understood that or not.

His mother's consternation followed Ezra out the door as he left half an hour later. She was sitting at the table eating—if pushing her food around on her plate could be called eating—when he palmed the truck keys and said his good-bye.

She didn't even utter a grunt in response, and he hated himself all the more for continuing on his way. He opened the truck door, got inside, then leaned his forehead against the steering wheel. Why did everything have to be so hard where she was concerned? He hated the fact that he hated how she treated him.

Where had all the forgiveness gone that she had been taught her entire life?

He sat back and started the engine, knowing there were no answers to those questions. He backed out of the drive and headed down the road, each mile bringing more relief from his mother's attitude.

He was not going to feel guilty tonight. A friend had invited him to dinner. A friend who could potentially be more than a friend. But he was meeting more than just Sadie. He was going to eat dinner with Cora Ann and Daniel and maybe even Melanie and her husband Noah, if he understood Sadie right during the invitation. She'd said they were eating together as a family. And he was looking forward to it. Trying the food that Cora Ann had made, eating the bison meat that he had produced.

He really didn't eat a lot of his own product, simply because his mother didn't like the taste of the bison meat. She thought he was wasting his time by raising the big creatures and thought he should focus more on being a dairy farmer. But he had wanted more when he had taken over the farm. He wanted to do something different, something that stood out among the crowd. Something that no one else in Taylor Creek or in Wells Landing had done. That was how Hein's Exotic Animal Ranch came into being. And he was expanding all the time. It was challenging and fun and he loved it, whether his mother understood it or not. Still, it would be nice to enjoy the fruits of his labor for once. And the fact that he didn't have to cook the meal? Even better.

By the time he pulled his truck to a stop in front of the restaurant, the tension had left his shoulders. Mostly, anyway.

He looked in the rearview mirror to make sure his hair was in place, grimaced at his reflection, made sure his teeth were clean, then got out of the truck. He was being ridiculous, he knew. But he wanted everything tonight to be great. Maybe because he knew that the people around them didn't understand their relationship. Didn't understand what drew them together, an Amish woman and a Mennonite man. But how could anybody explain the laws of love? Well, he backtracked, this wasn't love. But this was where things like that started. Strangely enough, he liked the idea. Never before had he thought about having a family of his own. But as the thought settled around him, he realized that having a wife would bring so much joy into his life as well as ease the chores that he had both around the house and on the ranch. The only problem was his mother.

He pushed himself into the restaurant, the bell on the door jingling as he came through.

Cora Ann came bustling up. "Can I help you—" She stopped. "Ezra! Come on, let's eat." She grabbed his arm and dragged him into the restaurant, back to a table that was a little larger than the others. Daniel was already seated there coloring a picture. Ezra had seen him do that many times before, and he figured that coloring was Daniel's go-to activity when nothing else was going on around him.

"Hey there, Daniel."

"Hey." Daniel did not look up from his artwork. In fact, he dipped his head even farther, his nose almost touching the paper on the table.

Ezra smiled to himself. When Daniel colored he went to his own world. There were times when Ezra wished he could do the same.

"You're here." Sadie's words were nothing more than a gush of air in the wind.

He turned to face her, a smile on his lips. "I'm here."

She stood for a moment just looking at him, and he took a minute to look back. There really was something about Sadie Kauffman. She wasn't a beauty like he had seen, those girls that drew people to them like flies. That didn't mean her face was hard to look at. It was small with a petite nose and big hazel eyes. A few freckles danced across her nose, and her mouth was bracketed with small dimples. But there was something more about her, something that shone from within her that no one else around had. He didn't know what it was, but he wanted to. He wanted to know what made her so special, what drew him to her.

"You look really nice tonight."

She frowned and looked down at her dress. She was still wearing black, all black from shoulders to toe. Only her prayer *kapp* was white. And he couldn't wait to see her in something other than that dark color. Maybe a green that would bring out the blue in her eyes. Or maybe it would bring up the little flecks of brown. "I do?"

"Yeah." Ezra nodded. "You do."

The blush that rose into her cheeks put a smile on his lips. Had no one ever told her that she looked nice? Or that she was pretty? What was wrong with the men of Wells Landing?

"Are you ready to eat?" Sadie seemed to have intentionally changed the topic of conversation, and he let her.

"Yeah, I am."

"Ezra!" Cora Ann rushed up and grabbed his hand, jumping up and down a little as she squeezed his fingers. "I'm so glad you're here! I'm so glad you're here!"

Ezra gently extracted his fingers from her grasp, then nodded toward her. "I was promised a meal, you know. Something special."

Cora Ann smiled. "You are going to love this."

"I hope so. I'm hungry."

"Did you have problems on the ranch today?" Cora Ann led him to the table and pointed to the seat next to Daniel. "Sit right here, and I'll go get your food."

"What about—" He broke off as Cora Ann hustled from view. He turned back to Sadie. "Is everyone else eating too?"

"Of course." She turned to walk away, then stopped and turned back. "I should help get the food. Would you wait here with Daniel, please?"

"Of course."

A few minutes later Cora Ann and Sadie bustled out of the kitchen carrying platters of food.

"These are stuffed bell peppers," Cora Ann explained. "But instead of using green peppers you use red ones, and instead of using ground beef you use—"

"Bison meat," he supplied.

Cora Ann set his plate in front of him. "Then there's au gratin potatoes with scallops and scallions. Those are both different things."

He was glad she told him that because he had no idea what either one of them were.

"And here's a squash casserole and a small salad. That's today's special for New Food Tuesday."

He looked at the plate of gourmet food, and his stomach growled. He might not be familiar with all of the ingredients, but it smelled delicious. He unwrapped his silverware and placed his napkin in his lap. "It looks great." He glanced around at the girls, who stood above him, staring, watching as he went to take his first bite. "Aren't you going to eat with me?"

Cora Ann jumped. "Oh!" She pulled out a chair and slid into it, then propped her elbow onto the table and her chin in her hand.

That wasn't exactly eating.

Sadie took a seat across from him, but at least she grabbed the plate as if she were truly about to eat as well.

"I've never eaten a stuffed pepper before. And I'm not really sure how," Ezra confessed.

"Well," Cora Ann said, "some people do it differently than others. But I like to eat all the filling out, then eat the bell pepper at the end, using my bread."

He wasn't sure about eating nothing but pepper and bread.

"Don't listen to her," Sadie said. "This is how you do it." She took a knife and cut the pepper down the middle, then proceeded to chop it into pieces, each one with part of the filling stacked on top. "Then you fork up a bite like this and eat it."

He watched as she put the bite in her mouth, then looked back down at her plate. It was better by far than watching her chew and staring like an idiot. "You want to trade plates now?"

She laughed. "Don't trust your knife skills?"

"Exactly." She'd cut the pepper like she had been doing it for years. He had the feeling that instead of little bite-size morsels of pepper and bison meat filling he would end up with something resembling a mutilated casserole.

"My pleasure." Sadie handed him the plate as he handed his over to her.

Cora Ann looked from each of them to the other. "Is it good?"

"You haven't tried it yet?" Ezra asked.

"Oh yeah." Cora Ann nodded so fiercely her prayer *kapp* strings danced and bobbed. "But I like everything. I want to know what you guys think."

"Well," Sadie started, swallowing the bite as she surveyed the food on her plate. "It's good, but it needs something."

Cora Ann sat back in her chair. "I knew it. I knew I should've added some basil."

Ezra wasn't sure exactly what basil would do for the meal, but he was enjoying himself nonetheless. He was sitting across from what had to be the prettiest girl in Wells Landing with her sister, who loved to cook, and their little brother, who still hadn't stopped coloring long enough to eat.

"Is he going to eat anything tonight?"

"He only eats things like peanut butter with apple jelly."

"It's a color/texture thing," Sadie explained. "He only eats tan foods."

"Tan foods?"

Sadie nodded. "You know, graham crackers, peanut butter, wheat bread, tan-colored things."

"I see." He had never heard such a thing.

"Oh," Cora Ann said, jumping up from her chair so quickly she almost knocked it backward. "I forgot to get the iced tea." She hustled off before Ezra had a chance to say even one word.

"That girl." Sadie shook her head. "I wish I knew what I wanted as clearly as she does."

"You don't know what you want?"

There came that blush again. And Sadie ducked

her head. "You know, from life. All she wants to do is cook, make recipes, and try out new foods. Who knows what she'll ask for next week. Maybe alligator meat."

Ezra chuckled. "I'm not raising alligators. No matter how cute she is."

Sadie laughed. And he loved the sound. "No, but if we don't watch out she'll have us going down to Louisiana to buy one."

"That's interesting that your mother allows her to pick out foods for the restaurant."

Sadie nodded again. "It is. But Cora Ann has always loved to cook. And the restaurant is all we do. Plus . . ."

"Plus what?" he asked.

Her eyes flickered ever so briefly to her brother, then she lowered her voice to where she knew he couldn't hear. "Since *Dat* died, she has been pretty lenient. You know, my sister even left go live with the *Englisch.*"

"That's right. You told me about that."

"At first *Mamm* wasn't very happy about it, but later she came to realize that Lorie had a different path to take in life. And she didn't hold that against her."

"And you don't know what your path is." He meant for it to sound like a question, but it didn't. Sadie frowned a bit, but he could see the wrinkles on her smooth brow and the flicker of the corners of her mouth as they turned down, then pulled back into place. "I thought I did. But now I'm not so sure."

That was a loaded statement if Ezra had ever heard one. But he didn't have time to ask as Cora Ann bustled back in with two glasses of iced tea.

"Here you go." She sat one glass in front of him and one in front of Sadie, then returned to her seat and the same position she had been in before.

It was a bit unnerving to have the cook stare at him so intently while he was eating her food, but it really was delicious. And he didn't think it needed anything at all. But for now, he was eating, taking in everything that Sadie had told him, and he would tell the chef later what a wonderful meal it truly was.

Sadie could not believe that she was sitting across the table from Ezra, eating bison meat and talking about her sister. Sure, she didn't have a lot of experience where guys were concerned, but surely she could find a better topic of conversation than her sister leaving to go live with Zach Calhoun in Tulsa. But it was better by far than talking about the rest of the things that happened around her father's death, like them finding his tattoo, and Lorie painting pictures in the storeroom and not telling anybody. The whole thing had been so hard on them.

Sadie felt that wearing black every day dragged it out even more. She missed her dad terribly, but did she have to wear black to prove it? She did it because that was what she was supposed to do. But if she could shed the black, put on something pretty and colorful, something that her father would have liked, she might be able to see him smiling down from heaven.

She took another bite of her stuffed pepper and wished it had more flavor. She had long since realized that it wasn't anything that Cora Ann had done to the recipe, but it was more about being across the table from Ezra and catching sight of those brown eyes every so often. Each time he looked at her, her heart stuttered in her chest. What exactly did that mean?

Maybe she was just nervous. *Mamm* had made no

secret that she didn't think Sadie should be hanging out with a Mennonite guy. But what was the harm in it, honestly? Sure, they said they were dating, but that didn't mean a whole lot at this point. They hadn't been out even one time yet. Not really. She didn't count the two visits to his ranch. Or meeting him at the market. No, this was really their first date, and they had two people hanging out with them.

What could *Mamm* find wrong with that? Still, the thought made Sadie a little nervous.

Mamm would read too much into it. Just because Sadie was spending time with Ezra didn't mean anything more than they were spending time together. They had said they were going to date, but no one else knew that. How could they get to know each other unless they did just that? Who knew, they might not like each other after the second date. Her father had always said never date a man you wouldn't marry, but would she marry Ezra Hein?

She looked up and caught that brown gaze. Once again her stomach dropped two inches, and she found it hard to swallow the bite that she had been chewing for who knew how long.

She couldn't say if she would marry him or not. Could she? She barely knew him. And the only way she would get to know him any better was to date him.

It made logical sense in her head, but she had a feeling that if she said those exact words to *Mamm*, the understanding would be a long time in coming.

They finished their meal, and somehow Sadie managed to get it down without a grimace. Again, it wasn't because it wasn't tasty, she simply had an awful time trying to eat with Ezra right across from her.

Cora Ann took up their plates and came back a few

minutes later with a cheesecake for dessert. Sadie would've rather had something a little more tradition- ally Amish, like shoo-fly pie, but this was Cora Ann's night to try out a new menu.

Sadie had eaten cheesecake once, and it wasn't bad. She liked it when they put cherries on top, and Cora Ann had used some sort of blackberry sauce. Where the girl had gotten blackberries in late January Sadie had no idea.

She forked up a bite and was about to put it in her mouth when she caught Ezra's expression of pure bliss.

"Wow," he said around his mouthful of cheesecake. "What is this?"

Sadie couldn't tell if his expression was one of pain or extreme pleasure. "It's cheesecake."

He forked up another bite and shoveled it into his mouth before the first one had been swallowed. "Just regular cheesecake?" he asked. "I've had cheese- cake before, but not like this."

Sadie laughed. He ate the cheesecake with such joy that she offered him her piece.

"You don't want it?"

"I'd rather have pie. You can have this piece." She offered it across the table to him. He didn't hesitate and took it from her, eating it in three bites.

Cora Ann took that moment to walk back with two cups of steaming coffee. She stopped short, noticing that both plates of cheesecake were empty and both were on Ezra's side of the table.

"I brought you coffee, but your cheesecake is gone. Would you like another piece?"

Ezra smiled. "Do you have another piece?"

Sadie had never seen anyone eat with such joy on their face. "Get him some more, will you, Cora Ann?"

Cora Ann set the tray of coffee down next to Sadie and well out of Daniel's reach, then hustled back to the kitchen to get some more dessert.

But instead of bringing one slice out on a plate, she brought the entire pie plate and set it in front of Ezra. "Eat what you like. I'm not sure anyone else here really enjoys it."

"It's good," Sadie said.

"But?"

"It's too sour," Sadie said. "I like a sweeter dessert." She looked over at Ezra. "Don't you?"

He looked back up at her, a strange expression on his face. "What was that?"

Sadie shook her head. "Never mind." He was too far gone in the cheesecake to pay attention to much else.

After three pieces of cheesecake, Ezra sat back and patted his stomach, apparently full.

"Did you get enough to eat?" Cora Ann asked.

"More than enough."

"Why don't you walk it off in the park?" Cora Ann suggested.

Sadie whirled around to stare at her sister. "Are you going with us?"

Her sister shook her head, a mischievous gleam in her eyes. "No, I've got work to do, and Daniel is still here. Why don't you two go on ahead?"

"That sounds like a good idea," Ezra said. "I haven't eaten that much in I don't know when."

How could she say no? "Daniel, do you want to go with us?" Sadie asked. There was something bothersome about being alone with Ezra in the approaching darkness. It wouldn't be long before the whole town was blanketed in the midnight-colored sky.

"No." Daniel shook his head, not bothering to look

up from his coloring. He had gone into one of his zones and would have to finish before he would interact fully with them again.

Sadie pulled on her coat and her scarf and bundled up to keep from getting too cold outside. Surely they would take one lap around the park, then they would come back and it would be time for Ezra to leave. Not that she wanted him to. But the whole situation was making her so nervous she could hardly stand it.

They started out of the restaurant, Ezra as bundled up as she, though he had on a black coat and a baseball hat like she had seen Luke Lambright wear. The ends of his blond hair curled up around the edges, and Sadie had to squelch the urge to reach up and straighten the curl out to see if it would pop right back into place when she released it.

So not appropriate. What was it about this man that had her wanting to do things that she had never thought about in her life?

"You know, I've been to this town I don't know how many times, and I never really noticed the park."

"How could you miss it? It's right smack in the middle of town."

"I know. Kinda silly, isn't it?"

"Not if you've got your mind on work, I suppose. Isn't that why you come to Wells Landing?"

"Yeah, usually. Sometimes the grocer lets me put an ad up on the bulletin board for meats and things. And I bring some stuff down occasionally to the compounding pharmacy. But mostly it's families from Tulsa who want fresh meat who come to get my products. And I sell it at a butcher shop there."

"I had no idea." Sadie bumped against his shoulder as they walked along. They were almost in front of the bakery now. It was only a step across the street, and they would be at the park. No one was around; after all, it was late January. It hadn't been extremely cold lately, but it was cold enough that most people didn't want to go out and swing at six o'clock at night.

Sadie headed across the street to the park. A small patch of sunlight still shone, though most of the sky had turned a shade somewhere between dark purple and dark blue. The park was illuminated with tall street lamps that buzzed and hummed as flies flew around them. She sat down in a swing, fully expecting Ezra to sit in the one next to her. Instead he walked around behind her and started to push. How long had it been since someone had actually pushed Sadie in a swing? She couldn't remember. Maybe when she was in school?

"That's too much, Ezra!" She felt like she could reach out her toes and touch the setting sun. "Slow me down now, please." Along with the feeling of freedom, she had a pitch in her stomach that had nothing to do with height and everything to do with the man she was with.

"Baby," Ezra teased. But still he moved around in front of her and caught her swing, easing it back slowly again and again until she was barely moving. He moved his hands up the chains as Sadie stood, trapped somewhere between his arms and the swing.

A heartbeat passed between them and then another. And another, until Sadie wasn't sure how long they had stood there, just staring at each other.

"Ezra," she started, her voice shaking and unsure. What was happening between them? Was this the beginning of true love? Whatever it was, she never wanted it to end.

"You know what I think?" he asked, his voice a whisper in the fading light.

"What?" Sadie asked. It could be anything, but she had her hopes. She wished he was thinking about her and him and how they should take things slowly, not rush into anything. Give them both some time to decide what they truly wanted from each other.

"I'm thinking about kissing you."

Chapter Ten

Sadie's heart pounded in her chest. Kiss her? He was thinking about kissing her?

The night stood still. Even the Oklahoma wind stopped as Sadie waited, breathless. The January sky had been painted indigo, and a million stars twinkled above their heads.

Ezra took a step closer, and Sadie's indrawn breath sucked in the clean smell of him, detergent and after-shave. He seemed to be moving at a snail's pace, as if he was allowing her time to tell him no. To stop him. Like she could find those words in her heart.

Suddenly nothing else mattered. Nothing was as important as the two of them and right now. Not their families, not their faith, not their friends.

He took another step toward her, and Sadie shivered. Not from the cold, but from anticipation. How had she only known Ezra such a short time, yet she felt so connected to him?

Her dad used to say that there was someone out there for everyone, that God made someone special for them all. Up until tonight, she had thought that Chris was her someone special. Even after he told her he was flying away to Europe, probably never to return. But now, *now*, she knew her special someone was Ezra Hein. Another step closer and she wanted to shout at him to hurry. Not the most romantic thing she could say, but the anticipation would be the death of her. She had waited her entire life for this kiss.

"Sadie!" Cora Ann ran down the sidewalk toward the park. She didn't have on her coat, though the tail ends of her scarf trailed behind her, a base for the trailing prayer *kapp* strings.

Sadie took a step back, noticing that Ezra did the same as Cora Ann drew closer to them. Suddenly, the night didn't seem quite so magical, and she wondered if perhaps it had ever been.

"*Mamm* wants you." Cora Ann looked from one of them to the other as if she could sense the anticipation that still hung in the air around them.

"What does she want?" Sadie asked. Her voice held a trembling edge as unsteady as her feet. If she felt this way in anticipation of Ezra's kiss, how would she feel when he actually touched his lips to hers? The thought made her light-headed. She resisted the urge to sit down in the swing again.

"I don't know. She said to come in now." Again Cora Ann looked from one of them to the other, as if somehow she knew what she had interrupted.

Ezra cleared his throat. "I guess we should be getting back, then." His voice rasped, and she hoped it was from his own feelings for her and not that he was coming down with something. She would feel terrible if he caught a cold because he had traipsed out into the park to push her in the swings on a cold night.

"*Jah*," Sadie agreed.

Cora Ann turned on her heel and started back

toward the restaurant, pausing every so often to turn around and make sure they were still following her.

Sadie walked next to Ezra, so close, and yet there was such a distance between them now. As if the interruption had placed a chasm in the middle that couldn't be scaled.

They were silent on their way back to the restaurant. Sadie didn't know what to say anyway. She walked along next to him, wondering if his mind was as full of churning thoughts as hers was.

"I guess I better be getting back home," Ezra said. He stopped at his truck, as if his feet had been dipped in glue.

Sadie couldn't blame him. If *Mamm* had sent Cora Ann after her, then surely she wouldn't have a warm reception for Ezra. Her mother made no secret that she didn't think that Ezra was fit to court her. But Sadie thought the reasons were ridiculous. What was wrong with him? He was a great guy, kind and loving. Yet *Mamm* couldn't see past his being a Mennonite to the person he was in his heart.

"*Jah*," Sadie agreed. "I'm glad you came to dinner tonight."

Ezra smiled, a flash of teeth in the indigo night. "Me too. Your sister is quite a cook."

Sadie smiled. "That she is. She'll make some man a fine *fraa* one day."

Ezra shifted from one foot to the other, as if he wasn't sure what to say next.

Sadie had no idea either. As far as dates went, this was pretty much her first one. She and Chris tended to hang out with other members of their group and didn't do a whole lot alone, maybe a walk here and there, but never in Chris's presence had she felt like she did when she was around Ezra.

"Well," Ezra started again. "I really should be going. Thank you for dinner."

"You're welcome." Was this how it ended? She knew he wouldn't dare kiss her in front of the family restaurant. Plain people didn't go in for a lot of public displays, and certainly not where their overprotective *eldra* could see.

She tried not to deflate with the disappointment. It was probably too soon anyway. They needed to take things slow. What happened if, a few weeks down the road, they decided that they weren't as compatible as they appeared right now? No, it was better this way, regardless of how disappointed she felt.

"When can I see you again?"

Sadie's heart soared. He wanted to see her again! Those had to be the sweetest words she'd ever heard.

"I don't know." It was Tuesday now, and they would have to work through the week. She knew Ezra was really busy on his ranch. Having him come to Wells Landing during the week would take more effort than she would've liked.

"Someone usually rents the rec center in Taylor Creek on Friday nights. Everyone gets together and plays volleyball. How about then?"

He wanted to take her to play volleyball? She hadn't got to do anything like that in a long time. "I think that sounds like a lot of fun."

"Pick you up at five thirty? Six o'clock?"

Sadie smiled. "Better make that five thirty." She didn't want to go a minute longer than she had to before she got to see Ezra again.

* * *

Chris walked to the edge of the field, looking out across the tiny green sprouts of winter wheat. It would be a while longer before they came out of their dormancy and started to grow again. Until then, there was more than plenty to do on the farm. There was always something. Never a day off, never time to rest—the farm sucked the energy out of him. It stifled him, made him feel like he was drowning. He couldn't wait to get away from it all.

A couple more days and it would be February. He was counting down the months until June. He hadn't said a word to his folks about going to Europe. They wouldn't understand. Not at all. How could he even explain it?

It wasn't something that he had taught himself. He just had this longing down deep inside, the urge and desire to see places, places that some people only saw in books. There was the huge Eiffel Tower in Paris, and Big Ben, the clock tower in London. There were the cliffs in Ireland and Scotland, beautiful rivers in Germany, and all the wonderful things the Romans left behind in Italy. He wanted to see it all. After all that, he might even go farther. Maybe over to Greece and beyond. There was so much to see, so much he wanted to witness with his own eyes.

It was nothing he could explain. It was a part of him as much as his eye color or his hair color, and he couldn't change either one of those even if he wanted to.

He continued around the edge of the field and swung himself back up onto his tractor. The fields were in good shape. It didn't look like the deer were munching on the sprouts, and that was a good sign. There were scarecrows posted all around in the woods that butted up against the Flauds' fields. Hopefully they would keep most of the critters out. But he knew that it would still have to be watched constantly. It was all part of a farmer's life. And he hated it.

He turned his tractor onto the highway and putted back toward the drive to his house. Well, his parents' house, the one that he shared with them and his younger brother, Johnny. As was Amish tradition, Johnny would inherit the house and the farm one day. That was perfectly okay with Chris, because that gave him the opportunity to get out. Johnny liked to farm well enough. Some men were cut out for that. Chris wasn't one of them. For twenty-plus years he'd been working side by side with his father, plowing, planting, hoeing, weeding, spraying, irrigating, and planting again. It was a never-ending, vicious cycle that he wanted no part of. How could a man look at a farm, look at mere plants, and think that they had done something worthwhile? He just didn't understand.

He wasn't trying to say that farming wasn't a valuable endeavor; it just wasn't the job for him. He was more than ready to set his boots on a different continent instead of this dusty Oklahoma farm.

He parked the tractor to the side of the barn, then went in to wash his hands before heading into the house. The screen door banged behind him as it always did. It was one of the few things that he would miss when he left. He didn't hate his family or want to be away from them, but he felt so closed in. Even out in the open fields full of green and growing wheat, he felt like the sky was low, sitting right on top of his head, and the plants were jerking at his arms, pulling him this way and that when all he wanted to do was get away.

"Just in time, brother." Johnny came up out of nowhere and smacked him on the back. A few years younger than him, Johnny was everything that Chris wasn't. He was jovial, always had a smile on his face and a joke on his lips. His eyes twinkled merrily. Chris didn't know anyone who enjoyed life more than Johnny.

"I know when dinner is."

"Then get on in here and get a plate." His mother stood at the doorway of the kitchen. As usual when she cooked, she had a dish towel thrown over one shoulder. Her cheeks were pink from the heat in the kitchen, and the little wisps of her hair that had managed to work free during the day had curled around her face. He would miss her most of all. She was the one ray of brightness they had on the farm. Her and Johnny. He would miss them both. But his father . . . Chris pushed that thought away. His father was his father, and there was no changing that. But they had never been able to see eye to eye. On anything. No matter what he did, or how hard he tried, it was never good enough for Merlin Flaud.

Chris knew that most likely his father had grown up the same way, with stern parents who wanted what they wanted when they wanted it. He could barely remember his *dawdi* on his father's side, but he remembered enough to know that his father was a walking image of that man. Every time Chris looked at his *dat* he saw what he would one day become. It wasn't what he wanted. He didn't want to be old, gray, and bitter, with his mouth turning down at the corners as he stomped around in the dirt and tried to grow wheat in impossible climates.

Oklahoma had the craziest weather of any state in any country he'd ever read about. They had earthquakes and floods, blizzards and tornadoes. Anything weather related that could happen, happened in Oklahoma, and it happened with a vengeance. No wonder his father appeared so downtrodden all the time. Trying to grow something on this land was next to impossible. It was stressful, constant, and wearing on one's soul. Chris couldn't wait to get away.

"Come on," Johnny said, nudging him toward the table. His mother sat the pan of biscuits down next to the rest of the food and wiped her hands on that ever-present dish towel.

"Where's *Daf?*" Johnny asked.

Chris felt a stab of guilt. He should've asked where their father was, but he hadn't. Truth was, he really didn't care.

He closed his eyes and said a small prayer for forgiveness for such a mean thought about the man who brought him into this world. Yet these days, the times between their differences was growing shorter and shorter. Chris saw that one day soon there would be a time when they couldn't get along at all. He was getting out before then.

He'd told Sadie that he'd be back. Aside from his mother and his brother, he would miss Sadie most. She had been his friend for so long he couldn't imagine life without her, but he knew she wouldn't go with him. She'd joined the church long ago, and he felt more than guilt at the thought that she had been waiting on him to join the church and ask her to marry him. She deserved better than the likes of him. She deserved a man who wanted the same things that she wanted: a farm, a house, kids, and a green tractor to drive around the fields. She wanted Sunday in church, Sunday night singing. All that and more should be hers.

He had made his plans, and as much as he cared for Sadie, they didn't include her. He didn't blame her for breaking up with him, but he couldn't stop the stab of jealousy when he heard that she had been running around with a Mennonite boy from Taylor Creek. He had no claim to Sadie Kauffman. Not anymore. He couldn't even say they were friends any longer.

"There he is." *Mamm* sat the bowl of applesauce on the table and plunked a spoon down next to it as Chris heard the door open and close, then the swish of fabric as his father removed his coat and the thump of his boots as he came to the head of the table.

His father pulled his chair out and sat down, not saying a word as he bowed his head and expected the others to follow for the silent prayer.

Chris had no words for the prayer. He should be asking for forgiveness for his unkind thoughts, forgiveness for putting Sadie through so much when all she wanted was to get married, peace for his family, then the months to speed by quickly so that he could move on. But none of those things would come to his mind. All he could do was sit, hands clasped in front of him, head bowed, as he waited for his father to end the prayer.

An eternity passed before his father raised his head and reached for the first bowl of food.

Chris passed the biscuits to Johnny, who smiled and thanked him, then started telling the story about one of the horses in the barn. Chris half listened, just enough that he could nod every so often and at least appear like he was following the conversation. But his mind was in other places. Off in Europe, wondering about Sadie, what to make of this Mennonite man who had attached himself quite nicely to her.

Even more guilt swamped Chris. Suddenly he realized that in keeping Sadie as his best friend for all these years, he had shielded her from any other suitor in

the district. Maybe even the whole entire settlement.
She had never dated anyone, never been out with
anyone, and he was quite sure that she'd never kissed
anyone. Now she had taken up with some racy Mennonite who drove a truck and wore patterns. Who
knew how the man would treat his Sadie.

Chris resisted the urge to push his chair back and
excuse himself from the meal even though he had not
eaten a thing. He needed to talk to Sadie, and soon,
before this Mennonite took more liberties than he was
entitled.

Sadie was a good girl, but she didn't have any experience in the ways of the world, and Chris was terrified
that the Mennonite would take advantage of her. The
thought sent ice water running through his veins.
Tonight, he vowed. He would head over and talk to her
tonight. Before this thing with the Mennonite went any
further.

It was after seven and long past the dinner rush,
but Sadie heard the bell on the door and looked up to
see who was coming in. This time of day it was most
likely a regular coming in to pick up a snack or a pie
for the next day. The tourists had long since gone
home to their families, made themselves dinner, and
were settling in for a night of whatever tourists did
when they weren't being tourists.

Instead it was Chris, coming in for . . .

"Hi." She hadn't talked to him for a couple of days.
She tried to pretend that he had been the one that was
busy, but in all actuality it was her. Somehow she had
been drawn in by Ezra Hein and all the things he
had mentioned the other day. She could hardly think
of anything else but kissing him, dating him, and not

worrying about what their families thought. Somehow she knew if she saw Chris, she would spill it all, and she wasn't sure how he would feel about that. So she kept her distance to keep from having to tell Chris anything.

"Can I talk to you for a little bit?" Chris asked. He shifted in place, uncomfortable, as if the situation was delicate as a spiderweb.

Sadie nodded. "*Jah*. Of course." She bustled over to where Cora Ann was wiping down the high chairs in preparation for an early closing.

"Cora Ann, I'm going out for a minute to talk to Chris. Do you have everything here okay?"

Cora Ann looked from her to Chris, then back again. "*Jah*. I've got it." She leaned in closer, her eyes flicking toward Chris before settling back on Sadie. "Unless you don't want me to have it, and then I don't."

Sadie tried not to laugh at her sister's antics. Instead she shot her sister a quick smile. "I don't believe that will be necessary. But thanks."

With a small shake of her head, Sadie left her sister and went to grab her coat and scarf by the door. In no time at all, she and Chris were walking down the street where Main Street narrowed and led to a residential district.

Sadie loved the little town. It was a hub of excitement, the park in the center and shops all around. She loved everything about it. Except for tonight. But it wasn't the town that was causing her those feelings, but the man at her side.

"What's the matter, Chris?" He had been acting so strange lately. She remembered his voice the other day on the phone when he canceled bowling. Strange that she hadn't talked to him since then. Before his announcement they had talked every day. She supposed it was understandable, this change in the dynamics of their relationship. But she missed him. He had been her friend for so long. "Are you okay?" she asked.

"Of course I am. It's you I'm worried about."

"Me? Why are you worried about me?"

"I've been hearing you're going around with some Mennonite guy."

Sadie stopped in her tracks. Chris took two more steps before he realized she wasn't next to him and backtracked to where she stood. She folded her arms and waited on him. "Some Mennonite guy? That's what everyone is saying about me?"

Even in the shadows of Main Street, she could see the confusion flickering across Chris's face. "*Jah*," he said. "Is it not true?"

"I've been hanging out with Ezra Hein, and he's Mennonite. But I wouldn't call him 'some Mennonite guy.'" She couldn't quite explain the uncharacteristic anger she felt at Chris's words. Was it because he had said them? Or because everyone in Wells Landing was talking about her and Ezra behind their backs?

Still, she should've known. She just didn't expect this from Chris.

"That's what I said, some Mennonite guy."

"I happen to like Ezra very much."

"He's Mennonite."

"I wish everyone would quit saying that." Sadie propped her hands on her hips and coldly eyed him. "So what?"

"Really, Sadie?" Chris frowned at her. "What would your mother say if you ended up dating a Mennonite guy?"

"I cannot answer that." She'd had about enough of this. She had thought Chris had come to talk to her about something important, but all he wanted to do was point fingers and make accusations against people. Accusations that had no meaning other than trying to find fault in another for their religious beliefs. Somehow that didn't set right.

"I don't want to see you get hurt," Chris said. His voice had changed from stern to soft, and Sadie couldn't tell if he was trying to persuade her or if he was sincere.

"I'm not going to get hurt." She had already been hurt enough. And at Chris's hands, no doubt. He hadn't meant to hurt her, but he had. He'd broken her heart and destroyed the dreams she held for the two of them. It was hard having dreams that involved another person who didn't share them. But this time, it was different. Ezra was different. And she knew what she was getting into. She had her eyes open and her heart closed. She was going to get to know Ezra better and then see what would happen from there. Then, maybe, just maybe, if Ezra stuck around, she might give herself the chance to fall in love with him.

He'd made a mess out of it, Chris thought as he drove home on his tractor. He'd tried to help Sadie and all he succeeded in doing was making her angry at him. He was only looking out for her. Wasn't that what friends did?

He pulled his tractor to the north side of the barn where they usually left it, cut the engine and the lights, and got down. He might have made a mess of it, but that didn't mean he was stopping now. Sadie was his friend, and he would help her in any way he could, whether she knew she needed that help or not.

He marched to the house, trying not to let his frustration get the better of him but feeling it seep

into his very being at the same time. The last person
Sadie needed to be dating was a Mennonite guy.
Couldn't she understand that? There were plenty
enough Amish guys around Wells Landing. Why did
she have to go all the way to Taylor Creek to find a new
boyfriend? He stopped in his tracks.

Was that what the Mennonite was to her? A boyfriend? Had it gotten that serious? He might not ever
know, since he'd blown trying to talk to her today. Now
all he could do was pray.

He shook his head and continued on to the house.
The lights were on in the front room, and smoke
puffed from the chimney, its smell permeating the air
around him. Between the woodsmoke and the cold,
there was no other smell like wintertime.

He stumped up the stairs and into the house, wiping
his feet before his mother started hollering for him
to do so.

"I'm glad you're home."

Chris looked up, for the first time noticing they had
company. He had to have walked right past their
buggy, but somehow in the darkness, with his frustration over Sadie, he had missed it. The bishop, the
deacon, his dad, his mom, even his older brother
Joshua sat around. Waiting for him. He didn't know
how he knew they were waiting for him, somehow he
just knew. He swept the bottom of his shoes one more
time against the entryway rug, keeping an eye on them
as he did so. He took off his hat and his coat and hung
them on the pegs by the door before walking across
toward the fire to warm his hands. He wasn't sure what
this was all about, but he had a feeling that before he
walked in they had been talking about him. He kept
his back to the room as he warmed his hands. The
waves of anticipation rolled off everyone in the room.

Why? He had no idea. But he was certain he was about to find out.

Unable to stay facing away from them for much longer, Chris turned toward them, warming his backside. He let his gaze rest on each one of the people seated there and waited for someone to speak. No one did.

"Did someone die?" he asked.

His mother shook her head, even as tears rose into her eyes. Everyone else sat with frowns on their faces as they surveyed him as if he were some poor lost soul brought in from the storm.

"No, Chris," *Mamm* said.

Before she even finished, his *dat* stood. "Now, son," his father started in that tone that set Chris's teeth on edge. Why couldn't they get along? Life would be so much easier for all of them if the two of them could get along. He supposed most would say that his relationship with his father was all part of God's plan, but that didn't stop him from praying about it every night. "The bishop here has come by to talk to you about joining the church."

A stab of guilt pierced his heart. He didn't want to join the church. Not now. Maybe someday. Maybe when he could figure out why he wanted to wander all over the world and see all the sights, backpack over mountains, ride bicycles in hills and valleys, sail on a boat across the ocean, ride a camel in the desert, and a hundred other things that he'd seen in *National Geographic* magazine. Maybe after that he could settle down and join the church.

The bishop stood. "That's right. Your father came to me, and I agree that it's time you started taking your faith seriously, Chris. It's time you thought about settling down."

Settling down?

"You and Sadie Kauffman have been happy for a long time now," his mother said. "Wouldn't it be nice to join the church and marry Sadie this fall?"

Whoa. Join the church and get married all in the same year? The same year that he had planned to travel to Europe? He had been saving his money for nigh on five years. He had scrimped and scraped, skipping lunch when he had money to eat in town. He had taken on odd jobs here and there, fixing porch steps and anything else that would make him a couple of bucks. He had squirreled it all away, stuffed in a slit in his mattress upstairs. No one knew it was there. Not even Johnny or Sadie.

"I guess you've got your mind made up for me." Chris did his best to keep his tone level and smooth without a trace of his mounting frustrations. It would do no good to yell and scream and shout to the rooftops that he didn't want to join the church yet. He didn't want to marry Sadie yet. Give him a couple years was all he asked. Was that too much to ask? He didn't know why God had laid it on his heart to travel, to see things that other people hadn't seen. It would've been much easier if he had had dreams and aspirations of being nothing more than a farmer in tiny Wells Landing, Oklahoma. But he didn't. It was something he had to deal with, a cross he had to bear.

He looked over to Joshua. His brother was studying his fingernails as if somehow the answer to every question in the world was written there.

As the oldest, Joshua had moved away a long time ago. He'd found himself a wife and a house, but instead of farming like their father, he went to work for an *Englisch* shed company.

He was sure to the outsider that the idea of passing

land and vocations from generation to generation sounded quite charming. He'd heard all the words the tourists used to describe the Amish culture: sweet, innocent, wholesome. But that wasn't what he wanted. It was a dead end and led to nowhere. And nowhere wasn't where he wanted to go.

"It's time, don't you think?" His father raised one eyebrow at him in a look that Chris had seen too many times to count. It was like a punctuation mark. *This is the end and this is how it will be. I have spoken and you will obey.*

Frustration and anger bubbled in the back of his throat like acid. He wanted to tell them all to leave him alone. They didn't understand. He didn't know where these dreams came from, but they were his and he was keeping them. He was nurturing them and soon, so very soon, he was going to live them to the fullest.

He swallowed that back and managed to bite his tongue as he formulated his answer. "I've got some time, right?"

The bishop nodded, and the deacon followed suit.

"Until Easter, right?"

"I think you should decide now." His father's tone brooked no argument, but his mother stood and wrapped one arm around his, pulling him closer to her so she could whisper in his ear.

No one knew what she said, but Chris made a mental note to thank her later.

"Easter, then," his father said. "I expect you to be in baptism classes."

Baptism classes in the spring, no trip in the summer, and married in the fall. Chris nodded. He had no choice but to agree. If it came down to it, he would start baptism classes after Easter if only to keep his family from knowing his plans. He hated to deceive them, but what choice did he have? If he told them now, his father would kick him out and forbid his brothers to talk to him, and Chris would be left floundering until he agreed to his father's demands.

His *maam* took one of his hands into both of hers. "Why don't you go on upstairs and clean up. Then have a good piece of pie before bed." She smiled, that same smile he'd seen his whole life through. It would be one of the main things he missed in Europe. Perhaps he should buy a camera and take a picture of his mother smiling like that so he would have it with him always.

"Okay," he said. He moved past his family and started toward the stairs. He put his foot on the first step when his father spoke behind him.

"Easter. And that's it. No more stalling. No more procrastinating."

Chris didn't bother to look at his father. He merely nodded and started up the stairs.

Chapter Eleven

"Are you going somewhere?"

Sadie nearly jumped out of her skin and whirled around to face her sister. Melanie stood framed in the doorway of the bedroom that Sadie had once shared with Lorie. The room Melanie had shared with Cora Ann was down the hall, with another one on the other side reserved especially for Daniel.

"Melanie!" Sadie exclaimed, clutching one hand to her chest. "You scared me."

"Obviously," Melanie said, taking a couple of steps into the room.

"What are you doing here?" Sadie asked.

"I think I should ask you the same thing." Melanie settled herself down on one of the twin beds in the room and tucked her feet underneath her. "Well . . . are you going to tell me?"

"I asked you first." Sadie stalled.

"Fair enough. I came to see what you were up to tonight. You've been acting really strange lately, and I'm worried about my sister."

"Worried about me?" What was it with everybody these days? Why couldn't a girl sneak around and meet a boy every so often without everyone thinking something was wrong?

"Word around the district is that you're still seeing that Mennonite boy."

Sadie spun toward her sister. "What does it matter if I'm still seeing him?"

"Sadie, you're going to have to stop this. You can't go around with a Mennonite boy."

"Why not? Everyone talks like he's some kind of *Englisch* ax murderer when he's just a guy."

"A guy who happens to be Mennonite."

"Is that so terrible? That he's Mennonite?" She had heard terrible stories about women whose husbands beat them and their children, of men who drank, smoked, and did all sorts of other sins that would make any normal person cringe.

"You're avoiding the question."

"So what if I am?"

Melanie shot her a look. "Avoiding the question or seeing the Mennonite?"

Sadie grabbed up her scarf and her coat and started past Melanie. Maybe she could get her sister to leave before Ezra came.

The plan had been perfect. She was supposed to take the night off from the restaurant, say she was going out with friends, and come home to get ready. Then Ezra would pick her up, and no one would know.

Sadie made her way down the steps with Melanie close behind. Ezra would be there any minute, and Melanie showed no signs of going anywhere anytime soon.

"Where's Noah?" Sadie asked.

"He and his brothers are off doing something.

They said they were going to a singing, but you know those boys."

She did. All of Bishop Treger's sons acted as righteous as they could when eyes were watching, but took every chance they had to kick up their heels and have some fun. "I guess the wives weren't invited?"

"You know it."

Sadie pushed her arms into her sleeves and started to button up her coat.

Maybe Melanie would take the hint. She hated to blatantly make her sister leave. But she also didn't want Melanie to know that she was going out with Ezra tonight. Everyone was making such a big deal out of it, and frankly she didn't want to hear it.

"Shouldn't you be getting back home?" She hadn't meant for her words to sound so hateful, but she really needed Melanie to leave. Soon.

"Fine, sister." Melanie shook her head. "I'll let you keep your secrets. But I'll tell you one thing. If you're going out to see Ezra, you need to really think about it. If you're having to sneak off to meet a boy . . ." She frowned. "Just like Lorie."

Without another word, Melanie let herself out of the house. Sadie stood in the living room, stock-still with shock, hardly believing the words her sister had said to her.

Then she heard the tractor start up outside and Melanie chug away on the big green machine.

Everyone was so worried about Sadie and what she was doing with Ezra, but no one was worried that Melanie was out driving tractors after dark all by herself.

She was deflecting the situation, but Melanie's words made her heart hurt. Lorie had left last year to go live with Zach Calhoun. Well, to get ready to marry Zach this summer. Sadie was so very happy for her sister, but that didn't mean she didn't miss her. Especially when Lorie had to leave because their mother kicked her out of the house, telling her to choose between the *Englisch* world and the Amish world. When Lorie had refused to choose, *Mamm* had made her leave anyway. Sadie had been so very sad to see her sister go, not knowing if she would ever talk to her again. Was that what *Mamm* would do? Make her choose between Ezra and her family?

The choice was clear. How could Sadie do anything but choose her family? But it wasn't a choice she wanted to make. Why couldn't she have both? It didn't make sense.

A few moments later she heard Ezra's truck pull up outside. At least, she thought it was a few minutes. She really didn't know how long she'd been standing there in the living room with her scarf in one hand and her gloves in the other, her coat all buttoned up as she waited for him.

His knock on the door startled her out of her trance and she raced to open it, so happy to see him.

"Are you ready to go?" he asked, looking at her gloves, scarf, and coat. "I thought . . ."

"You thought what?" Sadie grabbed her bag and nudged Ezra back onto the porch. She shut the door behind her, quickly wrapping the scarf around her head and pulling her gloves on.

"I thought maybe I would talk to your mother tonight." A small frown burrowed its way across his brow.

"Maybe another night." She nudged Ezra down the steps and out into the yard.

"Sadie, did you tell her that we are going out tonight?"

She shook her head as he walked with her over to the passenger side of the truck and opened the door. Without another word, she slid inside and waited for him to come around to the driver side and slide in beside her.

"Why not? I thought you said she would be okay with this."

Sadie shrugged. "I don't really know how she would feel and . . . I don't know. I just don't know. I didn't tell her, that's all." And now that Melanie had said what she had about Lorie, Sadie was doubly grateful that she hadn't mentioned going out with Ezra to her mother. She wasn't sure how *Mamm* would have handled the revelation.

Ezra started the engine and backed up into the side yard, then pulled the truck out onto the road.

"So volleyball, huh?"

Ezra rolled his head over toward her and then turned back to face front. "Changing the subject?"

"Yes," Sadie said. "I don't really know what to do."

"Is this a good idea? I mean, I don't want to cause problems between you and your family."

"And this isn't causing problems with your family?" Sadie would forever remember the stern look of consternation on Ezra's mother's face when she saw her sitting at the table eating cookies and drinking coffee. She didn't know why his mother didn't approve, and but it was evident that she didn't. And that was all that mattered.

Ezra turned down the next side farm road that they came to and parked the truck. He left the engine running and the lights on. Sadie could see the little bugs dancing in the beams, a sure sign that spring was coming early this year.

"I guess we should figure this out now, before it goes any further."

Sadie nodded. "I guess so."

Ezra turned to face her, one knee braced on the bench seat between them, and flung his arm across the back. "I'm not sure I care what people think."

"You're not?" Sadie looked at him, her eyes wide as she searched in the dim light of the truck to read his expression.

"I don't know." He tapped his fingers against the back of the seat as if somehow that would make his thoughts clearer. "It's all so dumb."

Sadie sighed in relief. "I know. I feel the same way. Don't date him, he's a Mennonite." She lowered her voice as if mimicking the bishop. So Bishop Ebersol had never really said those words to her, but she could sure hear them come out of his mouth. He was a good man, fair and honest, but it was his duty as the bishop to make sure that the church's rules were followed. Amish married Amish, and that's the way it had been for a long time, hundreds of years. If a person was Amish and didn't marry Amish, then they had to leave. If they had joined the church, they were shunned. If they hadn't joined, then technically they weren't shunned, but it was hard to come back. Look at Lorie. She had only come back a handful of times in the four months since she had left. Sadie knew that she was busy working and planning her wedding, but she had a feeling that it was more than that.

You can never go home again. She'd seen that quote somewhere, maybe at the library on one of the posters they had hanging up in the foyer. She passed those every time she had to fetch Cora Ann from the small brick building. Now she understood what it meant.

Ezra shook his head. "Maybe we should forget the whole thing." He reached for the gearshift, and Sadie scooted across toward him and grabbed his hand.

"Don't do that. I mean, I don't want to forget it all." Her heart thumped in her chest. This was about more than getting married and having a family. This was about her and Ezra and the potential that she felt between them. There was something there, something extraordinary God had given to them, and she felt as if she would be doing a disservice to the both of them if she didn't try to find out what it was.

Ezra looked at her hand to her face and then back again. "You mean that?" The air around them turned thick, tense and heavy, but not in a bad way. It was full of expectancy and hope. Sadie nodded. Swallowing hard, she looked up and met Ezra's gaze. The moment held, suspended between them. Or maybe it was an hour. She really couldn't tell. It was the two of them, all alone, in a moment so special it almost brought tears to her eyes.

He turned toward her. Reaching out a hand, he ran the back of his fingers across one cheek.

Sadie's eyes drifted shut, then opened again. Something exceptional was happening, and she didn't want to miss a second of it.

As if in slow motion, he moved toward her. Sadie felt herself leaning toward him as well as if they were pulled together by some invisible force she couldn't name. Closer and closer still, until their lips were almost touching. She could feel his breath across her cheeks and the expectancy that hummed around him, anticipation and a bit of longing.

Then he raised both hands to cup her cheeks and pressed his lips to hers.

It was the sweetest thing she'd ever known, being kissed by Ezra. She felt cherished, precious, as if in that moment in time no one in the world existed except for the two of them. It was sweet and soft and forbidden all at the same time, and she never wanted it to end. She'd waited her whole lifetime for a kiss like this, and she nearly cried out when he moved away from her.

Ezra turned back to face front, and Sadie wondered if perhaps she had done something wrong. She touched her fingers to her lips as she watched him, just staring out the windshield, his hands fisted on either side of the steering wheel. She knew in that moment why her father had said to never date a man she wouldn't want to marry. Because if guys went around kissing girls like that all the time . . .

Ezra's kiss had awakened something in her that she had never known existed. And it had less to do with all the dreams she had thought she had about raising a family and getting married and more to do with the man sitting beside her.

"Ezra?" She didn't want to speak his name and risk breaking the moment that was lingering between them. "I'm sorry." She'd never kissed anybody before. And she hadn't been expecting this. Not really. He hadn't warned her like he had the night in the park. But he hadn't kissed her then. Just tonight. She'd probably done it all wrong.

The Mennonites were as conservative as the Amish when it came to relationships. But she didn't know if Ezra had a girlfriend before. He might have kissed a dozen girls. The thought made her stomach hurt.

"You're sorry?" Ezra turned to look at her, though

his hands were still white-knuckled, wrapped around the steering wheel.

"I mean, I'm not a good kisser. I've never done that before."

She hadn't realized how tense he was until his shoulders slumped and a small laugh escaped him. "You think you're a bad kisser?"

Sadie nodded. "But it's something I can learn, right?"

Ezra pulled her close once again, but this time he planted a smacking kiss in the middle of her forehead. He pulled away, laughing. "Sadie Kauffman," he said, still chuckling, "you are most assuredly not a bad kisser."

"You mean that?" Sadie couldn't believe she was having this conversation now, in the middle of a field in Ezra's truck with darkness all around. But the thought made her a teeny-weeny bit happy. It was good to know she wasn't a bad kisser and that she hadn't disappointed him.

"I mean that." He chuckled again, then refastened his seat belt. He waited until she had fastened hers as well, then he pulled the truck back to the highway.

She thought she was a bad kisser. Ezra tried not to chuckle all the way to Taylor Creek. Of course, laughing about it was surely better than melting into a puddle at her feet. He had only kissed a couple girls in his lifetime. It was no big secret why. *Rumspringa* for the Mennonites started at age seventeen, the exact year his father left. Ezra hadn't had too much running-around time before he had to buckle down and start deciding a direction for the ranch. Seventeen years old and he didn't have time for girls. Or maybe God was saving him for Sadie.

She wasn't a bad kisser. In fact, he'd had to make

himself stop. He had to pull away from her and wrap his hands around the steering wheel so tight that his knuckles turned white to keep from reaching for her again.

This was why the elders told them not to be alone with each other. The temptation was so great. Especially when he felt like he had just kissed the one God had made especially for him.

Oh, would Logan have a time with that one. But it was the truth. There was something special about Sadie Kauffman. Ezra couldn't say what, and maybe he didn't even want to know. Finding out could take away the beauty of the mystery and make it common instead. No, for now he'd just go with it, and know that he'd better not kiss her again anytime soon. Especially not when they were alone.

He pulled his truck up to the front of the rec center and found an empty parking spot.

"Are you ready to go in?"

"It's going to be okay?" Sadie asked. She was cute when she worried. But there was nothing to be concerned about. So the Amish had a few hang-ups about the Mennonites. His mother's issues with Sadie had nothing to do with the fact that she was Amish, but that she existed at all. With time he was certain that his mother would get over that. She needed some time to adjust to the fact that there was a new woman in her son's life, another person other than herself. And Logan? Ezra didn't know what to do about his cousin, and frankly, he didn't care. Logan had found his happiness. No one should begrudge Ezra his own.

"It's going to be perfect," Ezra said, flashing her a quick smile before releasing his seat belt and hopping out of the truck.

Sadie must've been a little nervous, for she didn't

wait on him to let her out, but slid to the ground and slammed the door before he even got around the back of the tailgate.

She took a deep breath as if fortifying herself for some type of battle. "Okay," she said. "Let's do this."

Ezra was nearly bursting with pride as he walked into the rec center with Sadie at his side. He led her into the gym where volleyball nets had been set up, one on either side of center court. They played four to a team but never boys against girls, always couples against couples. It made the matches more even. He liked playing with the girls as well. It tended to make some of the guys a little more humble. And humility was always a good thing.

"Hey, Ezra, you got here." Logan jogged up, wearing long basketball shorts and a T-shirt with the arms ripped out. If a person didn't know he was Mennonite, they would think he was like any other *Englisch* guy at any other basketball court at any other rec center in the world. Mennonite girls were more easily identifiable with their small black head coverings and print dresses. They looked like a slightly less conservative version of most Amish girls.

See how the same we really are?

"Are you going to play in that?" Logan pointed to Ezra's jeans and boots.

"I've got some shorts and tennis shoes right here." He indicated his gym bag, though he doubted he would put on the shorts. It was strange to think about playing with Sadie while only wearing half a pair of pants. He couldn't really say why. Maybe because the rest of the couples there were married and they weren't. "I'm just going to change my shoes," he said. For now.

Logan nodded, then looked to Sadie. "It's good to see you again. Sally, right?"

If he'd been a more violent man, Ezra might have punched Logan in the face. But as it was, he simply said, "It's Sadie," and let the rest of it go.

"Come on, Sadie. I'll introduce you to the girls." Logan hooked one arm over his shoulder in that age-old gesture to follow him.

Sadie looked from Logan to Ezra then back again.

Ezra wanted to tell her that she didn't have to go. But maybe it was better this way, to have her jump in and meet the girls on her own terms. He knew they were interested in her. And she them. He had known most of these couples his entire life.

Instead, he sat down on the bottom bleacher and started putting on his athletic shoes. He kept a close watch on Sadie as she followed Logan around. She laughed and smiled and appeared to have a really good time.

He had known it would be like this, he thought as he tied his shoes. Her friends might not be as accepting of their relationship, but he knew his would be. In time, he was certain that they could convince all of their friends and family they belonged together.

Chapter Twelve

By the end of the night, Sadie wondered if she would even be able to remember three of the girls' names. There were just so many of them. Aside from remembering their names, she had to remember the boys' names and then what girl belonged to what boy. It was enough to make her head swim. It didn't help that the gym was loud and every time the ball hit the ground it echoed four times through the building. Or maybe she was just nervous. She wanted them to like her so badly. And that kiss.

Ezra had kissed her, and she felt like she was walking on clouds. Now she was here with his friends playing volleyball and having the best time of her life.

Clapping erupted on the other side of the net as the ball went out of bounds.

"Okay," Ezra said. "We can do this." He clapped his hands encouragingly, and Sadie wanted nothing more than to go over and wrap her arms around him. He was cute when he was being athletic.

She shook her head at her own fanciful thoughts and moved up to the front of the net as Ezra's cousin moved back to serve. She and Ezra were playing with

Logan and his girlfriend Mindy. Against another couple. If she remembered right it was Peter and Mary and Mose and Amanda. Or maybe it was Peter and Amanda and Mose and Mary. She couldn't remember.

Logan served the ball high and true. Peter went back to hit it and bumped it up for Mary to hit. The ball went high and Mary spiked it down, hitting Sadie in the face.

It happened so quickly that Sadie hadn't seen the ball coming. One minute she was standing there, and the next minute her face throbbed with pain and stars filled her vision.

"Oh my gosh!" someone hollered, but she didn't know who. The only thing she knew was that it wasn't Ezra. She would've known his voice anywhere.

His voice was soft and next to her. "Sadie? Are you okay?"

She tried to nod, but it hurt too bad. Instead she turned toward him. "I think so," she said.

"Oh no, you're not." He said the words gently, in that sweet Ezra way that he had. Then he helped her to her feet and over to the bench.

He reached into his gym bag and pulled out a towel. Only then did Sadie realize that her hands were covered in blood. Her blood. "Is my nose busted?"

"It's just bleeding," Ezra said. "Here." He held the towel gently to her nose, then nudged her head back. "I'll help you to the restroom. Okay?"

"Okay," Sadie said, but she didn't recognize her voice, as muffled as it was by the towel.

"Don't worry. I'll lead you there."

Sadie tried to relax and follow his lead as Ezra helped her toward the restroom. She couldn't see where she was going, so she closed her eyes, but that only made things worse. She opened them again, watching the ceiling as she walked down the hallway of the rec center with him.

"Here," Ezra said. "Do you want me to go in with you?" He released the towel into her hands.

Sadie tipped her head back straight. "No, I think I'm fine," she said and started into the ladies' room.

She blinked a couple of times as she walked into the brightly lit room, then went over to the sinks to survey the damage. It looked worse than it was. She had blood on her face and blood on her hands, but her nose was only slightly swollen. The ball must've hit just right to make it bleed but not break it. Still, she thought as she cleaned up, that was one good thing about mourning. Any blood that she got on her dress was hidden, though she would have to make sure come laundry day that she soaked out the stains.

She had less than three more months to wear the black, but she couldn't go around stained up for even that long. She wet the towel in the sink with cold water, pressing it to her face to eliminate any other swelling. She tried to hurry since he was out there waiting. His voice had been filled with worry as he led her to the restroom. She wanted to make sure that he knew she was okay.

She wrung out the towel again and rinsed the blood that was left in the sink, then held the towel over her face one more time.

"Did you see her?"

At first Sadie almost answered, thinking the disembodied voice was speaking to her, but then another voice joined the first one.

"I cannot believe he brought an Amish girl here."

Sadie didn't recognize the voices, but she didn't need to know who they were to know that they were talking about her.

"I don't understand. I tried to get him to go out with my sister. Logan has been trying to set him up with Annie K. Then he brings that."

The words were so mean that Sadie could barely register them at all. Had she just called her a *that*? What was wrong with her? What was wrong with Sadie? She hadn't done anything wrong. She surely hadn't done anything to the unknown girl in the bathroom stall.

"I know. I mean aside from the fact that she's plain and not really very pretty and in mourning wearing all that black, she's Amish. What was he thinking?"

That was the worst thing the unknown girl could say about her? Sadie knew she was plain, she knew she was dressed in black, and yet the worst thing the woman could say about her was that she was Amish? What was wrong with these people?

Suddenly Sadie wanted out of there as fast as she could get. Bile rose in the back of her throat, her stomach churned, and a sob threatened to escape. She pushed it back, stifled it with one hand, and with the other pushed her way out of the restroom.

Ezra was waiting there for her, as he had promised. "Are you okay—" He stopped as he saw the look on her face. "Why do I have a feeling this doesn't have anything to do with your nose?"

She shook her head. "Can you take me home now?"

"If that's what you want."

"*Jah.* Yes," Sadie corrected. "I'd like to go home now."

Ezra led her back to the gym door. "Are you going to tell me what happened in there?"

"Not right now, okay?"

"Okay," Ezra said. "But you need to tell me. I don't want secrets between us."

How could there be secrets between them when

everyone had made it their personal goal to discuss them whenever and wherever they wanted to? But Sadie didn't say that. She nodded and stayed outside the gym as Ezra went to retrieve his bag.

He was fairly certain that one of the hardest things he'd ever done was leave Sadie standing outside those gym doors not knowing what had happened in the bathroom. She had only been in there five minutes, tops. Her nose didn't look nearly as bad when she came out as it did going in, so why were those hazel eyes swimming with tears when she stepped back into the hallway?

He hustled over to where he left his bag, not bothering to put his boots back on. He shoved them inside the bag, wanting to get back to Sadie as soon as possible.

"Is she okay?" Logan asked.

Ezra zipped his bag and looked up to see not only Logan and Mindy waiting on answers, but Peter, Mary, Mose, and Amanda as well. Mary looked near tears.

"I didn't mean to hurt her," Mary said.

"I know you didn't, and she'll be fine. I'm going to take her home now."

"Will you tell her I'm sorry?" Mary asked.

Normally Ezra would have said for Mary to tell Sadie herself. But somehow he got the feeling Mary would be one of the last people that Sadie wanted to see right then. "I'll tell her," he said.

Ezra slung his bag over his shoulder and started for the door. The girls fell back, leaving Peter, Mose, and Logan to walk with him. They got halfway to the door of the gym when Ezra turned around.

"Is there something you guys would like to talk

about?" He would've liked to have said that he was surprised when Logan nodded. But he wasn't.

"Why did you bring her here?" Logan asked.

"Because I like her."

"She's Amish," Mose said.

Ezra closed his eyes for a moment and shook his head, trying to free those rattling thoughts from his brain. Was that such a bad thing that she was Amish?

"We are Mennonite," Peter said.

Ezra had known them all since they were in grade school. Logan was his cousin, Peter was his neighbor, and once upon a time Mose's mom and his mom had been the best of friends. But that was before his dad had walked out and everything had fallen apart.

Ezra had managed, he had moved on, but at times like this he felt as separated from them as he had the day his father had walked out the door.

"Does that really matter?"

The three men looked at each other, then turned back to him. "There's a reason we have two religions."

That had to be one of the dumbest things Ezra had ever heard anyone say. But he had no rebuttal. He gave them a curt nod and started for the door. They were fine, but Sadie needed him.

He pushed the door to the gym open so hard it hit the wall behind and snapped back. Sadie jumped, and he immediately regretted the action. He couldn't remember being this mad ever in his life, not even when her friends had questioned him at the bowling alley. These were *his* friends. How dare they? Some people had a lot of gall.

"Are you ready to go?" Ezra asked. He did his best to make his voice sound calm and collected when inside he was anything but. His emotions churned like an angry storm. What was wrong with everybody?

"*Jah.*"

The last time she had corrected herself and said yes, but this time she left it in the Pennsylvania Dutch. It was a start, as far as he was concerned. He didn't want her changing for him.

He walked back out to the truck. "Do you want some Tylenol? I think there's some in the glove box."

"That would be good," Sadie said. "My head is really hurting."

Ezra looked around the cab of the truck. Usually there was a stray water bottle hiding out somewhere, but he didn't see anything. He started the truck and put it into reverse. "Hold on a second. I'll get you to a store. You can get something to drink and take some then, okay?"

"That'd be great."

He found a Love's Country Store, one of his favorites. They were a little smaller than some of the other convenience stores in the area, but they made good sandwiches and had a place for people to sit inside the building and relax for a few minutes. Right now, relaxing was something he and Sadie desperately needed.

He led Sadie over to the booths that sat near the front windows of the store so she could watch the traffic drive by. He got them both a Coke and a chicken Italiano sandwich.

"Are you going to tell me what happened?" He took her hand into his, hoping the gesture gave her strength and confidence. He had a feeling she needed it.

"There's really not a lot to say."

Ezra released her hand and took a bite of his sandwich. "I think there's probably a lot to say. But I don't think you want to say it, and I don't know why."

Sadie picked up her sandwich and started to eat as

well. Maybe if they got some food they would feel better. . . .

She popped the pills into her mouth and uncapped her drink, taking a long swig before she spoke again. "Thank you. That was really sweet of you."

To his dismay, tears welled in those hazel eyes once more.

He reached across the table, squeezing her fingers in his own. "Don't cry."

"Give me a minute, okay?"

"Okay," Ezra said. "As long as you know I'm here for you."

Sadie nodded, but she was about to cry again, so Ezra looked away. He thought that might be best.

Girls were such a mystery to him. He'd spent most of his life around girls of another sort, bison and deer, bovine and ostriches, and all the other creatures on the ranch. But not the ones like the one seated across from him. He really didn't know what to do with *them*. Maybe once upon a time he thought he did, but now he was so out of practice he felt like he was playing a different game.

"Do you feel better?"

"*Jah.* I think I'll be all right."

"Are you going to tell me what happened in the bathroom?"

"It doesn't matter really."

"If it makes you cry, then it definitely matters." That possessive streak in him rose to the surface. Anything to do with her mattered. But how could he tell her that? Would she even understand something he didn't understand himself?

"There were some girls in there." Sadie looked away, out the window at the cars passing by.

"What girls?"

She shook her head. "I don't know. I didn't see their faces."

"So what happened?"

She shrugged. "I heard them talking is all. They couldn't believe you brought me to play volleyball."

Never in his life had Ezra wanted to smash something like he did in that moment. "Don't worry about those girls. They don't matter."

"How can they not? Your mother doesn't want us together. My mother doesn't want us together. Your friends don't want us together, and my friends don't think we should be together. Why is the whole world against us?"

Ezra sighed. "I don't know that. But I do know one thing."

"And what is that?"

"The decision is ours. This is our life. And the more I get to know you, the more I want to get to know you and the more time I want to spend with you. I don't care what anybody says. Not my mother, not my cousin or those girls in the bathroom. There's only one thing that matters. And that's what you want."

Chapter Thirteen

Sadie could hardly believe her ears. "You mean that?" Never in her life had she felt as special as she did in that moment. Maybe because Ezra was willing to go against everyone he knew to be with her, and yet Chris was dropping everything he knew to get away. She shook her head. Now was not the time to be worried about Chris Flaud.

"More than I've meant anything in my life."

She pulled her gaze from his and stared down at her half-eaten sandwich. It was the best thing she had ever eaten and yet it tasted like sawdust. Not sure what that meant, she shook her head again, then lifted her chin to meet his gaze once more. "So what do we do?"

He thought about it a minute. "If we can't hang out with your friends in Wells Landing and we can't hang out with my friends in Taylor Creek, then let's go somewhere we can hang out alone."

Sadie's heart jumped at the thought of being alone with Ezra. The implications, the temptations. Everything about it was wrong and yet right all at the same time.

"Let's go to Pryor and get something to eat next

week. Just the two of us. No hanging out with friends on either side, no hanging out with family. Nothing. Just us."

Her tears threatened again. Maybe she was over-tired from getting hit in the face and being talked about behind her back, or maybe the whole conversation was making her a bit fragile. But she would like nothing more than what he just said. Her and him alone, without outside forces pulling at them. Pryor wasn't far from either town. In fact, it was the next big town over, the place they took Daniel to the doctor when he needed to go. Pryor was close enough to Wells Landing and Taylor Creek not to raise eyebrows as she walked in with her black mourning dress and her prayer *kapp*, and surely not close enough to either one that anyone would care if a Mennonite guy and an Amish girl were having dinner together.

"Yes," she whispered. "I'd like that more than anything."

They finished eating and got back in the truck. All too soon Ezra was pulling down the road that led to her house.

"How are you going to explain . . ." He gestured around his face, indicating the injury to her nose.

Sadie shrugged. "I don't know. Tell them the truth, I guess."

It seemed as if there were going to be a lot of white lies in her future if she and Ezra started sneaking around. It'd be better to tell the truth now and in any instance she could.

"I'll tell them I got hit in the face with the volley-ball." They didn't need to know any more than that.

When they found out she had an injury, everyone would fuss over her and that would be that.

Ezra nodded.

They drove in silence a bit, then he turned, casting a quick glance in her direction. "I'm glad you came with me tonight."

Despite everything, she was glad she came with him too. He pulled up in front of her house and left the engine running. "What time next week?" he asked.

"I have Thursday night off from the restaurant."

"Isn't that your bowling night?"

"Well, not really. I mean, I would rather eat dinner with you than go bowling with them." She didn't have anyone else to bowl with except for Ezra. Maybe she should let Chris have that slot. He could take who he wanted to. But she knew he wouldn't take anyone. She'd let the couples worry about that.

Ezra nodded. "I'll see you Thursday, then?"

Sadie nodded in return. What was next? Would he kiss her again like he did on the way to volleyball? It was something she both anticipated and dreaded.

She waited to see what would happen. But he only reached out a hand and ran his thumb across her cheekbone. "I'll see you then."

Sadie tried not to be disappointed as she slipped from the cab of his truck. She walked up to the porch knowing he was watching to make sure she was safe. When she reached the door, she heard him put the truck in gear and back out of the driveway. She stood there and watched him go, wondering why he hadn't kissed her again.

* * *

Sunday afternoon Melanie came by for a visit. Luckily their two church districts held their services on the same Sunday, so she was off when they were off and they could visit together. Otherwise Sadie wondered when she would ever see her sister. She could understand Lorie's infrequent visits, seeing as she lived in the *Englisch* world and miles away. Melanie lived on the other side of the district.

They settled down in the living room. The day was overcast and looked like it might snow. But Sadie had heard the old-timers talk about it yesterday at the restaurant, and it was supposed to be cloudy for a couple more days and then clear up after that.

"I'm glad you came out today," Sadie said.

Melanie frowned. "I hear you've been seeing Ezra Hein."

The statement took Sadie aback, but at least Melanie used his name and didn't call him "that Mennonite boy."

"Maybe," Sadie muttered. It was no secret. Melanie had even gone bowling with them the one time. But everything else had been either out in the open or in Taylor Creek. She still had four more days before they went on their date in Pryor.

"Sadie, I know you're upset about Chris. But going out with a Mennonite boy to make him jealous is not a good idea. This can backfire on you."

Sadie bit back the harsh words that sprang to her tongue. Her sister had no idea, no idea about the situation with Chris. She had already told Lorie, but that was different, Lorie didn't live in town. She didn't talk in the sewing circles and gossip after church and everything else that the Amish tended to do to spread around the "news." If she told Melanie, it would surely get back to Chris and Johnny and maybe even their brother Joshua.

No, as bad as it spited her, she had to keep this to herself.

"I'm not dating him to make Chris jealous. I've gone out with him a couple times because I like him."

"He's a Mennonite." Melanie said the words clearly, pronouncing each syllable as if it were a word in itself.

"I'm aware. But what's wrong with that?"

Melanie sat back. "We're different. That's all. You know that. We don't go to church the same. We don't dress the same. They drive around in cars."

"Everyone around here drives around on tractors. They both have rubber wheels and both could take a person anywhere they wanted to go. Why is it so terrible to drive a car instead of a tractor?"

"I don't have the answer to that," Melanie said. "It just is. And don't forget that they have electricity."

"We have electricity in our restaurant. What's the difference in that and having it the house?"

"Electricity leads to TV and computers and radio and all the other worldly things." Melanie shook her head.

"I've been to Ezra's house, and there's nothing there like that. They use electricity to light the house and to have hot water and cold food, all the things that we use propane for. So they pay the electric bill to the city. Is that really ungodly?"

"They're not like us," Melanie said finally.

Sadie pinched the bridge of her nose. Her head was starting to pound, and the last thing she wanted to do was argue with her sister. Why were people so narrow-minded? Why couldn't they see past all the little things on the surface to the person underneath? What did it matter that he was a Mennonite? Was it really important that he cut his hair different? Or that he wore patterned shirts? And the whole electricity thing was so ridiculous she couldn't even laugh at it.

"I don't want you to get hurt," Melanie said.

"I've already been hurt. By a guy I've known my whole life. An Amish guy."

"Look," Melanie started. "I know it was hard when Chris broke up with you."

"Chris and I were never a couple and I told him that I wouldn't wait . . . I mean, that I couldn't marry him."

Melanie inhaled sharply. "You?"

Sadie nodded.

"Why?"

"I'd rather not say."

"Sadie . . . ?"

"It doesn't concern you, Melanie." She hated to be like that with her sister. But she couldn't divulge Chris's secret no matter how hurtful his abandonment. What happened between them and the secrets he'd confided to her were not something that she could share with her sister.

"Find a nice Amish boy. Can you do that?"

"The only available Amish boy I know is thirteen, and I think he likes Cora Ann."

"You are exaggerating."

Sadie snorted. "You know what I mean. This whole town has had me tagged with Chris since we were fifteen years old. You started going with Noah and Ruthie started going with Mark. Lorie started going with Jonah—"

"Look how that turned out." Melanie had been as hurt as Sadie had when Lorie left. But they had all been grateful when Lorie came back and made up with their mother. She might not have stayed within the Amish faith, but she had been there when Melanie got married. And they would be there in June for Lorie when she married the *Englischer* Zach Calhoun. They were family, and that was all that mattered.

"Well, Chris and I aren't going to work out either."

"He looks so miserable." Melanie shook her head. "I understand that you can't tell me why you broke up with him, but could you see fit to give him another chance?"

"Did he . . . Did he send you here to ask me that?" Was Chris having second thoughts about going to Europe? Her heart gave a funny flip-flop in her chest. He'd made it quite clear that he wanted to go to Europe. Was he having reservations about leaving? And if he was, why hadn't he come himself?

"Noah asked me to come."

"Why would your husband care?"

"I'm not sure that he does, really. But his father does."

Bishop Treger, Noah's father, was a much more conservative leader than Sadie's bishop. Bishop Ebersol was father to Emily, one of Lorie and Sadie's best friends. He had seen them through a lot of tough times over the last few years. She didn't think he would care that she was dating a Mennonite boy. Not like Bishop Treger would. Not like her friends and family. Everybody was more than willing to point fingers and show how different they were when they didn't take any time at all to look for all their similarities.

"Just think about it, will you, Sadie?"

"I'll think about it." How could she think about anything else? But thinking about it didn't mean it would change anything at all.

* * *

She probably should have waited until she knew that she could find the bishop at home. But she hadn't. She'd driven over to the Ebersols' only to find that Bishop Ebersol was visiting with the Riehls.

Sadie hopped back into her buggy and headed over to James and Joy's house. A couple of years ago, James Riehl had been kicked in the head by a cantankerous milk cow. The injury to his brain had rendered him somewhat childlike. He could hold his own in most conversations, but there was something so innocent and sweet about him. Everyone loved to be around him, especially Emily, his new daughter-in-law. Emily had more of an idea about what Sadie was going through than anyone.

Emily had loved Luke Lambright, but he loved race car driving more. *Kind of like Chris loves the thought of traveling more.* So Luke left the Amish, leaving Emily behind. Soon after that, Elam Riehl had come into the picture. Now her friend was the happiest she had ever seen her. Emily had a new baby girl.

Sadie pulled her buggy to a stop in front of the Riehls' house, thinking that maybe instead of the bishop, she should talk to Emily. Maybe her friend had some insight on what to do.

The bishop's buggy was still parked out front, so Sadie was in luck. She had her choice of who to talk to—Emily or her father. But Sadie had a feeling that the bishop would render the best advice in her situation. She hopped out of the buggy and skipped up the porch steps as the front door swung open. James Riehl stood on the other side of the threshold, baby Lavender in his arms. "Sadie Kauffman! I'm glad you're here!"

Sadie smiled. James's enthusiasm was contagious.

It was so hard to be around him without smiling. After coming back from such an injury, he showed them all how good God was and how precious life.

He looked up and down at her black attire. "Mourning still?" He nodded sagely. James had an adoration for the color purple and he always wanted to know about the purple things people around him owned.

"Is the bishop still here?"

"*Jah.*" James stood aside so that Sadie could step into the house. Since Emily and Elam had gotten married, they had moved in with James and Joy to help with the workload. It was an interesting situation because instead of the grandparents living in the *dawdi haus*, the kids were living there.

Sadie supposed that was the best plan for them. They could be close to James and Joy when they needed to be and have enough privacy to start a family of their own.

Just then Emily came out of the kitchen carrying her baby in her arms. Sallie Mae Riehl was a tiny thing, only two months old now. But she was shaping up to be the perfect combination between Emily and Elam. She had Emily's blue eyes and Elam's dark hair. Sadie knew the first time she had seen her that no one would ever call that baby plain.

"Sadie," Emily gushed, rushing over to give her a one-armed hug. "What brings you out today?"

"My visit is long overdue, but I really need to speak with the bishop today."

"And I thought you'd come out to see me." Emily smiled.

Elam came in the back door, dusting off his feet and pushing his leather work gloves into the back pocket of his pants. He was a big man, the kind of guy that made a girl feel safe and secure. And suddenly Sadie envied Sallie Mae for having her father.

"Next time," Sadie said. "I promise."

Bishop Ebersol took that time to come out of the kitchen, where he had no doubt been sitting at the table talking to Joy and perhaps the other Riehl children. It was a fun and happy household, filled with so much love that it nearly brought tears to Sadie's eyes.

"Did I hear my name?" the bishop asked. He glanced around at the faces staring back at him from the living room.

Sadie could only nod. "I was hoping to have a word."

The bishop tilted his head to one side, unanswered questions lighting his eyes. He gave her a quick nod and said, "Would you like to take a walk?"

Sadie swallowed hard and nodded. "That would be good, *jah.*"

She felt all eyes on her as she turned and headed to the front door. She waited on the front porch for the bishop to don his coat and join her.

Without a word, they made their way down the porch steps and across the yard to the milking barn. It was much cooler inside so they stayed out, allowing the sun to warm their faces.

"You have a serious look on your face, Sadie Kauffman."

"I've got something serious to talk to you about."

The bishop nodded. "Whenever you're ready."

Was she ready? In so many ways she was and in so many ways she wasn't. She didn't know where to start. "I . . . ?"

"Take your time," he encouraged.

"Why do we hold such animosity toward the Mennonites?"

The bishop blinked as if her question had been the

very last one he thought she would ask. "I do not have any animosity toward the Mennonites."

"Then why can't I date one?" Sadie cried.

The bishop led her over to the fence and propped his arms up on the rail, turning them away from the house. Sadie wasn't sure if he did that so she would be faced with the calming scene of the cows munching hay in the field or if he didn't want her voice to carry to those in the house.

"You want to date a Mennonite?"

"There's a boy, *jah*."

"What about Chris? I thought you and Chris Flaud were a couple. In fact, I've been waiting on him to come to me and talk about you for a while."

Sadie shook her head. "That's not going to happen."

He nodded. "Okay, then. Who is this Mennonite boy?"

"He lives over in Taylor Creek. He's this really nice guy, and I don't know . . ." She trailed off, uncomfortable telling the bishop how much she truly liked Ezra Hein. She might even be in love with him. Maybe she was in love if she was willing to sneak around and date him against everybody's wishes. "Why is it not okay?"

"There's a lot to think about, Sadie. You know the differences."

"But are they really that different from us?" she asked.

"*Nay*." He shook his head. "The Mennonites are not very different from us at all. We drive tractors. They drive cars. We wear solid colors. They allow prints. They have electricity. We don't. Those things can all be overcome. But to date a Mennonite . . . Well, that's not the real problem, now is it? The real problem is we have different churches. If a Mennonite boy comes to court you, one day that might lead to something else. He's going to want to get married. You're going to want to get married. Then comes the matter of the church. One of you will have to give up their church. You have to ask yourself, Sadie Kauffman, are you willing to give up your church for him?"

Chapter Fourteen

Was she willing to give up her church for Ezra Hein? The words haunted her on her way back home. And the worst part of it all? She didn't know. Didn't even want to think about it. Didn't want that hanging like a cloud over her time with Ezra. If they continued to see each other, fell in love, and wanted to join their lives, surely they could find a solution to that problem. It wasn't anything she should have to decide for herself.

Mind made up, she unhitched her horse and thought only about her upcoming date with Ezra.

She called Ezra Thursday afternoon. He answered on the first ring, his voice breathless as if he had hurried to answer it. She knew that was silly. He'd most likely had it in his pocket. But she liked to think of him rushing to the phone because he thought it might be her.

"Are we still going out tonight?" She hated to ask because the answer could be no, and her heart wasn't prepared for that.

"Of course."

She smiled. "Do me a favor?"

"Anything."

She felt that hitch in her breath. "Pick me up at the library."

"The library?" The confusion in his voice was evident.

"It's just that . . ." She traced the outline of the phone where it hung on the restaurant wall. She had taken a moment to come call him, hoping and praying the whole while that no one would realize who she was talking to. "I think we should keep things low-key. Don't you agree?"

"Yeah, you're right. The library it is. Six o'clock?"

"Six o'clock." She smiled, counting down the minutes until she could see him again.

Pryor was only about fifteen minutes from both Taylor Creek and Wells Landing. Sadie thought the idea of them going there for dinner was about as brilliant as they could get. Close and yet far enough away that they wouldn't completely stand out. They could blend in without having to change a thing. And no one there would care about whose church they were going to join and all the other stuff that was giving everyone around them such grief.

She rode beside Ezra all the way there, the anticipation building. Their first real date, not a hangout session with friends, but a real date like she'd heard the *Englisch* go on. They'd eat, then who knew what they'd do after that. Maybe they could go for a walk or to a movie. The idea was exciting.

The Amish didn't normally go to movies, but neither

Amy Lillard

did they sneak out to eat dinner with Mennonite boys. What was one more transgression on her record?

Ezra pulled his truck into the large parking lot filled with cars. The restaurant was busy for a Thursday night, but it was one of the most popular in the area. Of course, they didn't serve traditional home-cooked meals and Amish food like Kauffman's Family Restaurant did, but they had wonderful steaks and the best pumpernickel bread she had ever tasted.

The hostess seated them and brought water and bread as they looked at the menu. Sadie was so excited she could barely concentrate on the words. "Will you order for me? Please?"

Ezra looked up and caught her gaze, a small chuckle escaping him. "I was about to ask you the same thing. What sounds good?"

"I don't know. Everything. Anything." As long as she was with him, the world was a perfect place. She didn't care if she ate dirt or the most expensive meal the two of them could find.

The waitress came back, order pad in hand. "Have you decided?"

Ezra laughed. "Bring us two specials."

"How you want those cooked?"

They looked at each other and smiled and turned back to her. "Medium," they said together.

The waitress finished jotting down the order, then looked up at both of them in turn. She smiled. "Y'all make a cute couple," she said, then tucked her pencil behind her ear. "I'll have your salads right out."

They made a cute couple. Sadie loved those words. She had never heard anybody say that about her and Chris. But with Ezra she felt happier than she ever had with Chris. Her whole life she had thought Chris Flaud was the one God made for her. Now she was beginning to think that special someone was Ezra.

Worst bowling night ever. Chris pulled his tractor into the driveway and chugged over to its parking spot. It simply wasn't any fun without Sadie.

She had called him that afternoon to let him know that she wouldn't be able to come, and he really couldn't blame her. Their relationship had changed, but he still wanted to spend time with her. She was his best friend.

He swung himself down from the tractor and headed across the dark yard. He had taken his time getting home, not really caring, too much on his mind to make the trip speedy.

"I didn't think you were ever going to get here." His brother Joshua was sitting on the front porch.

"What are you doing out here?" Chris asked.

"Waiting on you." Joshua stood and stretched, smoothing down his pant legs back over the top of his black boots.

"Aren't you cold?"

"Nah, the fresh air does me good sometimes."

Joshua worked in an office all day on a computer. Not the most Amish sort of job, but he said he enjoyed his work. Chris supposed that a dose of fresh air every now and then was just what Joshua needed.

"Maybe I should ask why you are out here."

Joshua settled himself down in the seat again and patted the bench next to him. "Come here. I have something I need to show you."

Chris tromped up the porch steps and took the seat his brother indicated. He waited as Joshua pulled his cell phone from his coat pocket and started tapping on it with his thumbs.

"Does the bishop know you have that?"

"You know full well that it is for my job."

Chris nodded.

"Well, mostly it is." He sat back and handed his phone to Chris. "See the screen there?"

Chris nodded. His brother had his Facebook page pulled up. He was certain the bishop didn't know about that.

"That man in the picture works for the shed company. He's my friend on there."

"That's great." Chris started to hand the phone back to his brother. "Still not sure why you're showing that to me."

"Look what's behind them. Or should I say who?"

Chris looked at the picture again, more closely this time. The guy in the foreground was smiling, standing close to a girl with the same happy look on her face. It looked like they were in some sort of restaurant. There were tables behind them and other things that indicated they had gone out to eat. But at one of those tables . . . "Sadie."

"*Jah*, that's what I thought too. But who's that she's with?"

"The Mennonite." Chris knew that they had been seeing each other. But he didn't know it was serious. "I wish I could see this better."

Joshua took the phone from him and made some sort of pinching motion on the screen. Suddenly what had been in the background now filled the screen. It was grainy and hard to make out a few of the details, but the happy look on her face as she gazed at Ezra Hein was unmistakable. As was their clasped hands resting on the table.

"That was taken in Pryor," Joshua said.

She hadn't given him an exact excuse as to why she couldn't come bowling tonight. She had left a curt message on the phone shanty recorder about how she couldn't make it. He figured she didn't feel very good, or maybe trying to keep up appearances had taken its toll. But he had never in a million years dreamed that she had been sneaking off with the Mennonite.

He handed the phone back to his brother, unable to find any words to express how he felt. Betrayed, jealous, sad, angry, the list went on and on.

Joshua stood, stretching once again and pocketing his phone. "I really didn't want to be the bearer of bad news, but I thought you should know."

"We're not a couple, you know." He wasn't sure if word had gotten back to his brother. And if nothing else, those words served as a reminder to him.

"I'd wondered if those rumors were true." Joshua nodded.

"I'm leaving this summer." Chris wasn't sure what possessed him to make such a confession; maybe it was a pride issue. Sadie wanted nothing to do with him. She said she wouldn't wait. But that didn't mean their feelings for each other had died in that instant.

"I was wondering how long it was going to take you. Is that what happened between you and Sadie?"

"*Jah*," Chris said. "I told her I loved her and asked her to wait for me. But she doesn't think I'm coming back."

Joshua chuckled, but the sound lacked humor. "You told her that you loved her, you want her to wait, and then you told her you are headed off to who knows where."

"Europe," Chris admitted.

Joshua sat back in his seat. His eyes wide. "That's some trip."

"*Jah.* It is. But I've waited my whole life." And Sadie had waited her whole life too, a little voice inside him whispered, but what was a couple to do when their dreams just didn't mesh? "No one else knows. Just you and Sadie."

He nodded. "I won't say anything."

"I appreciate that."

"I guess I better get back home," Joshua said. He loped down the stairs, then stopped and turned back around to face Chris. "You really are coming back?"

He nodded quietly, but felt a pang of guilt in his chest. He had been thinking more and more about Greece and Turkey and all the other little countries over there. How exciting would it be to explore the whole continent?

Maybe this was best. He couldn't imagine staying away from Wells Landing forever, nor could he imagine not seeing everything that Europe and the Mediterranean had to offer when he had the opportunity.

Now if he could figure out how to tell his parents and find a way to get over Sadie Kauffman.

Sadie felt as if she were walking in a dream, like her feet weren't even touching the ground, as Ezra led her back to his pickup truck. They'd had a wonderful dinner sitting and talking.

They had made the rule that they couldn't talk about their families or the problems that they faced. They could only talk about happy things, and she was glad they had decided that. It was so refreshing to not worry about what her mother thought or his mother thought, or any of the other people around them who didn't want them to be together at all. It was only about her and Ezra, and it could not have been more special.

Ezra opened the truck door for her, then went around to his side of the vehicle. He slid behind the steering wheel and they were off again. "Where to now?"

Sadie smiled. There was so much she wanted to do that being in Pryor just made it harder. Because there was so much to do.

"Well," she started. "If it was a little warmer outside I'd say miniature golf."

Ezra chuckled.

"How about a movie?"

He shook his head. "How about an ice cream instead."

"Braum's?"

"Is there any place else?"

"Not as far as I'm concerned." Sadie smiled.

Five minutes later Ezra pulled his truck into the parking lot at Braum's Ice Cream and Dairy Store. It was locally owned and arguably the best ice cream in Oklahoma.

They went inside and over to the ice cream counter, looking through the glass shield at the available flavors.

"What'll you have?" Ezra asked, as the girl approached.

"That banana split sure looks good."

"After the big meal we just ate, you think you can eat a banana split?" Ezra asked.

The girl behind the counter smiled and patiently waited.

"How about we share one?" Sadie suggested. Ezra

was right. She could be completely empty and not be able to eat the entire banana split. Sharing one was the perfect solution.

"Banana split?" the Braum's worker asked, looking from her to Ezra.

Sadie nodded, and they moved down the line to wait for their ice cream to be made.

"I call the chocolate side," Ezra said.

"You can't call it yet," Sadie said. "We're sharing, remember?"

"This is chocolate we're talking about," he said. "You can have the pineapple part."

"I don't like the pineapple part."

"No one likes the pineapple part," Ezra said.

"And I want my share of the chocolate part," Sadie said. "And the strawberry part."

The young girl behind the counter stopped scooping ice cream and looked at them both. "So no pineapple. How about I add chocolate ice cream with marshmallow sauce?"

"Can you add chocolate ice cream with chocolate sauce?" Sadie asked.

"Of course," the girl said. She moved down to get the chocolate ice cream.

Sadie looked at Ezra. "That's my part."

They ended up sharing all the parts, like she had known they would. But it was fun playing with him, pretending to bicker back and forth about who got the chocolate. All in all the whole evening was the perfect date.

"Coming to Pryor was a really good idea," Sadie said as they approached the sign that said they were back in Wells Landing. It wasn't like she could do that all the time, especially not if she was dating someone who was Amish too. They didn't have cars to take them all the way to Pryor, and each trip would require a driver, which she didn't think would be quite as much fun as sitting next to Ezra, putting along in his pickup truck.

But they had been right. Pryor was far enough away that their families didn't haunt them there, and their differences weren't so obvious to the average onlooker.

"Yeah," Ezra said. "We need to do this again. Next week?"

"Next week?" Her heart thumped.

"Wednesday is Valentine's Day."

"Oh that's right." She had forgotten. "I guess it's dumb to ask if any of our friends are having a party."

"Not if you want to take the chance and see if they'll be accepting."

"Do you think anyone will eventually understand and let this go?" As soon as she said the words, she wished she could call them back. It sounded a little too much like forever, and they had only been on their first real date.

"We can do whatever you want to do," Ezra said. "If you want to go to the party, then we will go to the party. Or we can go eat."

"Tex-Mex?"

"You want to drive to Pryor and eat Tex-Mex when you have Ricardo's on the next street over and two blocks down from you?"

"If *Mamm* were to see us eating there, I don't think she would understand."

"Because she doesn't like Mexican food?"

"Because she thinks that we need to be eating in the restaurant and not the competition."

"You consider Ricardo's her competition?"

"*Mamm* considers everyone competition."

Ezra chuckled again. "So what do you say?" he asked. "Are we still on for Wednesday?"

Valentine's Day with a man at her side? It didn't get any better than that. "I would love that."

She saw the flash of Ezra's smile even in the darkness of the truck's cab. "Then it's a date."

"Where to?" He had picked her up from the library to help disguise their date, and he didn't blame her. After all the trouble both of them had gotten from friends and family, it was better this way. They wanted to spend time together and they wanted to get to know each other better, and sometimes a couple had to do what a couple had to do.

"Everybody should be gone from the restaurant now."

"You want me to take you home?"

"Would you mind? You can drop me off at the driveway. You don't have to come down the driveway or to the house or . . ." She was rambling, a sure sign that she was uncomfortable.

"I don't mind taking you home, and I don't mind driving down your driveway. It's not that long." Maybe a hundred yards. So what had her so upset?

"I don't want to run into any family drama tonight."

"Agreed."

"So drop me off at the entrance of the driveway, and I'll walk the rest of the way. No one needs to know that you and I were even together tonight."

Part of him hated that sentence. He didn't want to sneak around. He wanted to show Sadie to everybody. But keeping everything as low-key as possible was the way to go. The fewer people who knew they were going out, the fewer people there were to send them looks of consternation whenever they walked past.

"Okay, then." He didn't want to, but he would. "I'll leave you at the end of the driveway, as long as you acknowledge that I wouldn't have done this for any other reason."

Sadie nodded.

All too soon he slowed the truck to a stop on the road in front of her house. He didn't want the night to end. It had been so much fun eating and talking and enjoying each other's company. It was almost like a regular Plain date, only with great food and ice cream.

"So . . ." Sadie said from the seat beside him. She had unbuckled her seat belt and turned slightly so that she was facing him more than she was the front of the truck. "I guess this is where we say good night."

Good night. This was the part of the date where he would lean over and give her a good night kiss. But he couldn't. He shouldn't have kissed her the other day. Things were moving way too fast between them, and he needed to put a slow block on it as soon as possible.

"Yes. Well, good night." He hated the flash of hurt he saw in her eyes. And the next thing he knew she was frantically reaching for the door handle to get out.

"Sadie, no, don't." He grabbed her arm just as she was about to tumble from the cab. "Don't."

"I don't understand." She sounded close to tears. And he had to admit this whole journey had been nothing but a roller-coaster ride of emotion.

He smoothed a hand across the side of her face. Thankfully there were no tears. "I can't kiss you tonight."

"You can't? You won't?"

Ezra chuckled. The sound was derisive to his own ears. "Both. We need to take things slower. The other night . . ." He trailed off. "The other night I pushed things too fast, and I don't want to do that with you."

"What if I said it's not too fast?"

He shook his head. "I've made up my mind. This is how it's going to be." Unable to stop himself, he ran his thumb across the softness of her lips, then leaned in to kiss her forehead. "Now get on in there before someone decides to come see what's going on out here."

She swallowed hard, then gave one nod and slid away from him. She was out of the truck and the door was shut before he had time to protest. Not that he could. It had to be this way. As much as he hated it, as much as he wanted to kiss her until neither one of them could breathe, he couldn't. Maybe one day, maybe soon, when they convinced their friends and family that this love building between them was worthy and good. Maybe then they could get married. And when that happened, he was never letting her go.

Chapter Fifteen

Sadie knocked lightly on the office door and entered after her mother's summons. The room was as crowded as usual, boxes stacked up and paper records on every available surface, but Lorie's fiancé, Zach Calhoun, had started his own accounting business and was slowly doing his best to work through the tangle of papers in the office.

Mamm sat back in her seat and gave Sadie an un-comfortable once-over. "Well now, my Sadie, you seem to have something on your mind today."

Sadie nodded. "I need Wednesday off, please." She figured professionalism was the way to go. She had a request, and she delivered it. Now with any luck, *Mamm* wouldn't ask her where she was going.

"For what?"

"I just need off, please."

Mamm frowned. "I depend on you to work here on Wednesday nights. You already have Thursday night off."

"I'll switch, then. I'll work Thursday if you let me have Wednesday off."

"And where are you going again?"

"Just out." Why did she have to ask that many questions? Maddie Kauffman was one of the most protective mothers in the district, as far as Sadie and her siblings were concerned; why couldn't she have picked tonight to let things drop? After all, Sadie was nearly twenty-three years old. She should be able to go someplace without having to tell her mother every little detail of the outing.

"I'll consider giving you the night off, but I think you need to be honest with me."

"*Mamm*, I just need the night off. I will work Thursday. And Friday too, if you need me. But I can't work Wednesday."

Mamm looked at the calendar on her desk, then back up at Sadie. "That's Valentine's Day."

"We don't normally get any more traffic from Valentine's Day than we do any other time of the year. It's not like this is a romantic restaurant that people use to celebrate big events." They served home-cooked meals. The people they would be getting in would be girls wishing they had a Valentine come to drown their sorrows in mashed potatoes and gravy.

"I don't know, Sadie. I think I need you."

"I think you're being unfair."

"You do?" Maddie took off her reading glasses, a sure sign that she was serious about whatever she had to say. Then again, *Mamm* was usually serious about everything. "Fair has nothing to do with this. I gave you the schedule you requested. You are part of this family. That's what you work and that's what you will continue to work."

Sadie growled in frustration. "Fine. Forget it."

She left her *Mamm*'s office, fuming with her mother's stubborn streak. Sadie shouldn't have to detail her every move to her mother. She was old enough to make her own decisions and old enough to go out when she wanted to without having to have a hundred questions thrown at her. Was that too much to ask?

She hit the waitress station as Melanie came through the door. Her sister was all bright smiles, but that was typical. Being a newlywed, Melanie was always smiling. Of course, if she had so recently gotten married, Sadie would be smiling too, so she couldn't begrudge her sister that.

"Hey, sister. You look angry."

"I'm just frustrated." Sadie shook her head. "I have a dinner date Wednesday night, and *Mamm* won't let me have off."

"I can work for you."

"You will? I mean, it's Valentine's Day. Don't you and Noah have plans?"

"We're waiting till Friday to celebrate. I don't mind coming in and helping out."

"That would be fantastic, Melanie. You'll never know how much that means to me."

Melanie shrugged. "What are sisters for?"

Wednesday couldn't come quick enough as far as Sadie was concerned. She didn't tell *Mamm* that Melanie was going to work for her. She was still angry about the whole situation. She was a grown adult, and she should be able to ask for a night off without having to endure an interrogation. She was fairly certain murder suspects didn't get as many questions asked of them as her mother had asked her about Valentine's Day night.

Of course, it didn't help that she didn't want to answer those questions. If she told *Mamm* she was planning to go out with Ezra Hein, *Mamm* would probably lock Sadie in her room to keep her home.

Sadie smoothed her hands down her dress. It was her favorite, a pretty blue color somewhere between royal and the midnight sky. It was not her mourning attire, but she was tired of it and she was going on a date. Besides, her father wouldn't care. It was only a couple more months before their mourning officially ended, and just because she was wearing a blue dress didn't mean she didn't miss her father. She would miss him till the day she died too. But for now she wanted to look good for Ezra, and looking good meant not wearing that ugly black dress.

She smoothed her hair down one more time, checked her teeth once again to make sure they were sparkling white and clean, then let herself out of the bathroom. Everyone else was at work. They wouldn't miss her for another hour or two. By then she would be long gone to Pryor with Ezra Hein at her side.

Thankfully she had the house to herself so he wouldn't have to worry about picking her up someplace odd. It made her feel a little better to know that he was coming to her house like a real date, like people who had parents that approved of the person they were dating and didn't get hung up on things that weren't important like whether or not he was a Mennonite.

Everyone acted like she was going to automatically marry him. If she did, they would work through it all. He was Mennonite. It wasn't like he was *Englisch*. He could easily become Amish, and they would live together happily, side by side.

She scooped up her purse from the back of the kitchen chair, grabbed her coat, and headed out for the door.

Standing on the porch, she slipped her arms into the black wool and hoped that Ezra would get there soon. She was so excited to have such a date. Normally, she would've gone over to somebody's house and played games and exchanged Valentines, eaten heart-shaped cookies, and in general had a good time. But Ezra's plan was better. Dinner in Pryor and something fun afterward. After all, how fun would it be to go to a party where nobody wanted them there? Since his friends didn't want anything to do with her and her friends didn't want anything to do with him, they would spend the evening by themselves. Come to think of it, she liked it that way.

From the road came the rattle of a vehicle and the crunch of gravel. Soon Ezra's blue truck came into view. She tried not to jump up and down with glee; at least she was able to contain herself better than Cora Ann. He pulled up in front of the house and she rushed to the truck, not even allowing him to get it in park before she slid in next to him.

"Hi," she said. "I'm glad to see you."

Ezra smiled. "I'm glad to see you too. Happy Valentine's Day." He took a red envelope off the dash and handed it to her.

"Can I open it now?"

"Uh-uh, wait until we get to the restaurant." He put his truck in reverse and backed it up so he could head out the driveway nose first.

Sadie pouted. "Why would you give it to me now if you knew you were going to make me wait until I get to the restaurant to open it?"

"I'm mean like that."

"Well, I'm not going to be mean, and you can't have what I have in my purse for you until we get to the restaurant."

"You call that being nice to me? That's a teaser if I've ever heard one."

Sadie laughed. Tonight was going to be such a good night, she could hardly wait until they got to Pryor. Tex-Mex and Ezra by her side, everyone around them in love and celebrating Valentine's Day. How much better could it be?

They chatted all the way to Pryor, about this, that, and the other, nothing in particular. She didn't mention any of her friends, and he never mentioned any of his. She didn't want to talk about her mother, and she knew he didn't want to talk about his. So they kept it light. What they might eat once they got to the restaurant and how long they thought they might have to wait for a table since it was Valentine's Day.

"I take it your mourning is over?"

Sadie shook her head. "No. But I'm so tired of wearing a black dress that I just couldn't take it anymore."

Ezra frowned. "So you wore it anyway?"

"*Jah,* sure. Why not? It's not likely that I will run into anybody I know in Pryor on Valentine's Day. All my friends are together playing games and stuff."

Ezra shook his head. "Sadie, you don't know who you might see."

Posh, she wanted to say. But she bit her tongue and kept the word back.

"Let's not worry about it," Sadie said. "We're supposed to be having a good time tonight. I wanted to wear something pretty for you. And that black dress . . . It's not pretty."

"You wore that for me?" He shot her a grin that for all intents and purposes had a wicked gleam in it.

"I did. This is my favorite dress. And I can tell you one thing. My dad loved color. He wouldn't have wanted us to wear black any longer than necessary."

"But that's not the rules."

Sadie held up her hands. "We said we weren't going to do this. We are not to talk about it anymore. Agreed?"

"Agreed."

Sadie stared at the window as Ezra drove them through town. Pryor wasn't a big city by any stretch of the imagination, but it was so much larger than Wells Landing that it almost made her head swim. Ezra pulled up to the parking lot of the red-tile-roofed building. "This is it."

He took her elbow and led her into the restaurant. Sadie relished his touch. All her life she had been waiting for that undeniable something that two people in love have, and she found it with Ezra Hein. She'd been about to give up, thinking it was not even real. She was so glad that she'd listened when he came along.

He held the door open for her and escorted her into the building. Then he whispered something to the host, and before she knew it they were placed in front of all the people waiting for tables and were seated in a dark, secluded corner with a red bowl with a white candle flickering between them.

"This is so romantic."

Ezra smiled. "It's also the best Tex-Mex."

"It's perfect. What looks good tonight?" she asked.

"I always get the fajitas."

"That sounds good, but I'm thinking I want the enchiladas."

"Then you should have the enchiladas."

The waitress brought over chips, salsa, and glasses of water. They each told her what they wanted, then she left, leaving them time alone once more.

This was what Sadie had been waiting for. Time for her and Ezra. And it was miraculous.

"What's Logan doing tonight?"

Ezra shook his head. "I thought we weren't going to talk about our friends tonight."

"I thought it would be fine." That could probably be the most stupid thing she'd ever said. But she was quickly running out of conversation that didn't involve family, friends, religion, or any of the other taboo subjects they had come up with.

"Do we have plans for after dinner?"

"Not really. I figured we would play it by ear and see what you might want to do later. You have any suggestions?"

Sadie smiled. "I do, but we can talk about that later."

Their food arrived and Ezra tucked in as if he hadn't eaten in a year. It made Sadie smile, seeing him eat and enjoy himself. She knew he worked so hard on the ranch that he needed a diversion as much as she did.

Before long their dinner was done, their waters had been refilled a couple of times, and Sadie was so full she could hardly move. "I'm going to have to watch what I eat on the days that we don't go out or I'm going to get fat."

Ezra shook his head. "You're not going to get fat." He grabbed the check and together they walked up front to pay at the cashier.

Sadie slid into the truck and shot him a smile. "Want to hear my idea? Let's go to the movies."

Ezra frowned. "The movies?"

"*Jah*, what's wrong with that?" Sadie asked.

"A lot of things." Ezra had been about to start the truck, but instead he left the engine off and turned to face her. "We can't go to the movies. You're Amish, and I'm Mennonite."

"*Jah*," Sadie said. "And?"

"And nothing," Ezra said.

"I don't understand what's wrong. We're sneaking around, going against everybody's rules and the things that they want for our lives, and you think going to the movies is a bad thing?"

"The movies have always been off-limits. You know that."

"Not always," Sadie argued. "I know people who went to the movies on their *rumspringa*."

Ezra sighed. "Neither one of us are running around."

"Why does that matter when we are already breaking the rules?"

"Someone will find out, Sadie. Someone always does. I don't have a problem sneaking out to see you and not telling people that I'm dating you. But I do have a problem with something like going to the movies."

"That does not make any sense."

"You and I both know that the Amish bend rules much more than the Mennonites. I can bend the rules so I can see you, but that doesn't mean I'm going to go as far as to sit in a movie theater and watch a movie. My mother would have a fit."

"And mine wouldn't?" Sadie shook her head. "I've gone against everything in my life to be with you. I don't see how us going to the movies is any worse than anything else we've been doing."

"I don't know how to tell you why. It just is."

"That's the most ridiculous thing I've ever heard!" Sadie hadn't meant to yell, but this conversation was so unreasonable. It was okay to do all those other things against their communities, but going to the movies was taking it too far? It was about the dumbest thing she'd ever heard.

"Ridiculous or not, it is how I feel." His voice turned cold, hard.

Sadie wanted to cry. "It's Valentine's Day, we were supposed to go out on a fabulous date."

"I thought that's what we were doing. Until about ten minutes ago."

"Whose fault is that? I made a suggestion. You are the one who got all righteous on me."

Ezra looked like he wanted to say something in return, but instead he turned around and started the engine to the truck.

Sadie buckled her seat belt, but still continued to frown at him. "Where are we going?" she asked.

"I'm taking you home."

He was fuming. How had such a special night turned into ash? He hadn't thought about anything past going to eat dinner. Thinking about their impromptu ice cream dessert the other day made him realize that maybe some things were better left unplanned. Then they could have a good time doing whatever they wanted whenever they wanted.

As long as that didn't include going to a movie.

He didn't want to take Sadie home. He wanted to do something fun. Take a walk, get another ice cream, anything as long as they were together.

Anything but go to the movies.

He could feel the anger coming off her in waves as she sat next to him on the trip back to Wells Landing.

Some Valentine's Day this was turning out to be. After what seemed like an eternity he pulled up to her house. "Can I go down the driveway or not?"

"No need," she snapped. She grabbed her purse from the floorboard and slung it over one shoulder, then pushed the truck door open. She slammed it behind her and stopped in front of his headlights. He could see bright flashes of pink on her cheeks, one more testament to her anger. She looked as if she was going to say something else, then spun away. He watched her stalk out of sight, then he turned his truck toward Taylor Creek.

Chris pushed his way into Kauffman's Family Restaurant. He wanted to see Sadie. He had been thinking more and more about that picture that Joshua had showed him, and he needed to make sure that she was okay.

She had been his best friend for so long. It was more than a simple breakup with a girlfriend. He'd lost the one person he could truly talk to.

This was all his fault. If he hadn't told her that he wanted to go to Europe, then she wouldn't be acting so wacky. She had been through so much lately—losing her father, her sister moving away, and now this.

Her sister Melanie bustled over, no doubt alerted to his entrance by the bell's summons. "Why hello there, Chris Flaud," she said with a smile. "What brings you in tonight?"

"I thought I would come in and talk to Sadie. But I expected to see her, not you."

Melanie frowned. "I thought she was out with you. In fact, I worked for her today so she could go out."

Chris bit back a sigh. She was out with that Mennonite again. He couldn't blame her. He had practically thrown her by the wayside, asked her to wait. Even Joshua had told him that was a bad idea. What had he been thinking?

Melanie motioned him back around the counter and toward the row of booths off to one side. "But you can come back here to sit down. I'll come and join you in a second. Coffee?"

Chris nodded. What could he do? He had come to see Sadie, to talk to her, only to find out that she had gone out with someone else again. He wanted her back. If he couldn't have her back romantically, then he would darn sure take her back as a friend. He missed her terribly.

Chris slid into the booth and watched as Melanie bustled away. She stopped for a moment to talk to Cora Ann, who was filling glasses behind the waitress station.

Cora Ann looked up at him and nodded, her mouth pulled into a small frown. The way everybody was acting, he would've thought she had died. Going out with a Mennonite was almost as bad.

Melanie came back a few minutes later with two steaming cups of coffee. She sat down across from him and cupped her hands around her mug. "So," she said.

"So," he repeated.

Melanie shook her head. "I'm worried about Sadie."

"Me too."

"She lied to *Mamm* about where she was going tonight. She lied to me too."

"She's been sneaking around with that Mennonite guy."

Melanie's eyes grew wide. "Do you think that's where she is right now?"

"I'm pretty sure." He took a sip of his coffee and stared out over the restaurant. People were eating, milling about. No one was in too big a hurry, but he looked at those people and he couldn't help but think they had no problems. Not like the weight of his heart.

As much as he knew he was being ridiculous, it was still how he felt. "My brother found a picture of her online with him. Ezra."

Melanie shook her head. She stood. "I need to get *Mamm*. Don't go anywhere."

He didn't even have time to respond as she hurried away, returning moments later with her mother in tow.

Maddie Kauffman had never been one of his favorite people, but she was Sadie's mother. Still, the woman looked as if she'd been sucking on green plums. Her face was always tense and unhappy, and he couldn't help but wonder how she could produce such sweet, loving daughters when she herself seemed as sour as a persimmon.

"Tell her what you told me," Melanie said.

"My brother Joshua, he showed me a Facebook page. There was a picture of Sadie and that Mennonite boy, Ezra Hein."

"Facebook? Like on the computer?"

"*Jah.*"

He wouldn't have thought it possible, but her face grew even more pinched and her mouth flattened into a thinner line than before. "Show me."

She led them into the office. There was barely room for the two of them. She sat down behind the restaurant's computer and tapped a few keys. A few minutes later Facebook appeared on the screen. It didn't take long before Chris found his brother and tracked down the guy who worked at the shed company with him. He clicked on the picture then zoomed in, finally showing her the picture of Sadie and Ezra.

Maddie shook her head. "I don't know what to do. We can't let her continue like this."

Melanie nodded.

Chris stood, uncomfortable with the whole situation. He'd come here to find solace for himself and instead he'd only brought pain to the others around him.

Maddie Kauffman grabbed his arm before he could take even one step from the office. "Chris, help us," she beseeched.

He shook his head. "What can I do?"

"Something. Anything. We can't let her go on like this."

That was when he understood Maddie Kauffman was so worried about Sadie because she was afraid she would lose that daughter like she had lost her other.

"You could court her again," Melanie said.

Chris wasn't quite sure what to say. He would love nothing more than to court Sadie. He had made so many mistakes where she was concerned. He would like to correct all those. But he had already decided. He was going to Europe in a few months, and Sadie didn't want to wait for him. What was a guy to do?

"Please," Maddie asked, squeezing his hand in her own bony fingers. "I can't lose her too."

To his surprise, Chris found himself saying yes, that he would try to keep Sadie busy, go out with her, make sure she knew he cared. With any luck and God on their side, they could convince her that Ezra Hein was no good, and staying with her family and the righteousness of the Amish faith was the only way to go.

Chapter Sixteen

Sadie was rolling silverware at the restaurant the following afternoon when Cora Ann summoned her to the phone. Sadie was so excited she nearly tripped over her own feet trying to get to it. Cora Ann told her it was a guy, and she knew it was Ezra calling to apologize. His stern attitude about going to the movies was ridiculous. All he needed was a little time to understand how crazy dumb his thoughts on the matter really were before he would offer her his apology.

"Hello?" she said, then waited to hear his familiar voice.

"Sadie, is that you?" Not quite the familiar voice she had been expecting.

"Chris?" She hadn't heard from him in days, weeks maybe. They never talked anymore.

"One and the same. How are you doing?"

"Okay, I guess." She was frustrated and tired and heartsick all at the same time, but other than that she was fine.

"Good, good," he said.

"Is that why you called? To find out how I'm doing?" She was more confused than ever. But she had to admit that she loved hearing his voice. She had missed him since they had been arguing.

"I wanted to ask about bowling tonight."

"We settled that. You can go bowling. Find some girl and take her." The thought was not one she was comfortable with, so she pushed it aside.

"See, I have found a girl."

"Oh?" She hoped her voice sounded even and only mildly interested.

"You."

"Chris, this is not a good idea."

"I think it's a great idea. You're a good bowler. I'm a good bowler. Between the two of us, we could take them all."

"That's not what I mean and you know it." She looked around to see if anybody else was listening in on the conversation, then she lowered her voice where only he could hear. "You're leaving."

"And you're dating a Mennonite. I know."

Was she? She had been, but after last night she didn't know where her relationship with Ezra stood.

He had dropped her off at the driveway without a word and left. No good-night kiss or another date for the next week. Nothing.

"Chris," she started in protest.

"I miss you, Sadie. You're my best friend. Come bowling with me. That's all I ask."

How could she say no to that?

"The dynamic duo returns!"

Sadie wasn't sure who said the actual words, but she smiled, happy to be embraced back into their buddy bunch.

Jonah and Lorie still weren't among them and

never would be. Jonah had really taken Lorie's leaving hard. He hardly came out anymore. Sadie had even heard that he had been going to wild parties in Tulsa. But the rumor mill in Wells Landing was so extreme that there was no telling what they would've said about him or Lorie.

"It's good to be back."

There was a lot of back patting and handshaking. Even Ruthie and Hannah gave Sadie a hug.

"We asked Melanie to join us. And Noah too, of course," Hannah said. "I hope you don't mind. We needed a fourth since Lorie's gone now." As she said the words, Hannah looked off in the distance as if she didn't want to look at Sadie directly when she said them.

What was wrong with everybody? Couldn't they see how happy Lorie was now that she had gone *Englisch*? Did it really matter? Did it make her less of a devout person? Did it make her less of a Christian? Sure, the temptations of the world were great, but Lorie had to find out who she was now, not who her dad had turned her into by hiding her among the Amish to protect her.

"Of course I don't mind, Hannah. She is my sister, after all."

"And a much better bowler," Melanie added with a laugh.

"We'll see about that." Sadie got out her ball. She had gotten it back from Ezra after their second date and wondered if she'd ever get to use it again. It felt good to be back at the bowling alley, having a normal Thursday night surrounded by all her friends. That was just where she thought she needed to be.

* * *

Just before the ninth frame, Melanie sidled up and sat down on the bench next to her. "So how was last night?"

"It was fine, thanks for asking. And thanks for working for me too."

"So how's Ezra?"

"He's good, I—" Sadie half answered the question before she realized it was a trick. "That wasn't nice, Melanie Treger."

Melanie shrugged. "I'm your sister, I don't always have to be nice."

"I think you got that backward. You're my sister, so you should always be nice to me."

"All joking aside, Sadie, what are you doing?"

"I'm sitting here."

"I said all joking aside," Melanie repeated. "Why are you seeing him?"

"Ezra?" She had been about to say something about Chris, but thought better of it. She had a feeling she had pushed all her sister's buttons enough for one night.

"Yes, Ezra." Melanie looked around, then back to her sister. "There's so many nice guys here in Wells Landing. Guys that share your same beliefs. Why would you want to go out with a Mennonite when you can go out with Chris?"

Sadie shook her head. "There's so much more to the situation than you know."

"Then tell me," Melanie said.

"I can't. It's not mine to tell."

"Fine then. But do me this favor." She waited to continue until after Sadie had nodded her agreement. "Give Chris a chance. Whatever it was that happened between you before, I think he really likes you. And you wouldn't have to worry about all the rest—shunning, moving, and making *Mamm* cry."

A shunning. It was the one thing Sadie hadn't thought about. She had joined the church. Lorie hadn't. Lorie wasn't shunned. She could come and go in Wells Landing as she pleased. The only consequence she had was the fact that *Mamm* didn't want her to go *Englisch*. But once *Mamm* had gotten used to the idea, she had forgiven Lorie quickly and allowed her back into the family fold. But with Sadie, it was different. She had joined the church, and if she left to do something like marry Ezra, then she would surely be shunned. Most people didn't realize that a shunning was to bring someone back into the fold. But once she married Ezra, there would be no coming back. She would be shunned for life. There was no recovery from that. She would never be able to sit at the same table with her family and eat again. She could never take money from them or even ride in the same car with them. The thought broke her heart, especially when she thought about Daniel.

Sweet, sweet Daniel. He had such a hard time when Lorie left that he surely wouldn't understand why he couldn't spend time with Sadie.

"Think about it, okay?" Melanie asked.

What was there to think about? That she couldn't marry Ezra if she wanted to remain a member of the Kauffman family in good standing, or that she could date Chris for the next couple of months, and come June he was on a plane to Europe?

It wasn't much of a choice either way, now was it?

After spending the evening with Chris, Sadie was more confused than ever. Even prayer hadn't brought her any solace. All she wanted was a sign, for God to help her.

Ezra hadn't mentioned marriage, but she couldn't believe that both of them were going against their family and friends just to date. It had to be going somewhere.

She loved the sizzle she felt whenever she was near him. It was that spark she had read about in *Englisch* romance books during her *rumspringa*. Romance writers talked about that one special someone that made a heart sing. Sadie thought Ezra could be that person to her. But after Valentine's Day night, she wasn't so sure anymore.

And then Chris. She had known him all of her life. They had been through so much together. She loved him, but not with the same kind of love as she felt for Ezra. So it didn't have that zap and tingle, but it was steady and true, wholesome and solid as a rock. She would never have to worry about Chris. Well, she wouldn't after he got back from Europe. What was a girl to do? Wait on Ezra to propose and decide then? Put him off until Chris returned, if he returned? What would she do if she had both of them wanting to marry her at the same time?

The thought was silly. Two men wanting to marry her at the same time? She was just plain Sadie. And that was all she would ever be.

It was Friday afternoon and Daniel was due off the bus any minute. Sadie was staring out the window at nothing. The sun shone brightly with the promise of spring. It wouldn't be long before the crocuses started to come out, and the tulips that she had planted around one of the outbuildings. But staring out at nonexistent flowers was not helping her one bit.

She heard the roar of an engine and went out to meet Daniel's bus. But instead of Daniel, it was Ezra.

She stopped in her tracks as he pulled on the driveway, put the truck into park, and climbed out.

"Hi," she said. It was all she could manage to get through her numb lips.

"I've come to apologize," Ezra said. "Arguing with you and fighting with you on Valentine's Day was surely not part of my plan."

Anticipation rose inside her. Was this the sign she needed? Of all the days for her to be waiting at home for Daniel to come off the bus, and then have Ezra show up full of apology. She had asked God for a sign. Was this it?

"Does that mean you forgive me?"

Hope flashed in his brown eyes. "Of course." He took her hands into his and squeezed her fingers lightly. The touch was gentle but reassuring. "I know everything's not going to be perfect all the time. We're going to have a lot of adjustments, but I want you to know that I love you, Sadie Kauffman. As strange as it may seem, you're the best thing that's ever happened in my life."

She could hardly believe her ears. Ezra Hein loved her? "I don't know what to say."

He frowned. "I think if you don't know what to say, then that means you don't return my feelings." He nodded, but looked down as if he couldn't bear to meet her gaze again.

"That's not what I meant at all. I . . . I'm just so happy." Tears rose into her eyes. Yes, she was happy, but so very, very confused. She was hoping he would take her into his arms, maybe kiss her one more time and show her the love that he confessed. But another engine sounded, and this one most likely belonged to Daniel's bus.

They pulled apart as the bus stopped to let Daniel out. Sadie went onto the road to help him cross, then took his hand and headed back down the driveway. Ezra had climbed back into the truck cab.

"You're not staying?"

He shook his head. "I need to be getting back."

"I understand." She waited a heartbeat and then another. He had come to apologize. But he wasn't going to ask to see her again? Why was love so confusing?

"When is your next day off?" he asked.

"Tuesday." *Mamm* had changed it. She had the day completely off, and Thursday night off so she could bowl with her team.

"So Tuesday I can come by?"

"I-I . . ." she stuttered, then tried again. "I don't think coming by here is a good idea."

He nodded. "Right." Then he looked down at Daniel.

Sadie knelt down next to her young brother. "Daniel, why don't you run on in the house? I'll be there in a minute to get you some cookies, okay?"

He looked from her to Ezra, giving them both a big grin. "Okay, but I wanted to talk to Ezra."

"You can do that next time, buddy," Ezra said.

He nodded, then ran for the front door, his backpack slapping against his tiny back all the way there.

Yet for all the promises that Ezra had made, how was he going to talk to Daniel next time? The two of them couldn't even eat dinner together without everybody causing a big fuss. And if it came to pass that the two of them did get married, they would be shunned. How was that supposed to work out for him to spend time with Daniel? How was that supposed to work out where *she* could spend time with Daniel? There were too many questions and not enough answers.

"Pick you up at the library?"

"Are you going to tell me where we are going?"

"That's a surprise." He smiled, a dazzling flash that she wondered might perhaps be that sign from God she'd been asking for. One thing was for certain: Tuesday couldn't get there quick enough.

Sunday morning dawned, perhaps the prettiest day they'd had all year. Though the winds still held a chill, the sun shone brightly, holding promises of what it would be like come June.

Sadie loved the summertime so much more than winter, and she could hardly wait for the summer to get there. When she said that, she had to remember that Chris was leaving in June. Could she trust that he would come back, or was he going to be gone forever?

Sadie was helping put away the last of the benches after the church meal when Melanie came up beside her. "A bunch of us are going over to Millers' Pond. You want to go?"

"It's too cold to swim."

"Who said anything about swimming? We want to go have a good time. Sit around and talk."

"Who's all going?"

Melanie shrugged. "Me and Noah, Ruthie and Mark, Will and Hannah. You know. The group."

"And I'm going to be the only single girl there." It wasn't really a question. But Sadie had the feeling that Melanie had something going on that she wasn't telling her about.

"Well . . . Chris is supposed to come." There it was.

"Melanie, I don't think this is a good idea."

"Why not? You and Chris used to be quite a thing."

"Well, that was before . . ." She really couldn't say. Chris hadn't told anybody about his trip to Europe, and she was walking around having to keep his secret from all her family. It really wasn't fair. "We're not a couple, you know."

"About that . . ."

Sadie shook her head. "There are things you don't know, Melanie. Things that I can't tell you."

"But I'm your sister."

Sadie shook her head. "It has nothing to do with that. It isn't mine to tell. Just know that Chris and I are not a couple and we are not getting married."

"If you say so. But will you come to Millers' Pond with us?"

How could she refuse?

In addition to the group of young people that Melanie had mentioned, Jonah Miller also joined them, along with Sarah Yoder. Sadie supposed it was only natural, considering the pond was on his parents' property. But the fact that he was with Sarah Yoder was something of a surprise to Sadie.

Not too long ago, Jonah and her sister, Lorie, had been quite a thing, though their relationship was on again-off again. Lorie and Jonah argued a lot and did not see things the same way more often than not. Then Lorie met Zach Calhoun and everything changed.

Everyone had brought quilts and blankets and spread them out on the banks of the pond. Sadie could hardly wait until it was warm enough to swim again. She loved coming out here on her days off.

Sometimes it was girls only and sometimes her and Chris and other couples. Though now Chris would be leaving, and Ezra wouldn't be welcome. Who knew when the next time would be that she would be able to come out here and enjoy herself like she had in the past?

Melanie plopped down next to her. "Why don't you look like you're having a good time?"

"I'm having a great time." She hoped God didn't strike her down for the lie. But Melanie was so happy these days, loving life and being married to Noah. And here was Sadie, wanting everything her sister had and not able to have it. She added that transgression to her mental prayer list. "Who is that?" She nodded toward the quilt on the opposite side of the pond from where she and Melanie sat.

"That's Abbie King. You remember her, right?"

Sadie searched through her memory, trying to pull up what she knew about Abbie King. "It was her brother that was killed in the car wreck."

Melanie nodded. "That's her."

"We haven't seen much of her lately."

"Noah said that she had a hard time after Alvin died, so they sent her to some family in Missouri to stay for a while. She's only been back in town a couple of weeks."

Suddenly Sadie didn't feel quite so sorry for herself. Sure, she had lost Lorie to the *Englisch*. But she hadn't lost her completely—she could still visit, but Abbie King had lost her brother forever.

"I'm glad she's back," Sadie murmured.

"And did you see Mandy Yoder is here?" Melanie leaned a bit closer to deliver that piece of gossip.

"Sarah's cousin?"

Melanie nodded. "I guess it's Mandy Burkholder now."

"She married Levi Burkholder, didn't she?"

Melanie nodded again. "Right after Titus Lambert went to prison."

It was funny how her own problems had her forgetting the trials of others. A few years back Titus Lambert had been involved in a car accident that killed Alvin King and another boy, an *Englisch* boy. Because of that, Titus had been sent to prison; his girlfriend, Mandy, had married another; and Abbie had gone away to deal with her grief. It was so sad really.

Sadie shook her head. "We really shouldn't be gossiping about this."

"Then let's gossip about you." Melanie's smile was infectious.

"There's nothing to gossip about."

"Really?" Melanie nodded off to one side.

Sadie looked up to see Chris headed their way.

Melanie pushed to her feet. "Okay then. I'll catch you later." And with that, she disappeared.

Sadie waited for Chris to come closer.

"Mind if I sit down?"

Sadie shook her head without looking at him. She really didn't know what to say, but she couldn't turn him away.

"I miss you, you know." His words were so quietly spoken she almost didn't hear them.

She swung her gaze in his direction, searching for any evidence that he was telling her the truth. There was nothing but sincerity written on his face.

"I miss you too." And it was the truth. She missed Chris, her friend, her steady, her rock. He had been the one thing she could depend on all these years. And she hated that they had a falling-out.

"Does that mean you'll go bowling with me again on Thursday night?"

It was on the tip of her tongue to tell him no. She didn't want him to get the wrong idea. Chris knew her true feelings, and she knew his. Sure, if they were to get married they would make a great couple. Not in a completely *Englisch* romance kind of way, but look at how some of those turned out.

Maybe her argument with Ezra was getting the better of her. They were on their way to reconciliation. But everything around her was so confusing these days. Chris wanted to make up, she and Ezra had argued. It was almost too much.

But what was the harm in spending time with her best friend?

She nodded. "I would like that very much."

Chapter Seventeen

Sadie tried not to let her confusion get the better of her on Monday. She'd had a nice afternoon with Chris sitting by Millers' Pond, talking and visiting with the other members of their youth group and buddy bunch.

But she was waiting for her special date surprise on Tuesday with Ezra. Then she would have a day off in between to collect herself before she and Chris went bowling on Thursday night.

That was the hardest part of it all. She loved spending time with Chris and the other people she had known practically her entire life—Ruthie and Hannah, even Abbie King and Mandy Burkholder. Unfortunately she couldn't do things like that with Ezra.

Yet spending time alone with Ezra, just the two of them without the pulls of community and family, was special in itself as well.

But she couldn't figure out where she belonged in all of that.

* * *

"So where are we going?" Sadie asked for what had to have been the eighth time since Ezra had picked her up that morning. As best she could tell, they were headed into Tulsa, but Ezra had gotten off the highway. Now they were driving on unfamiliar streets. She tried to see if there were any road signs announcing the sights coming up from the exit they had taken. She thought she'd seen Mohawk Park, but she couldn't tell if it was this exit that led to the park or the next one.

"Be patient." Ezra smiled. "We'll be there in a minute." Two more miles and she figured out where they were headed.

"The zoo?"

Ezra nodded. "I thought it might be fun."

Sadie couldn't stop the grin spreading across her face. She hadn't been to the zoo in years. Since before she was even Cora Ann's age. "I think it'll be great fun too."

Ezra parked the truck and the two of them made their way to the zoo's entrance. He bought the tickets and led them through the turnstile and into the main area of the zoo. "What do you want to see first?" he asked.

Sadie shook her head. "I want to see everything."

"Everything it is." He hooked her arm through his and led her toward the right. First up were the monkeys and the rest of the primates.

The weather was good for February. Being a Tuesday, there weren't many people milling around the zoo. Sadie felt as if the animals were giving a show just for them.

They walked through the reptile house and into the rain forest section with its little poison frogs and all sorts of exotic creatures that she had never seen before. The penguin habitat and the polar bears, everything was magical and wonderful. She felt as if she had stepped into another world. Then they took the train around over to where the Galapagos tortoises were housed.

"It says here this turtle is almost a hundred years old," Ezra said, pointing to the little stand that contained information about the creatures.

Sadie shook her head. A hundred years was a long time. The tortoises were wrinkled and slow, but they were somehow beautiful in their own special way.

"Do you want to see the giraffes now?" Ezra asked, pointing toward the penned-in fields where the giraffes were kept.

But Sadie was drawn to the other side. The elephants. "Can we go . . ." She gestured toward the giant creatures.

"We can do whatever you want," Ezra said.

"Then I want to see the elephants."

This time, Ezra grabbed her hand and together, fingers entwined, they made their way toward the elephant habitat.

"They're beautiful."

Ezra chuckled. "You really think so?"

"*Jah.* I do." She leaned against the fence, not so much to get a better view, but to be a little closer to such magnificent creatures.

"Even prettier than the zebras?"

Sadie nodded.

"And the tigers?"

"*Jah.*"

Ezra tilted his head to one side as if he was trying to get a better angle to view the big beasts. "Don't get me wrong. They're great. But what do you see in them?"

Sadie stared at them, trying to find the words to describe how the elephants made her feel. "They're so big and beautiful, a little cumbersome and yet graceful all in the same moment. Can you see the intelligence in their eyes?"

Looking at the elephants was like seeing a reflection of something bigger than herself. Not in true size, for there was no mistaking the elephants were gigantic compared to her, but somehow bigger at an internal level, as if they held a special place in God's eyes.

"Okay," Ezra agreed.

But Sadie had the feeling he was saying that just to appease her. It upset her that Ezra couldn't see what she saw in the elephants, couldn't see love and compassion and all things beautiful wrapped up in big feet and wrinkly gray skin. It was as if God was playing some sort of trick on mankind to put something so special in an unlikely package. Sadie wondered if God was waiting on man to discover this specialness that He had hidden.

"I feel sorry for you, Ezra Hein."

"Sorry for me?" Ezra asked. His eyes were alight with surprise.

"*Jah*. I feel sorry that you can't see what I see in them."

He thought about that for a minute, then smiled. "I guess it's a good thing I have you here to point it out to me."

Ezra had the feeling that Sadie could sit and watch the elephants all day long. In fact, he made a mental note to bring her out to the zoo again with the intention of just going to the elephant habitat and sitting for as long as she wanted and watching these creatures that she had fallen in love with. But for now it was still February and cold. Not terribly bad. Spring was starting to warm the air.

That was the way of Oklahoma. A February day could be seventy or ten degrees, depending on the whim of nature. But for now he thought it best that they get someplace warm, at least for a little while.

Sadie said a sweet good-bye to the elephants, and he led her into the nearby gift shop. There was a café adjacent where they could get something warm to drink. He bought them each a cup of coffee, then they wandered through the gift shop, checking out all the animal-related items for sale there.

There were plastic-molded animals that looked realistic, though they were miniature. There were stuffed animals and postcards, coffee cups and drinking glasses of all sorts. There were even T-shirts and hats and all sorts of clothing for people to buy.

Sadie started looking through the many shirts there on display, while Ezra wandered into the section that housed some of the smaller items.

He wanted something for Sadie to remember today. It had been perhaps the best time they'd had together. When he had set up this date, he wanted someplace they could go and perhaps not be found out or be worried about being found out. After the trouble in Pryor, he felt it was better to go someplace where they would blend in even more. Not that they blended in completely. He supposed to the average person he looked like the average person, but Sadie in her black and prayer *kapp*, thick stockings, and walking shoes was so obviously Amish that a few people had stopped to stare. She seemed not to notice, or maybe she didn't care, as she wandered through the zoo's trails beside him.

He looked at the coffee cups, but there was nothing with an elephant on it. There were ones with the zoo's logo on them and some that had pictures of some of the newer habitats and creatures, the dinosaur exhibit and the penguins, but nothing with her majestic elephants.

There were postcards, but they didn't fit the bill. He wanted something beautiful for her to remember today by. Something as beautiful as she considered those big gray elephants out there.

Then he found it. It was the only one left, and he wasn't sure how he even saw it. But there it was: a silver necklace with an elephant pendant. It was fairly small, maybe no bigger than a dime, with this small indentation for an eye. Its trunk was raised up in salute, and it was perfect. She could wear it everywhere she went and have an elephant with her always. It was beautiful and he knew she had to have it.

"Ezra, look at this." She held up a pink nightshirt— at least he thought that's what it was—in front of her. It reached down to her knees. On the front were the intertwining trunks of two elephants that formed a heart. Below that it read I HEART ELEPHANTS.

"Would your mother care if you had that?"

He saw that rebellious light in Sadie's eyes flash, then she seemed to think about it without that surge of emotion. "I don't see why not. There isn't anything in the *Ordnung* about nightshirts with elephants on them."

"Then you should have it."

He hustled her to the counter, not giving her even a second to change her mind about the nightshirt. He handed the necklace to the cashier and gave her a look that he hoped the gray-haired lady behind the counter could understand. He wanted the pretty silver trinket, but he didn't want Sadie to know about it. Some things needed to be a surprise.

With age came wisdom, and the woman gave a small nod before slipping the necklace into a small bag, then putting it inside the larger bag where the T-shirt was now stored and ready to go.

Ezra paid the bill while Sadie gushed. "Thank you so much."

"You're welcome." His heart swelled at the sight of the pure happiness on her face.

Together they left the gift shop and headed out of the zoo park, back to the parking lot.

"Next time we need to buy a camera."

Sadie's eyes grew wide. "Oh my goodness! I didn't even think of that."

"I think it would be fun, don't you?"

"Maybe we can buy one of those disposable ones that they have there in the shop."

Ezra nodded. "That sounds like a great idea. Then you can take all the pictures you want of those silly elephants."

"They aren't silly." She shot him a mock-serious look.

"I know, I know, don't get your dander all up."

Sadie crossed her arms and gave him a stern look. "Never joke about elephants again."

"Never," he promised with a smile.

"Do you want me to drop you off at the library?" Ezra asked.

Sadie nodded. She hated having to sneak around and see Ezra like this. But after the day they had spent together, she felt as if she would do anything as long as she could spend time with him.

Did that mean that she loved him? Probably. But now the thought didn't fill her with dread and anxiety. She loved Ezra Hein. A Mennonite boy. The idea warmed her from the inside out, and she wanted to climb to the highest place she could find and shout it to all of Wells Landing, hoping that even the people of Taylor Creek could hear. So what if he was Mennonite and she was Amish? They would figure out a way.

Ezra wasn't like Zach Calhoun. Zach could've never become Amish. It would have been too hard for him, but they were so much alike, the Mennonite and the Amish.

And it would all work out. She knew it.

He pulled his truck into the library parking lot and eased it into one of the spaces. Leaving the engine running, he put it into park, then turned to face her. "I'm glad you came with me today."

"So am I." Sadie smiled at him, her heart growing bigger each time she looked at him. He was perhaps the most handsome man she had ever met, and he wanted to spend time with her. It was a beautiful thought. And if God put them together, then surely there wasn't anything wrong with it.

"Do you have your sack?"

Sadie nodded.

"Let me see it." Ezra held out his hand for her to give it to him.

"Why do you need it?" she asked, even as she offered it to him.

"Maybe there's a surprise in here." He grinned.

"Another surprise?"

He didn't answer with words, just stuck his hand into the bag and pulled out another small paper sack that had been tucked inside. She had no idea how it had gotten there. She hadn't noticed it when they were at the gift shop, but she had been so wrapped up in happiness and elephants that she hadn't been paying a great deal of attention.

"Today was special," Ezra said. His smile had dimmed and his eyes turned serious, but in a good way. Intense, and dare she hope, loving . . . ? "I wanted you to have something to remember today by."

"I have a shirt."

Ezra shook his head. "You need something more special than that."

He pulled a small box from inside the little paper sack and opened it.

Sadie held her breath as he lifted out a thin silver chain. A small pendant hung there, an elephant with smooth curved lines and a soft shiny finish.

He opened the clasp and reached around her neck to place the necklace there.

Sadie used every bit of energy she had not to pull away. She was torn. She wanted that beautiful necklace so badly, that memento of today, the one thing that Ezra had picked out in the store just for her, but . . .

"The Amish don't wear jewelry." Her words were barely a whisper. But they felt heavy in the air around her.

Ezra sat back and stared at her for a moment. "I don't understand."

Sadie wanted to touch the necklace, finger its smooth lines, claw it from her body. It felt fiery and hot through the fabric of her dress. She wanted to take it off, but she wanted to leave it on forever. Confusion had become her constant companion.

"It's okay to go to the movies, but it's not okay to wear jewelry?"

Sadie shook her head. "It's not okay to do either one of those things."

Ezra snorted. "Now I really don't understand. So it's okay to go against the *Ordnung* and go to the movies, but it's not okay to go against the *Ordnung* and wear a necklace. You Amish have entirely too many rules."

Sadie felt like she'd been punched in the stomach. "It's beautiful."

"But?" he asked.

She had a decision to make, and she had to make it right here. Right now. She and Ezra had so many differences, ones that they would have to see through to the end of their relationship.

"Do you love me?"

He stared at her for so long she wasn't sure that he would answer. It was on the tip of her tongue to take back her question when he sighed. "Yes."

She hadn't realized how thick the tension hung in the air until he said that one word and effectively dispelled it.

"I love you too," she breathed. They loved each other—surely that meant something. "I'm sorry," she said. "Sometimes I get confused and lose sight of what's important."

Ezra nodded. "It happens to all of us."

Sadie smiled. "Tell me it's going to be okay."

"It's going to be okay," Ezra said. He reached out a hand and touched her cheek.

Sadie closed her eyes, absorbing every detail of his skin against hers.

"Does this mean you accept my gift?" He seemed to be holding his breath as he waited for her answer.

Sadie nodded.

His smile was wobbly, but filled with hope. He reached up and tucked the beautiful silver chain and its charming little elephant under the neckline of her dress. Despite the February temperatures, the pendent felt hot against her skin.

"No one has to know it's there."

She wanted to nod, know that it was all going to be okay, and despite his words from a few moments ago, her own confidence was waning. "I have to go."

Confusion wrinkled his brow, but he didn't protest. "Next week?"

Sadie swallowed hard, then gave a quick nod. "Next week." She reached for the door handle, fumbling as she tried to get out of his truck. She wasn't sure what she was going to do with the nightshirt as she walked to the restaurant. She supposed she could tuck it under her coat. Hide it away like she had that tiny elephant necklace.

She slid to the ground, suddenly needing to be away from him and all the churning emotions that he brought out in her.

"Sadie?"

She turned to face him, shaking her head to stay his words. "Thanks for a lovely day, Ezra." Then she slammed the door on anything else he might've said.

Chapter Eighteen

One more week and it would be March.

Chris dusted off his hands and climbed down from the hayloft. One more week and he had three months to figure out how to tell his parents that he was going to Europe. That he had been secretly squirreling away money to make a trip of a lifetime, one that no Amish man had ever made before. At least not that he had ever heard.

The secret was tearing him in two. But he couldn't tell them yet. No doubt his father would toss him out on his ear. For all the talk of the Amish being forgiving, there were some things a man couldn't come back from. And Chris was certain this was one of those, as far as his father was concerned.

He had to tell them now or start baptism classes. He crossed to the wall where all the tools were hung and grabbed up the pitchfork. He stabbed one of the big bales of hay and dragged it down to the stables. As much as he would like to unburden his heart and tell his parents of his plans, the best thing to do was carry on like everything was the same. Even when it wasn't.

He stopped spreading the hay as a weird sound came from above him. Was that . . . ?

He leaned the pitchfork against the wall and headed out into the yard. Shielding his eyes from the noonday sun, he peered up at the roof of the two-story barn.

"Johnny?"

"Yeah?" His brother's voice drifted down from somewhere on the back side of the barn.

Chris started through the double Dutch doors, 'round to the other side. He stepped into the corral and peered up at the roof once more.

Johnny was crawling around like some *Englisch* superhero, nailing down pieces of the corrugated tin.

"I thought you were going to wait for me to help you," Chris hollered up to his brother.

Johnny finished pounding down the nail, then hollered back. "You were busy."

Chris shook his head. "Never too busy for you."

Though the sun was to his back, Chris saw Johnny shrug. "No worries."

"Want me to come up and help?"

"That's all right. I'm almost done. I'll be down in a minute." Without another word he went back to work.

Chris shook his head and started back to the barn. His brother was one of the hardest-working people that Chris knew, and he admired him for his dedication to this piece of dirt. He was glad Johnny liked the farm, because he wouldn't be able to get away from it fast enough.

From outside the barn he heard the sound of an angry dog barking. He recognized one of the dogs as his own blue heeler, Beau. But the other dog did not sound familiar. He hustled through the barn, wondering if the stray had come up and Beau was simply defending his turf or if something else was afoot.

When he came out on the yard side of the barn, Beau had definitely proven ownership of the property. The black and tan mutt that had wandered up was on the run as Beau chased him through the yard and toward the road. Before they got to the narrow driveway lane, another dog rushed up. This pooch had short tan fur and a vicious growl.

The mutt rushed the dogs from the side, hurtling them toward the side of the barn. Chris took his hat off and headed toward them, thinking he would wave them away.

Before he got there, they crashed into the ladder Johnny had set up against the side of the barn.

And everything happened at once. Beau managed to get the upper hand on both dogs and chased them clear to the road. Chris barely registered his dog's victory as a strangled cry rent the air. A dull thud sounded and Chris whirled around as the tall aluminum ladder crashed into the yard with a metallic crunch, missing his brother's broken and crumpled body by inches.

Sadie rushed through the swooshing glass doors at Pryor Medical Center. She had to find Chris, and she had to find him now.

Tears ran in hot trails down her cheeks as she searched the waiting area and the drawn faces of the patients and loved ones sitting there. In her frantic state, she had to survey the room twice before she saw him, sitting in a dogleg corner all by himself. His hat was gone and one of his suspender galluses had fallen off his shoulder. But he was there, her Chris.

She rushed over to him, nearly falling in her haste to reach him as quickly as possible. She dropped to her knees before him, grabbing his hands.

"Chris?"

His eyes fluttered open, and he appeared to be in some type of daze. Surely he hadn't been asleep, not with what just happened. He blinked a couple of times as if to clear his thoughts.

"Sadie?" The word was tentative, unsure and testing.

She nodded, and the gesture seemed to put him into motion once more.

He gathered her in his arms and held her close.

"Shush," she said, trying to calm him.

Deep sobs racked his body, and his hot tears burned her neck as he held her as if she was the lifeline to the world.

Sadie couldn't stop her own tears. But more than anything, she let Chris cry it out. She simply held him while he sobbed, uncaring about the staring eyes and frowns they received.

After a few moments, he pulled himself together and pulled away.

Sadie wiped one hand against his face, whisking away the last of his tears. "What happened?"

"It's all my fault. If I'd been helping him . . ."

Sadie shook her head. "You can't blame yourself." She said the words even though she didn't know the entire story. Whatever happened, she couldn't believe that Chris was to blame. He loved his brother more than anything and would have done everything in his power to keep him safe.

Chris recounted the tale of how Johnny had climbed up onto the barn to repair the roof. How the dogs had unsettled Johnny's ladder and he fell to the ground.

"Where is he?" She said the words as gently as

possible. No one in Wells Landing knew exactly what had happened or how Johnny was. She had grabbed the first person she knew who had a car, demanded and begged they take her to Pryor to be with Chris, instinctively knowing he needed her now more than ever.

"They took him in a helicopter to Tulsa." Chris squeezed his eyes shut and shook his head. "But I don't know what good it will do."

Sadie squeezed his hands. "Don't say that."

"He was bad, Sadie. He was out for a while. Then he kept saying 'I can't move. I can't move.'" Chris's tears started again. "It's all my fault."

Sadie squeezed his hands tighter. "Quit saying that. There was nothing you could have done to make this different."

"I don't know what I'll do, Sadie. I don't know what I'll do if he dies."

Sadie managed to talk Chris into going back to Wells Landing with her. His parents had taken a driver to Tulsa to follow Johnny to the hospital there.

Sadie didn't bother to ask if Chris had left the hospital at all; his shock and grief was enough of an answer.

He was uncharacteristically quiet all the way back to town. He leaned against the door and stared out the window, watching the world pass by.

Sadie directed the driver to take them out to the Flaud farm. From there, she should find somebody to come and stay with Chris so he wouldn't have to be alone.

She managed to get Chris into the house and seated

at the kitchen table, though he still appeared to be in deep shock.

She made a couple cups of coffee though she knew he wouldn't drink it, then set out to the barn and the phone the Flauds had there to find someone to stay with him.

She made several calls, left messages, then decided to ring Abe Fitch's furniture store.

Andrew Fitch answered on the second ring.

"Andrew," Sadie started. "There's been an accident. Johnny Flaud fell. I don't know how bad he is. They've taken him to Tulsa. His parents went with him, but Chris is here by himself."

"I'll be right there," Andrew said without wavering. She didn't even have to ask. That was the kind of person Andrew Fitch was. Two little kids at home, and he was willing to drop everything and help out a friend.

"Thank you so much, Andrew. I would stay but . . ." She didn't bother to finish. Andrew knew how inappropriate it would be for her to stay with Chris past dark alone in his parents' house.

"You'll stay until I get there?" Andrew asked.

"Of course," Sadie said. "I'll see you in a few." She hung up the phone and headed back into the house.

She wasn't even sure if Chris knew that she had left. Other than the first initial reaction he had when she'd seen him in the hospital, he appeared stoic and in some sort of weird trance. She knew that eventually he would get back to being closer to the Chris she knew, but she had a feeling it wouldn't happen until after he knew that his brother was okay.

Sadie called the restaurant to talk to Cora Ann, who

promised to call Melanie to come out and get her, but she would only leave after Andrew promised to let her know as soon as they got word on Johnny.

Lord, please . . . she started, but the words for her prayer wouldn't come. *Just please.*

God knew they were hurting. He knew who needed help. She trusted that even without a full prayer, He would see them all through.

Amen, she said, hoping her words hit their mark. One thing was certain, Johnny and his family were going to need all the prayers that they could get.

Sadie knocked on the door of the Flaud house the very next day. It was Thursday, and she was off from the restaurant, but she wasn't sure what was worse: sitting at home waiting for word about Johnny or being at work and worrying about the same thing.

She packed up a basket of bread and headed over to check on Chris and Andrew. She scanned the front room looking for him.

Andrew shook his head. "He's still in bed. I can't get him out. I figure he'll probably come around in a bit."

"That's not acceptable," Sadie said. "I'll call Lorie. Maybe she can help us find out something quicker." If she remembered right, Zach Calhoun's sister was a trauma nurse. They had explained that she helped people who had traumatic injuries. What was more traumatic than falling off the barn?

"Can you stay a bit longer?" she asked Andrew. "I'll go out to the barn and call to see what I can find out about Johnny."

Andrew shook his head and fished his cell phone out of his pants pocket. "Let me call Danny to come get me," he said, referring to his cousin who helped him at the furniture store. "Then you can keep my phone. That way you don't have to keep running back out to the barn."

Foolish tears rose into Sadie's eyes, but she blinked them back. "Thank you so much, Andrew."

He shook his head again as if it was nothing, then made the call to his cousin.

It took four calls, but Sadie finally found out that Johnny was in stable condition. She had to ask and make sure that it was a good thing, but Zach's sister, Ashtyn, assured her that it was better than a lot of the people they had treated that very same night.

They would have to do some more testing to find out the extent of Johnny's paralysis, but it was widely thought among the doctors and nurses who had treated him the night before that the fall would definitely leave its mark on him.

Sadie thanked Ashtyn, then ended the call. Despite the bold and forward action, she headed up the stairs to Chris's bedroom. She knocked on the door and waited a moment for some type of response. Getting none, she eased her way in, hesitantly glancing around to make sure that it was okay for her to continue into the room.

Sometime between when Andrew had checked on Chris and now, he had managed to get up and get dressed. Sadie hadn't thought to ask about the farm chores, but she was sure Andrew had taken care of most of those for Chris. Still, him being up and dressed was at least a baby step in the right direction.

"Chris?" She eased into the room. "I just got off the phone with the hospital. Johnny's going to be okay. He's stable. They said that was good."

Her words appeared to hit some chord within him. He looked up. "He's going to be okay?"

"*Jah.*"

"Can he move now?" The haunted look in Chris's eyes was nearly her undoing.

"They don't know yet. It'll be awhile. They explained it to me, but I didn't understand all of it. As best as I can tell, when a person falls it can take the body awhile to recover and for any lasting injuries to turn up. But for now he's alive and safe, and he's not in any pain."

"It's all my fault, Sadie."

"Would you stop saying that?"

Chris shook his head. "You don't understand. I hate this farm. I hate everything about it, and all I wanted to do was leave. This is God's way of punishing me."

Sadie sucked in a sharp breath. "That's not true. God wouldn't give you those dreams, then punish you for having them."

"What if my dreams aren't of God?"

"Chris! Would you listen to yourself? This was an accident. God's not trying to punish you. The devil has not taken over your life. It was merely an accident."

"I wish I could be that certain."

Sadie reached out and grabbed his hand, tugging him reluctantly to his feet. "Come on," she said. "You can't stay in here all day. The last thing your brother would want would be for you to hide yourself away."

Chris swung himself down from his buggy and took a deep breath. The bishop's house. This was the first step.

His heart had almost stopped in his chest when they told him that his brother would most likely be paralyzed from the neck down. Over time, he might gain back some of the use of his arms, but most likely his legs would never work again.

No matter how many times Sadie told him that the accident was an accident and that it was not his fault, he found it next to impossible to believe her. God had to be punishing him for wanting to get away from the farm and leave Johnny behind. No matter what Sadie said, he couldn't help but believe that it was true.

One thing was certain. He couldn't go to Europe now. He had to stay and run his brother's beloved farm. He had to carry on for his father. He couldn't spend a dime on anything other than his brother's treatment.

Stiff-legged, he made his way across the yard and up the porch steps. He rapped on the door twice, feeling the formality of the summons was just another part of this occasion.

Helen Ebersol opened the door. Chris had always liked Helen. He'd heard many people complain about the bishop and the bishop's wife in their district, but he had no problems with his. They were fair and kind, and right now, that was exactly what he needed.

"Is the bishop home?"

Helen nodded, then stepped back as if she had known he was coming all along.

Chris moved into the room, his eyes adjusting from the sun to the dim interior of the house.

"I'll go get him for you."

A few moments later, the bishop stepped from the kitchen. He gave a small nod to Chris as he motioned toward the sofa behind him. "Why don't you sit down, Chris Flaud? I've been expecting you."

Chris nodded and sat down, though he felt as if he wanted to pop right back up as soon as his legs touched the sofa. Instead, he managed to take a breath and ease himself back into the cushions.

"I wanted to say that I'm ready for baptism classes."

The bishop raised one eyebrow in question. "I thought we had already discussed this."

Chris nodded. "We had. But now I'm really ready."

To the bishop's credit, he didn't make Chris explain. Chris had come here on bended knee, so to speak, needing forgiveness and redemption. The bishop was not going to make him beg for it.

"Easter comes late this year. Classes start in about five weeks."

Chris stood and reached out to shake the bishop's hand. "I'll be there."

"Sadie, the phone's for you."

"Thanks." She stepped behind the waitress station and pushed the flashing button at the bottom of the multiline phone. "Hello?"

"So you are still alive?" Ezra's voice held a note of laughter. But she could hear the buried confusion in there as well.

"It's been kind of hectic around here the last few days." It had been six days since Johnny Flaud had taken his tumble from the top of their barn. He was still in the hospital in Tulsa and would be for a couple more weeks. When he got home, things would never be the same.

Sadie had spent nearly every minute she could over at the Flauds' trying to help out. She had cleaned the house from top to bottom, baked bread and cookies, and put as many things as she could into their propane-cooled freezer.

In general, she made sure Chris ate each day, got up

and got dressed, and managed to take care of any of the farm chores. He had male help as well. Elam Riehl, Jonah Miller, and Andrew Fitch and his cousin Danny came out in the rotation, each helping as much as they could, spending the night with Chris to keep him from being alone until his parents came back from the hospital.

"So it's true?" Ezra asked.

"I don't understand."

"I heard that a boy fell off the roof there in Wells Landing. Also heard that he was your boyfriend's brother."

"I wouldn't call him that. We're friends, you know? I've been trying to help out there. They're not sure that Johnny will be able to walk again. He may not even be able to use his arms."

"I don't have the words to say how sorry I am to hear that." She could tell by the tone of his voice that Ezra was being completely sincere.

"Don't be sorry," Sadie said. "Just pray for him. And his family."

"You know I will." From the other end of the line she heard Ezra clear his throat. "Are we still on for to-morrow?"

Sadie's hand flew to where the little elephant necklace lay against her skin. She kept it tucked under her dress, not wanting to take it off for anything. She knew it was wrong to wear jewelry. But how could she expect Ezra to hold a compromise with her if she couldn't compromise herself?

"I'm not sure. It's just that—" She broke off, unable to find the words.

"You've been spending a lot of time over there."

She could hear the edge of jealousy in his voice. She wanted to tell him not to be worried. But that was not a very smart thing to say. He'd told her that he loved her and she'd told him that she loved him. Of course he was going to be worried to some degree that she was spending all of her time with someone else.

"It's the right thing to do. Chris and I have been friends for as long as I can remember. I can't abandon him now when he needs me the most."

"I understand. I just wanted to spend some time with you. I know you're off tomorrow. So . . . Never mind. Maybe next week?"

She wanted to see him so badly, face-to-face and breathing in that wonderful smell that was Ezra. But she knew she couldn't spend time with him, enjoying herself off to where no one could find her, when Chris needed her right now.

"Please," she asked. "Next week would be great."

"I'll see you then," he said. And then he was gone.

Tuesday was quickly becoming his favorite day. Chris stood up from the table and smiled as Sadie let herself into the house that morning. He was already up and dressed, and he had done the farm chores for the day. There wasn't a whole bunch to do right now. But in another month it would be time to hit the field.

Sadie's eyes widened with surprise, and she smiled in return. "It's good to see you out and about."

"I thought it was time." Past time, he was sure. But he had to have time to grieve, to come to terms. His brother might not have died in the accident, but all of Chris's dreams had. He needed time to adjust, to think, to replant, to get his mind ready for what he had to do and accept it.

"*Mamm* called," he continued.

She faltered as she stepped across the living room. "Johnny?"

Chris shook his head. "He's fine. They think they'll release him in a couple of weeks. But he'll have to spend a lot of time in Pryor. For physical therapy and things like that. But *Mamm* and *Dat* are coming home today."

"That's wonderful news."

It was. And it was one more step toward the end of the tragedy and the normalcy that they all needed to regain in their lives. Everything would settle to a new normal, and of that he hoped everyone could be accepting.

"They should be home pretty soon," Chris said. "Will you stay until they get here?"

She nodded, that smile he loved so much working its way across her face. Today was going to be a big day. Bigger than she or his parents knew. But that was a surprise for later. For now he was sure Sadie would have something she wanted to do, darn Johnny's socks or sew buttons back on his father's shirt. She had worked nonstop in the days since the accident, trying to get everything in the house in order for his parents to come back home. He loved her all the more for it.

"I love you, you know." It was something that was always understood between them. And he felt now was the best time to say them again.

She stopped unloading the grocery sack she'd brought in with her. She had grapes and oranges and all sorts of fresh vegetables that no one could get this time of year unless they bought them at a grocery store.

"Oh, Chris," she said with a small shake of her head. His heart stuttered a beat and went back into its normal rhythm. "I love you too."

* * *

Four hours later he heard the car door slam outside and knew that his parents had come home. He turned to find Sadie watching him. He nodded. Everything was going to be okay. He had come to terms with the changes the accident brought in his life. They weren't anything compared to the changes that Johnny would suffer. So Chris would accept those changes with happiness and grace.

Still, his mouth turned to ash as he watched Sadie cross to the front door and open it.

She stepped out onto the porch and waved. "Welcome home!" she called, continuing her greeting.

He could hear the muffled voices of his parents and the Mennonite driver who had brought them home from Tulsa. But he couldn't make out any of the words they were actually saying.

It was probably not important anyway. More than likely the words were those of greeting and how are you doing, what are you doing here, thank you for staying, and all the other niceties that people said when they found themselves in a situation such as they had found themselves in today.

His mother stepped into the house first, turning around to give Sadie a big hug before she rushed to Chris's side.

He hadn't talked to her since the accident. In fact, he hadn't talked to anyone in his family. He had so badly wanted to talk to Johnny, but they told him that the painkillers he was taking made him loopy and hard to understand. Somehow they convinced him that he didn't want to talk to his brother when he was like that and it was better to wait until Johnny had a clear head. As much as Chris hated it, he had to agree.

He had apologies to make, and something that important needed to be said with clarity, not on a whim.

His mother took his hand and squeezed his fingers in her strong grip. "He's going to be fine, Chris."

Chris swallowed back the lump in his throat and managed to reply, "I'm so glad, *Mamm*." But he almost choked at the uncharacteristic tears that had risen into his father's eyes.

"Can you come in here and sit down, please?" Chris asked. "I have something I need to talk to you about." He wasn't looking directly at Sadie, but he did notice that her eyes widened and she shook her head. She had no idea what was coming next.

His parents settled down around the table. Chris turned to Sadie. "Can you get them some coffee, please, or something to drink?"

His mother gave a nervous laugh. "I feel like a guest in my own home."

Sadie still hadn't moved. "Please," Chris asked again.

"Chris," Sadie started with a shake of her head, but he cut her off.

"I'll be right back," he said, turning on his heel before she could protest and heading for the stairs. He knew that she wouldn't follow him up there. And for that he was grateful. He had things to do, and he didn't need her behind him interrupting the entire time.

He pulled his bed away from the wall and eased the mattress off to the side so he could reach the slit he had made there. He reached into the envelope-sized hole and pulled out the zippered bank bag where his money was stored. Then he pushed his bed back into place and started down the stairs once again.

His parents were right where he left them. Sadie

too. No one had moved at all in the time since he had been gone.

"I'm not sure how to say this," he started. In his dreams he had told them a hundred times he was going to Europe. He told them he was off to see the world, they didn't need him on the farm, and he was headed for a grand adventure. And a hundred different times they reacted a hundred different ways. Never before had he played out the scenario that was about to happen. "I've been saving some money for a while. Just a dollar or two here and there. And since this happened . . ." Chris stopped to swallow the lump in his throat. *Lord, give me strength to get through this.* "But now the family needs this money for something more important than anything I had planned for it." He took another step forward and laid the bank bag on the table in front of his *dat*. His father sat back in his chair away from it as if it had been tainted with some type of poison that couldn't be contained.

"It's okay," Chris said. "It's money. Johnny needs it more than I do."

His mother looked from his *dat* to the bank bag and then back to his father's face. *Dat* didn't move an inch. He stared at the bag like he wasn't sure if it could be trusted or not.

"Oh, Merlin." His mother took the bag and unzipped it. She looked inside, and her eyes grew wide. "Chris, where did you get all this money?"

In that moment Chris was glad that he hadn't managed to buy the plane ticket to Europe yet, so that money was still amongst the thousands he had stashed. "I've been saving it for a while."

"What were you going to do with it, son?" His father kept staring at the table. Even though the money bag wasn't there any longer, his gaze did not move from that spot.

Chris should've known that he couldn't give them such a grand sum without explaining how he came to have it. Or what he intended to use it for. "I was going to take a trip," he said.

His mother continued to thumb through the bills, all neatly stacked in order. "You were going far."

"I was coming back." Behind him, Sadie stifled a sob. He couldn't look at her, knowing that if he saw tears in those hazel eyes, he would surely fall apart himself. "I was."

"And now?" his father asked.

"Johnny needs it."

His father pushed back from the table and stalked out the front door, slamming it behind him. He left his coat hanging on the peg inside the door and his hat right above it.

For a moment Chris thought his mother might rush after him. She half stood from her chair, then sat back down. Sadie came around and eased down in the chair opposite his mother. They sat there like stoic bookends, staring at nothing in particular.

"I was coming back," Chris said, though he wasn't sure if either one of them believed him. He hoped they understood that it didn't matter anymore. His brother was paralyzed, and he was not leaving. Not ever.

Chapter Nineteen

Ezra waited on the phone for Sadie to answer. How many times in the last week had he called the restaurant only to be told that she was busy or over with Chris or some of the other excuses that whoever answered his call gave him? Sometimes he talked to Cora Ann, sometimes to Melanie, and other times it was their mother. Occasionally he got the young girl who helped out at night. Millie he thought her name was. But mostly he got excuses.

She was slipping away. He could feel it. He wasn't sure how, but something had happened. And he was desperate to get her back again.

"Ezra?"

It had been so long since he heard her voice he almost didn't recognize it. "Sadie?"

"I'm glad you called."

That sentence could have a hundred implications, none of which he liked except maybe she missed him too.

"Can I pick you up at the library tonight?"

"Tonight?"

"It's Monday. You don't normally work on Monday

nights. I . . ." He ran his hand through his hair. "I just really want to see you. I miss you."

"I know. It's been—"

"Hectic," Ezra supplied. "You've mentioned that before." Every time he called, as a matter of fact.

"I'm sorry."

"Don't be sorry. Just meet me there. We don't have to go anywhere. I'll come to you. We can sit and talk. Anything you want to do, okay? Please." He had resorted to begging to see her. The thought made him feel weak. But he couldn't help himself. He loved her. He loved her more than anything he had ever loved in his life. He was losing her. And he didn't know how to stop it.

Silence met his ears. And she finally answered. "Okay. I'll meet you."

"Six o'clock?" he asked, his breath held as he waited for her answer.

"*Jah.* Six o'clock," she agreed. "I'll be there."

He hung up the phone and stared at it a moment. This was what love did to a man. It made him pathetic. And he gained a little more understanding of his mother and her bitterness toward everything that her father had put her through.

Love was supposed to be a happy emotion. It was supposed to make a person feel like they were walking on clouds and all those other wonderful things that people said about it. What they didn't say was how bad it hurt, how confusing it was, and how it was anything but simple.

"Where are you going?" Somehow in his mental rant he had overlooked the sound of her chair coming into the room. He whirled around to face his mother.

"Just out."

"On Monday night?"

"Yes." He didn't want to explain it to her. She wouldn't understand anyway.

"It's that Amish girl again, isn't it?"

Ezra felt as if his patience was about to snap in two. "Tell me, Mom. Does it bother you that she's Amish or that I love her?"

"Don't talk to me like that," she said, her voice firm, unyielding. "I'm still your mother."

"I know that." He propped his hands on his hips. She was his mother and he loved and respected her, but he was not backing down this time.

"Did you hear what I said?" he asked.

"I need you here tonight," she said.

Ezra shook his head. "I'm going out."

"Not tonight."

Ezra felt like he was beating his head against a brick wall. "I love her, and I'm going out tonight. And with any luck, I'll come home engaged."

His mother acted as if she was going to push herself up out of her chair. "Engaged? You can't get engaged to an Amish girl."

"And why can't I? I love her, and she loves me."

"I loved your father too, and you see where that got us."

"That has nothing to do with this."

"You are so naïve. You think love is going to solve everything. You have no idea how many problems you'll have to face. Where will you live? What about the ranch? You surely can't go to Wells Landing and live there. Can you be Amish, Ezra? You won't give up your church. Do you think she'll give up hers?"

"Why would she not?" He'd thought about this many times. He had a beautiful house here. Of course, he shared it with his mother. But one day it would all be his. He had a ranch with organic domestic and exotic meats, a thriving business. Why would she not want to come here and live with him? They loved each other. And love could overcome anything they wanted it to. Of that he was certain.

"You're not going anywhere."

"I am twenty-four years old. I have devoted the last seven years of my life to taking care of you, and I am willing to devote the next seventy years of my life to taking care of you. But tonight I'm going to see Sadie. I'm going to ask her to marry me, and there's nothing you can do about it."

She stared at him, mouth gaping, as he whirled on his heel, grabbed his jacket up by the door, and headed out the front. Luckily the keys were in his pocket. He hopped into the truck and started the engine before the door had even shut. He loved his mother, but he'd had enough. Enough of her self-pity and drama. It was time that they all started living again. That was her problem. She was jealous that he had found someone he loved and who loved him back. He felt sorry for his mother. His father was a cad, but that wasn't Ezra's fault. And Ezra deserved to be happy, as did his mother. And tonight he was going to find his happiness.

He threw gravel up as he spun his tires out of the driveway and headed down the road. He barely got a quarter of a mile toward the highway before he pulled over. He fished his cell phone from his pocket and dialed Logan's number from heart. His cousin picked up on the second ring.

"Hey," Logan said.

Ezra sucked in a deep breath, trying to calm his nerves as he collected his thoughts.

"Ezra?"

"I'm here." He took another deep breath. "Listen, I

just had it out with Mom." He was embarrassed to say the words. He shouldn't argue with his mother. She was all he had left in the world.

"It's about time," Logan said.

Ezra didn't ask him to qualify that remark. He had other things to discuss. "I left in sort of a hurry. Can you go by and check on her? Please."

He almost heard his cousin smile on the other end of the line. "You know I will."

"You're a good nephew," Ezra said.

Logan scoffed. "I bet you say that to all your cousins."

Ezra hung up and started the truck back toward Wells Landing. He couldn't believe he was going to propose to Sadie without a ring at hand. But with her reaction over the elephant necklace, it was probably better this way. They would figure out all the details later, where they would live and all that. But he felt confident she would want to come to Taylor Creek with him. The thought brought a smile to his face as he continued down the highway toward the girl he loved.

Sadie looked at the clock one more time. Five fifteen. She still had forty-five minutes to go before she got see Ezra. She'd missed him so much in the last couple weeks. She almost felt selfish, missing him when she was trying to help a family get back on their feet. But it was true. She missed Ezra terribly.

"That's the third time you've looked at the clock in just as many minutes." Cora Ann came up beside her, carrying a stack of the trays they used to take drinks to the tables.

Sadie sighed. "I'm sure you're mistaken." She turned to look at the clock again.

"You did it again!"

Sadie shook her head.

"What are you waiting for?" Cora Ann asked.

Sadie wasn't sure how much to tell her sister. She didn't know how much Cora Ann knew. Probably not much, since she and Ezra had been keeping their relationship completely hidden.

"Are you going to see Ezra?"

Maybe they hadn't been keeping it as hidden as she had thought.

"I like him," Cora Ann said.

Of course she did. An exotic animal rancher was a foodie's dream, though Sadie didn't say as much. "I do too." But she more than liked him. She was crazy about him. Crazy in love.

"Why don't you go ahead and leave now?" Cora Ann glanced around the restaurant. "The dinner crowd is hitting, but it's Monday. We won't be that busy today. And Millie will be here soon."

She didn't have to ask her twice. Sadie reached behind her and started untying the cook's apron she wore. In short order they would be able to take off the terrible mourning black and wear their colors again. That time couldn't come soon enough. With the spring came renewal. A time to start over. A time to wear bright colors and rejoice and maybe start a new life with someone she loved.

She smoothed her hands down the sides of her regular apron. "Thank you, sister," she said.

Cora Ann smiled. "Anything for you."

Sadie made her way to the back office and grabbed her purse out of the desk drawer where her mother kept them. For once, *Mamm* wasn't in the office doing bills or trying to weed through the papers for Zach Calhoun to enter all their business transactions into his many spreadsheets he had started for them. She must've gone down to the bakery to see if she could figure out Esther Lapp Fitch's new piecrust recipe. Rumor around town was she was using a vinegar piecrust, but Sadie wasn't so sure.

She slung her purse over her shoulder and started winding her way between the tables, just as Chris came through the restaurant doors. He was perhaps the last person she thought she'd see now.

"Chris, what are you doing here?"

Please let him say he came to get something to eat. But something in the soft look in his eyes told her that he'd come for her.

"Can you walk with me?"

Sadie wanted to protest. She wanted to tell him that she had plans, that she was on her way to . . . She couldn't tell him any of those things. Besides, she was early for meeting Ezra anyway. She had a few minutes to talk to her best friend before she got to see the man she loved.

"In the park?" Sadie asked.

"If that will make you happy," Chris said.

Sadie smiled. That was Chris, a gentleman to the end.

She nodded, and in tandem they walked back through the restaurant doors and out to the street. Side by side, they made their way to the park that sat in the middle of Main Street.

Traffic in Wells Landing was quite busy for an early Monday evening. Sadie loved the bustle. It was just enough. Not so slow that it felt like it stood still, but not nearly as busy as Tulsa or even Pryor. Wells Landing was perfect.

They made their way across the street, but instead

of settling in the swings, Chris led her over to the picnic table. They sat, their elbows braced on the table, across from each other.

"How's Johnny?" She had asked that very same question this morning, when she had called out to the farm to talk to Chris's mother, but she had to ask Chris. She had to know as often as she could that Johnny Flaud was going to be okay.

"He's okay. He's wanting to get up, even though his legs don't work. And he can't do much with his arms. But they're thinking that maybe . . ."

Sadie nodded, then gave a slight start as Chris reached across the table and took her hands into his.

"I didn't come here to talk about Johnny."

Sadie's mouth went dry. "Then why are you here?"

"I came to ask you to marry me."

"Marry you?" It was the last thing Sadie expected him to say.

"I know that's what you wanted. You wanted a family and a house and kids. I can give you all that. I'm not leaving. I'm not going to Europe. I have my family's farm. I'm staying right here."

If only she had heard those words four months ago. That was all she ever wanted. But now things were different. "What happens if Johnny gets better?"

"You know he's not going to ever walk again. I will need to be here to take care of the farm. It's my job now."

Sadie wasn't sure what to say. She had loved Chris her entire life, but it wasn't a romantic love. It wasn't what the romance authors talked about in their books. She only felt that zip and zing when she was with Ezra. But would something like that last? She had no idea. And she didn't know who to ask. Caroline? Or maybe Emily, or Lorie? She didn't know. They all had found their loves, but did they feel that tingle when they were with their husbands? She had no way of knowing. It wasn't something the Amish normally talked about. She had so many questions and no answers. She was twenty-two years old and clueless when it came to affairs of the heart.

"I take it this is not what you expected."

"I-I—" she stammered, unable to find the words. What could she say to him? That she didn't want to be a second choice? That she loved him but she wasn't sure if that love was the end-all be-all love? Or that the love was just friendship—how did a person know? Was it possible to love two men?

She pulled her hands from Chris's grasp and pressed them against her temples. A headache was starting to pound. She had thought way too much about this. Was that the problem? Should she be listening to her heart? What did her heart even have to say on the matter? She just didn't know. "I'm confused," she said.

She closed her eyes as she waited for Chris to respond. But he didn't, so she opened them again to find him staring at her.

"I know you're confused," he said. "I've been confused for a long time. But I saw what happened. This is a sign. A sign from God that my choices were leading me wrong."

"Are you saying that God paralyzed Johnny to keep you here?" He had said something like that before, but she'd thought that was only grief talking. He'd had enough time in between to get a handle on his thoughts, perhaps even sort through them to the truth underneath.

"Could be. I don't know. But I know that if Johnny hadn't fallen, I wouldn't be staying. I promised you that when I came back I would marry you. Isn't that what you wanted?"

"What do you want?"

He shook his head. "What I want doesn't matter anymore. This is what I need. A farm, a house, a wife. I'll make you a good husband, Sadie. You have been my best friend my whole life. And I will do everything in my power to make you the happiest woman in Wells Landing."

She had no doubt about that at all.

But was that enough? Was that what she wanted?

"I've already talked to the bishop about baptism classes. He knows I'm completely on board now. I'm serious this time. I'll go through my classes, join the church this fall, we'll get married right after that. I know Bishop Ebersol will let us. And then we can begin our life together. Like you've always dreamed."

Like she had always dreamed.

"I," she started again. But there were no words. "Can I have a little time to think about this?"

He frowned, a look somewhere between fear and confusion. "Of course," he said. "I'm not going anywhere. And I'll be here for you always."

Chapter Twenty

Sadie put one foot in front of the other and walked the three blocks to the library in something of a daze. The last thing she had expected when she saw Chris walk into the restaurant was a marriage proposal. Strange how things changed so quickly. Two months ago she thought that soon she would never see him again. Now he was saying he wanted to see her every day for the rest of their lives.

She truly loved him. But it wasn't the same as the feeling she held for Ezra. Which one was true? Which one was valid? She had no idea.

She turned into the library parking lot, immediately looking for his truck. She almost stumbled when she saw that familiar blue vehicle. She caught herself in time and managed to walk with a bit of dignity to where he waited for her.

He smiled when he caught sight of her, and her heart warmed. She'd missed seeing him these last couple weeks as she helped the Flauds and did her best to help them adjust to the new life they now faced.

She walked around the back of the truck and let

herself into the cab, breathing in that familiar scent that was all Ezra. A combination of detergent, after-shave, and outdoors. How she loved that smell.

"I thought you might not come," he said, his eyes unreadable.

How could she stay away?

"I can't stay for long. I heard that Millie just called in sick. They're expecting me back at the restaurant in an hour."

He didn't bother to hide his disappointment. "I understand. I'm still glad you came, though."

"Are you okay?" she asked. An air of something hung around him, something a lot like sadness, maybe closer to despair, but she could sense it as if he had more worries today than he had the last time he had seen her.

"I'm fine. Glad to be here. Just a little tired." He sighed. "It's been a long week."

"I know that."

"How's the kid doing?"

Johnny Flaud was the last thing she wanted to be talking about with Ezra. They had so little time together now as it was. She didn't want to waste a minute of it on anything but them. And when she realized how selfish those words were, she shook them away. "He'll probably never walk again. They're still trying to decide if he'll be able to use his arms. But he's alive and God is good, right?"

Ezra nodded. But in times like this it was hard to say that God was good, even though they knew it deep in their hearts. On the surface they were all human, and tragedy was so hard to accept. Everything took time. And even then time didn't heal everything. Look at Ezra's mother.

"That's not why I asked you to come here," Ezra said.

Sadie nodded. "I'm glad you invited me, though."

"Do you have time to get an ice cream or something?"

"No, I wish I did." She wished she had the rest of the night to spend with him. Like the day at the zoo. The two of them enjoying each other, nobody pulling on them, nobody judging them. That had been paradise. What she would give to live it again.

"Walk with me?" he asked.

Sadie hesitated. Walking with Ezra through the streets of Wells Landing would only mean one thing, Amish people staring at the mismatched couple. It wasn't something that she relished the thought of.

"Please," he added. "I have something I want to talk to you about tonight, and I don't want to do it in the truck."

Her stomach sank. Whatever it was had to be important. And she was torn between telling him yes and refusing to get out of the truck so he didn't tell her whatever it was. Between the look on his face and the tone of his words, she was afraid that it was something terrible.

"Are you breaking up with me?"

Ezra laughed a choked sound that reminded her of the bark of a dog. "Breaking up with you?" He shook his head. "I don't want to break up with you. I want to marry you."

"M-marry me?"

"Why do you act so surprised?"

Sadie closed her eyes, trying to get a handle on the moment, on her emotions, on the whirling tornado that had become her life. "I didn't expect it is all."

"I'm sorry I don't have a ring for you, but all things considered . . ."

"I can't wear a ring, Ezra. I'm Amish." Hadn't they been through this already? She lightly touched the necklace he'd bought her at the zoo. She hadn't taken the little elephant off since Ezra had placed it around her neck. Thankfully no one had noticed. Or maybe with everything going on with Chris and his family, no one had actually looked.

"But after we're married you'll come live with me."

"In Taylor Creek?"

Ezra frowned. "That is where I live. And where my ranch is. All my animals. My livelihood."

"And my family is in Wells Landing."

"You want to live there and be Amish?"

"Of course. I mean, you're Mennonite. How hard would it be to become Amish? You can get baptized into the church, and . . ." She trailed off as Ezra began to shake his head.

"I can't become Amish. Can't move my ranch. I can't move everything to Wells Landing."

"But," Sadie started, yet she had no idea how she could finish that sentence. But what? But she thought they would live happily ever after in Wells Landing? But if he loved her he would move with her and become Amish? For her. He could say the same thing about the Mennonites.

Sadie shook her head. But it only succeeded in jumbling her thoughts more.

"But what?" Ezra asked.

"I don't know," Sadie said. She reached for the door handle and let herself out of the truck, no longer concerned about the good citizens of Wells Landing seeing her with "that Mennonite boy."

She shut the door behind her and started down the

street. She had no destination in mind, she just needed some fresh air. She needed to walk. She needed something to help her clear her thoughts. In less than an hour, she had received two marriage proposals. Each one of them had its own benefits and each had its own set of issues. Now she was more confused than ever.

She heard the truck door slam, and Ezra's footfalls behind her. He didn't call out, she was sure to keep from drawing any undue attention to them. And for that she was grateful. But he was taller than her and had longer legs by far. He caught up with her with ease.

"You can't run away from this, Sadie," he said. And as much as she wished he was wrong, he wasn't. There was no running away from the truth.

"I'm very confused."

"Do you love me? You told me once you did."

Sadie stumbled, and Ezra was there, catching her, studying her as they continued together down the sidewalk. But somehow in that moment he slowed her steps so that she was no longer fleeing from something she couldn't get away from. They were simply walking together down the street.

"This isn't something that can't be solved, Sadie." His voice was soft and reassuring, that same voice she remembered from the day at the market when she had ordered her bison meat for the restaurant. It seemed like years ago, but it had only been months. Somehow in that time, he had worked his way into her heart. And it would never be the same again.

"Tell me how," she begged.

"We turn *Englisch*?"

It wasn't funny, not by far, but Sadie found herself nearly doubled over laughing, standing on the sidewalk like some crazed person. Was it any wonder? It had been a record day for sure.

"Okay, it wasn't that funny, but at least you're not crying."

Sadie managed to pull herself together, wiping the tears of mirth from her eyes. Or at this point, were they tears of sadness? Never before had she realized that there was such a fine line between joy and sorrow. "What do we do?"

"We have to decide. Someone has to choose."

Suddenly the bishop's words had full impact and meaning to her. They would have to decide. Someone would have to leave their church.

"If I leave I'll be shunned," she said.

Ezra propped his hands on his hips and shook his head, but she could tell that it was more in amazement at the quandary they found themselves in. "How is it that our ancestors split over this hundreds of years ago and now we are paying the price for their decision?"

"I don't know." The situation was so ironic she could barely wrap her mind around it. "But if you leave, you won't be shunned. Is it that hard to live without electricity or to not have a car?"

Ezra led her over to a small wall at the edge of someone's property. The library sat on the cusp of a residential neighborhood, and they found themselves walking among brick houses that belonged to the *Englisch*.

He sat down and urged her to sit next to him. She did so readily, hardly able to stand anymore with all the emotions whirling around inside her. She felt like a bundle of nerves, somehow disembodied. Like a newborn colt trying to maneuver on wobbly legs.

He took her hand and wrapped her fingers in his. Despite the chilly air all around them, his touch was warm and comforting. "It's more than electricity, Sadie. Surely you understand that."

She shook her head, not because she didn't understand, but because she didn't know what else to do. How could she agree to leave her family behind? It was different with Lorie. Lorie hadn't joined the church. Neither had Luke Lambright. But Sadie had joined long ago, knowing that one day she would marry Chris.

Chris.

At the thought of his name she stood. "I can't do this right now."

"Can't do what?"

"I can't decide. I need some time."

Ezra had no idea that Chris had also proposed. Not that she was about to tell him. If she did, he would understand why she was so overwhelmed. But she wasn't sure how he would take the news, so she kept it to herself. "It's a big step," she said.

Ezra nodded and stood next to her, taking her arm and leading her back toward the library parking lot. "It is, I understand."

Sadie almost wilted in relief. They walked in silence back to his truck. Ezra got in, but Sadie walked around the driver's side door. He rolled down the window.

"I have to go back to work now."

He squinted at her as if examining every little piece of her face. She shifted, uncomfortably under his stare. "Are you sure you'll be okay?"

Sadie nodded. What else could she say? *No, I'm more confused than ever now. I don't know what I want to do. No, I've got two boys who are confusing me more than anything else in the world. No, right now I want to lay down and cry.* But none of those things were productive, and none would ultimately help her make a decision.

"I'll call you in a couple of days," Ezra said.

Sadie only nodded. She reached a hand in and touched his face, traced the strong line of his jaw. She wanted to lean in and steal a kiss,- but even as much as she wanted to, she didn't. She had a terrible feeling this would be the last time she would ever see Ezra Hein.

Numbly she walked back to the restaurant. She was a little late returning, but no one said anything. It was as if somehow her sisters knew that she was dealing with more than she could truly handle.

She tied the apron around her waist and headed into the kitchen. Cora Ann was taking another pan of meat loaf from the oven. Sadie came behind her and shut the door while her sister placed the pan on the warming tray.

"Can we switch tonight?" Sadie asked. It was Cora Ann's turn in the kitchen while Sadie took care of the waitressing. "I'm not up for out front."

For a minute she thought Cora Ann might refuse, but she merely nodded and handed the pot holder to her sister.

"*Danki.*" She would hide out in the kitchen until time to go home. There would be a solace in preparing food and not having to smile at the good tourists and citizens of Wells Landing, all the while pretending that everything in her life was not upside down. "Holler if you need any help."

Cora Ann smiled. "I'm sure I'll be just fine." She disappeared out the door, and Sadie was alone.

She checked the whiteboard for today's menu. It was Monday and everything was the same. The special was roast beef, mashed potatoes, and green beans.

There were biscuits, corn bread, corn, meat loaf, oven-baked chicken, and of course the made-to-order items for the kids: chicken nuggets and hamburgers and French fries. She had done it so many times she could do it in her sleep.

Tonight that would be a good skill, so she didn't have to think too much about the food, but that left her too much time to think about Ezra and Chris.

She had no idea what she was going to do. She slipped the corn bread into the oven. *Mamm* insisted that they make it fresh, but they didn't use the industrial pans some restaurants used. Instead they had cast-iron skillets, larger than ones in the average household. Sometimes three or four would go in at a time. Because that was the way *Mamm* wanted it. But more than that, Sadie knew that was the way that her father had wanted it. Despite his passing, they had held on to that tradition regardless of convenience.

Her father.

How she wished he was here with her now. She could sure use his calm ways and insight. He always had the answer to everything.

She could go talk to *Mamm*. But her mother wasn't the one she wanted to talk to. It could've been because her mother was available and her father wasn't. Or maybe it was just time to pray.

Tears welled in her eyes, but she blinked them back. She had too much to do to cave to the emotions now.

Cora Ann pushed into the kitchen. "Do you smell that?"

She shook her head "No, what's it smell like?"

"I don't smell it in here. Come out of the kitchen for a minute and see." She motioned for Sadie to follow her into the restaurant.

Sadie stepped out as smoke started seeping from the banquet room in the back.

Panic ripped through her. "Something's on fire!"

Mamm must've smelled it right about the same time. She'd been in the front, seating guests as they came in. "There's a fire," she said, rushing over to the two of them. "We've got to get everybody out. Now."

"I'll call the fire department." Sadie grabbed the phone and dialed 911 as *Mamm* and Cora Ann started going from table to table and informing the guests that they needed to leave.

It took forever before they got everyone out. Sadie's heart was pounding in her throat. She stared around at the people standing out in the parking lot and in the street in front of the restaurant. Toward the back of the building she could see flames rising. Surely by now the sprinkler system had kicked on. It had recently been inspected, but since it hadn't turned on already, Sadie was a little worried.

Cora Ann started to cry softly, the stress of the situation getting the better of her as they waited. What was taking the fire department so long?

Mamm wrapped her arms around Cora Ann and patted her shoulder. "It's going to be okay. At least everyone got out okay."

Everyone.

"Where's Daniel?"

Normally he would've been at home with Sadie. But since Sadie had been called into work, he'd had to come too. And now he was in the restaurant.

Alone.

Chapter Twenty-One

Sadie started toward the doors of the restaurant, uncaring about the fire. She had to find him. And she had to find him. Now.

Cora Ann grabbed her arm. "You can't go in there."

She shrugged off her sister's grip. "I have to." Where were the firemen? She didn't even hear sirens. Wells Landing only provided a volunteer fire department, but they still should have been here by now.

"I have to."

She rushed back to the double doors, thankful that they weren't hot to the touch yet. That meant the fire was still farther back in the restaurant. But where was Daniel?

She untied her cook's apron and wrapped it around her face, holding it in place with one hand while she ran through the empty restaurant. He wasn't at the booths coloring. He would've heard them telling everyone to get out if he was. And they surely wouldn't have overlooked him then.

How could they have been so careless?

But she knew it had to do with stress and the unusual circumstances they had faced tonight. Did it matter? She knew he was there. And she would get him out.

She could hear the fire crackling back toward the banquet room as it chewed through tables and chairs and walls trying to reach the rest of the building. He wouldn't have been in the kitchen. That left the office or the bathrooms.

The door to the office was warm to the touch. She grabbed up her skirt in her right hand and used it as insulation between her skin and the doorknob.

Lord, please let him be in here. Please.

She thought about the stories she had heard from some of the men who worked at the fire department, stories about backdrafts and things. She didn't understand all of it, but she knew that she was risking a lot opening the door. Yet if she didn't open it, she would never find him.

Lord, please let that be warm because it's so close to the banquet room.

She squeezed her eyes shut and opened the door, exhaling with relief as nothing happened. Nothing blew up, nothing came rolling out. Just an open door now.

She rushed into the office. There were two places to sit—behind the desk and on the cluttered couch. He was in neither place. What if he'd gone to the storeroom? He was so quiet and well behaved that no one would've noticed if he had gone around the side of the building and up the stairs.

No, she thought, he had to be in the bathrooms.

Lord, please let him be in the bathroom. I'll do anything. I'll do anything. Please. Her frantic mind went around in circles. *I know I've been confused lately, maybe even defiant. But that all ends now. Lord, help me find my brother, and I'll do what I'm supposed to do. I'll marry Chris. I'll stay here. And I will not leave my faith. Just help me find him, please.*

She rushed from the office to the bathrooms across the hall. She checked the women's first, thinking perhaps he had gone in there out of habit. He was so young the girls in his family usually made him go into the girls' restroom with them when they went. Poor boy, having to grow up with so many sisters. But he wasn't in any of the stalls. She checked all three of them twice, then ran out and toward the men's room. She pushed her way inside, frantically searching, but she couldn't see him anywhere. She could hear the fire crackling around her and smell the smoke coming through the ceiling tiles. It was overhead. She needed to find him and get out before the roof caved in. Her heart beat even faster in her chest.

Lord, please. I promise. Help me find him, please.

Somehow amidst the crackle and snap she could hear all around her, she heard a small sob. She looked through the stalls, making sure that he wasn't standing on the toilet for some reason. But they were still empty on the second trip around. She had to find him, and she had to find him now. She came out of the last stall and allowed her gaze to wander through the room. She took a deep breath, sucking in as much smoke as she did air. She had to get out of there, and she had to get out soon. Before they both perished.

She dropped to her knees. That was when she saw him, huddled behind the trash can, half-hidden with his head ducked between his knees. "Daniel?"

He didn't move. He was so small. Had he been breathing in smoke this whole time?

"Daniel!" she said, louder this time.

He jumped, raising his head and looking at her. "Sadie?"

"Yes! Yes, I'm here, Daniel."

He started crying openly now. "I didn't know what to do, Sadie. At school they made us do drills. I couldn't remember what to do. I put my head between my knees. I don't think that was what I was supposed to do, but I couldn't remember."

Sadie shushed him, rubbing a hand over his silky hair as her tears started to fall. "It's okay. You did fine, Daniel. Just fine."

He'd done the best he could. The adults around him had failed him. And she had made a promise. She would see them through.

Lord, please get us out of here alive. Please, please, and I promise I'll marry Chris. I'll stay in Wells Landing. I'll do everything I'm supposed to do. I'll live within Your guidelines and what You set forth for me to do. Amen.

"Hold on to me," she said, still on her hands and knees. "Get on my back, and I'll get us out of here." She said the words with as much confidence as she could muster, but the roar of the fire was getting louder and louder. In the distance, she could hear the wail of the sirens, but she had no idea how close the trucks were. It didn't matter. She had Daniel, and she had to get them out alive. It was all up to her now.

After Sadie left, Ezra sat in the parking lot at the library, trying to decide what to do. He couldn't make up his mind on anything. Should he drive home? Get something to eat? He sat there. Nothing was right; everything was wrong. So he remained in place. Like a statue. Or a man half-dead inside. He wanted to go to her, follow her to the restaurant and confess his love again. Tell her that they would figure something out. Somehow, there was a solution, a compromise between the two faiths. There had to be.

Why did things have to be so complicated? Why did God give him this desire to be with her, only to take her away? Were they so different after all?

The sound of sirens stirred him from his stupor. They sounded close and were getting nearer and nearer. Something was wrong. He looked up to see smoke rising into the sky, close to where the Kauffmans' restaurant was. Surely not, he thought. But he put his truck in gear and pulled out to the street.

It was only three blocks to Main Street. But he couldn't go all the way through. He parked his truck on the side of the street, breathing in the acrid air and knowing, somehow knowing, that Sadie was in trouble.

There were three fire trucks on the scene, which was probably the whole entire volunteer fire department crew. He could see the smoke coming out of the back of the restaurant, and his heart sank.

He looked around for the face he most needed to see. Tourists and *Englischers* and Amish people alike milled around. But he couldn't see Sadie. He couldn't see anybody that he knew or anyone in her family. Where were they all?

An Amish girl brushed past him and he grabbed her arm, not even knowing who she was. "Have you seen the Kauffmans?"

The young girl shook her head, then pulled out of his grasp. He realized he was acting strangely. But he had to find them, he had to find the Kauffmans. He had to find Sadie.

He pushed his way to the front of the crowd. Cora Ann was standing over to one side sobbing softly. Next to her stood Maddie Kauffman with one arm around her as they stared toward the front of the restaurant. Firemen dressed in fireproof clothing had their hoses turned toward the restaurant, dousing it with water in hopes of putting out the flames before too much damage had been wrought.

Down the street another fire truck was hosing off the roof that connected Esther's bakery with the restaurant. He was certain to keep the fire from reaching the entire building.

He rushed to Cora Ann. "Where is she? Where's Sadie?"

Cora Ann continued to sob and shook her head. He looked to Maddie Kauffman. Her frown was deeper than ever. Was she worried about the restaurant, worried about Sadie, or upset that he wanted to know?

Her eyes filled with tears. "She went inside to get Daniel."

"What?" He started toward the doors of the restaurant. He had to find them. He rushed past a fireman waiting outside.

What were firemen doing out here when somebody inside needed rescuing?

He got halfway to the door before somebody grabbed his arm and jerked backward.

"You can't go in there." He turned around and faced a big man with mossy green eyes. He looked vaguely familiar, and Ezra wondered if he'd ever seen him before. But the thought was quickly replaced with worry for Sadie.

"Sadie's in there. I've got to go get her."

"Jonah and Chris have already gone in. They'll find them if they're there."

If they were there? Where else would they be?

Ezra pulled against his captor's grasp and broke free as two firemen came through the doors of the restaurant. One carried Daniel cradled in his arms, and the other had his arm wrapped around Sadie as he helped her toward the waiting ambulance. She was limping, her dress smoldering, or maybe it was just smoke from being in the building.

The firemen held up one of her arms, and Sadie looked as if she was about to pass out from the pain. The burn looked bad.

Ezra wanted to rush to her, talk to her, hold her, tell her everything was going to be okay. But something secured his feet to the ground beneath them. Maybe it was the possessive way the firemen held her. Didn't the other guy say that Chris had gone in? Was that Chris, her one-time almost-fiancé, best friend who was going off to Europe? The way he was holding Sadie, Ezra had a feeling that man wasn't going anywhere.

He somehow managed to unstick his feet and started toward Sadie, but she was swamped by other people and he couldn't get through. Cora Ann and Maddie surrounded her, while the medic worked on her arm. Someone else put an oxygen mask over Daniel's face and then hers.

Ezra wanted to let her know that he was there, that he cared, that he loved her, but the words wouldn't come.

They loaded her into the back of the ambulance, and before he knew it, she was gone.

Without the restaurant open, Ezra had no way of getting in contact with Sadie. He waited two days for her to get settled before he decided to take a trip to her house. It was forward, but he had to see her. He had to make sure she was okay. He had to talk to her. That wasn't so much to ask, was it?

He pulled his truck into her driveway and turned off the engine. Sitting there for a moment with his hand still on the steering wheel, he collected his thoughts. He had practiced what he was going to say on the trip from Taylor Creek to Wells Landing, but now that he was there those words had flown the coop. He sighed and got out of the truck. As he did so, the front door opened and Cora Ann stepped out onto the porch.

"Ezra? Is that you?" Cora Ann flew down the steps and rushed him like a football player. She wrapped him in a warm hug, rocking him back and forth as if she'd never thought she would see him again.

Reluctantly he put his arms around her and hugged her back. It might not have been the most appropriate thing to do, but he had fallen in love with Sadie's little sister. It was a different sort of love, but he would've done anything in the world for her.

"I'm glad you're okay, Cora Ann."

She released him, but kept a hold on his arm, tugging on his sleeve as she dragged him toward the house. "Come in, come in. You have to see Sadie."

Before he could say another word she had hustled into the front door.

"Is your *Mamm* home?"

Cora Ann shook her head. "She's gone to town to meet with the insurance people."

Ezra had driven by the restaurant on his way there. It wasn't a complete loss. The building hadn't burnt to the ground, but there was enough smoke and water damage that it was going to be a long time before the restaurant opened again. He wasn't sure about the adjacent bakery.

The movement from the corner of his eye caught

his attention and he turned. Sadie stood, her arm wrapped in plain white gauze.

"You're okay," he breathed, wanting to rush toward her and wrap her in his arms. Instead, he trekked slowly over.

"You shouldn't be here." She said the words as if she were reciting from today's specials.

"You expected me not to come?"

Sadie shook her head, then turned toward Cora Ann. "I need to talk to Ezra alone."

Cora Ann narrowed her gaze in what looked an awful lot like distrust.

Sadie shook her head. "Let's go for a walk." She nodded toward the door, but Ezra didn't want to leave. What was so important that she needed to talk to him alone? If she was going to agree to marry him, then wouldn't she say so in front of her sister?

He pushed that negative thought away. It could be anything. She might want to announce it to her mother first before letting her sister know. Especially if she was leaving the Amish and joining him in Taylor Creek. Yeah, that had to be it.

He followed her out onto the porch, thankful that the weather had started to turn warm. It was early March. But in Oklahoma that could mean seventy-degree-plus weather. But the warm weather wouldn't get really steady until April hit, if then.

"Do you want to go for a drive?"

Sadie shook her head. "Let's walk."

"If you're sure you're up to it."

She nodded.

As far as Amish properties went, the Kauffmans' house was not typical. There was a small patch of ground to the south side of the house that would probably be used for a vegetable garden if one of the girls took a mind. But Ezra knew it took a lot of time, effort, and energy to run the restaurant, and things like vegetable gardens weren't as important to the Kauffmans as they were to the average Amish family.

The barn appeared almost empty. He was sure that it only served as a stable for the horses they used to pull their carriages. There was a tractor, but no other farm equipment, and the grain silo was overrun with ivy vines. They walked over to the fenced-in pasture and stood staring out at the crop of trees about a hundred yards away. Almost nothing stood between them and those trees but a few budding weeds and a couple of batches of tall brown grass.

"I can't marry you."

"I beg your pardon?" Those words were the very last thing he had expected to hear from her. Surely he had heard wrong. Surely she didn't just tell him . . .

"I can't marry you."

He studied her profile as she continued to stare toward those faraway trees. The oaks were starting to lose their dried brown leaves, the pines and cedars the only green among the bare branches of the shedding oaks.

His stomach clenched. "I don't understand." He started to reach out and touch her, but she moved away.

"What's to understand? I can't marry you because I'm marrying Chris."

"Chris?" Ezra said stupidly. He couldn't get his mind wrapped around the words she was saying to him. "But you love me, and I love you. How can you marry Chris?"

Sadie shook her head, finally turning to look at him. Her hazel eyes were dull, her mouth turned down at a resolute angle. "It's been hard since my dad died. I thought I wanted adventure, but I was wrong. And I should've never said those things to you."

"But . . ." Ezra started again, but he could find no argument. "Is this about the church? We'll figure something out, Sadie. You can't walk away from trouble in hard times. You have to figure it out. You have to work through it."

"I know all about hard times, Ezra. And I know all about working through it. I dragged my brother from a burning building two days ago. You don't need to be telling me about adjusting and adapting. I made a mistake. And I'm sorry. But I don't want to marry you."

Sadie turned on her heel, batting back the tears rising in her eyes. She'd managed to hold it together this long. Just a few more minutes and surely he would leave. Then and only then could she release the building sobs inside her. Surely one day soon she would stop crying, and her heart would heal. The most important thing was she had Daniel. He was safe.

She had asked God for help. She had told Him what she would do. Now it was time to uphold her end of the agreement. That meant staying in Wells Landing. Marrying Chris. And remaining Amish.

She remained calm and steady as she put one foot in front of the other, methodically walking back toward the house.

Please, let it go now, please.

She heard him say something behind her, but she couldn't make it out. Only his tone, which sounded angry and hurt. Her heart fell a few inches in her chest.

She might have saved her brother, but she had broken both of their hearts.

She continued on toward the house, praying the whole while that he would not follow her. He wouldn't demand more of an answer, and he wouldn't see the tears she was trying so desperately to hide.

She was reaching for the doorknob when she heard him get into his truck. The engine started, and dust flew as he backed out and left.

Unable to take a step farther, Sadie crumpled into the rocking chair sitting by the front door and wept.

Three days later Johnny Flaud came home from the hospital. Sadie packed a bag with cookies and bread, two jars of last year's blackberry pie filling, and a music player she found at the secondhand store in town. She had bought it with Chris in mind, thinking she might give it to him for his trip. She had downloaded the Bible from the library and had it ready to go. But now that Chris was staying and Johnny was hurt, she felt Johnny could benefit more from God's word than his brother.

"I'm going now."

Cora Ann was in the kitchen experimenting with a new recipe. This time she had chosen chicken, though Sadie had a feeling that since most everything in the restaurant had been destroyed, her sister would soon be wanting more bison meat.

Well, as soon as they settled with the insurance and started to rebuild. Most everything would have to be gutted, new tables and chairs purchased, stoves and ovens replaced, bathrooms redone, the works. But their father had insured the place well, and there would be no problems.

The last she heard, the fire marshal had said faulty wiring in the banquet room caused the blaze. What accounted for the malfunction of the sprinkler system, they might not ever know. Still, the lot would be replaced. And thankfully, aside from a little water damage, Esther's bakery and back room apartment had all been spared.

"Okay." *Mamm* peeked out of the downstairs bathroom, rubber gloves on her hands as she scrubbed. Sadie had never seen the woman clean so much in all her life. But without the restaurant to run and keep her mind off other matters, *Mamm* had taken to scrubbing the house top to bottom. Of course, it didn't hurt that church was at their house in another three months. The Amish took a long time to clean their houses in preparation for their church service, and Maddie was no exception.

Sadie let herself out, lightly touching the elephant necklace where it lay against her skin, under her dress where no one could see it. Despite what she had told Ezra, she couldn't take off his necklace. It was a gift from the heart and something she always needed to remember. Once upon a time a Mennonite boy had loved her, and she had loved him back. But things weren't meant to be. She had made her deal with God and now she had to see it through.

She climbed into her buggy. It would be good to go visiting today. She needed to see Chris, tell him of her decision. To talk to Johnny as well. She knew he would probably not be able to talk to her yet, but Sadie knew that one day he would get his speech back. At least that was what the doctors had told her. She turned the horse's nose west and toward the Flaud residence.

The day was turning out beautiful. Spring was in the air. The trees were starting to bud, and the birds had come out to bring their song to let everyone know that spring had come to Wells Landing. A couple of more weeks and it would be Easter. After Easter, Chris would start his baptism classes. After that, there would be nothing to stop them from getting married.

Half an hour later, she pulled into his drive. She was glad to see that the ambulance that had brought Johnny home had already left. Hopefully by now he was settled in his bed.

She parked her buggy and got out. She would need to unhitch her horse. She had no idea how long she was staying, and she didn't want to leave the mare attached to the wagon for hours on end. Not when the horse could frolic in the pasture.

Sadie had just turned the mare out when Chris came to the door. "I thought I heard you out here."

Sadie smiled. Chris. Her best friend forever. Her soon-to-be husband. It was what she had wanted for years. Now why did the thought fill her with sadness?

"Walk with me?" she asked.

"Don't you want to come in and see Johnny?"

"In a bit. For now I need to talk to you."

"How come when somebody says they need to talk to you it's usually bad?" He tripped down the stairs to her side.

She shook her head. "It's not like that. This is actually good, I guess." She tried a smile on for size, but it felt too tight.

"You guess it's good?"

Sadie nodded her head. "I've come to tell you that I accept your proposal. I want to be your wife."

Chapter Twenty-Two

He could hardly believe his ears! After all this time and all the trouble with the Mennonite from Taylor Creek, he had finally gotten what he wanted. Sadie Kauffman had agreed to be his wife.

He stopped there in the middle of the yard and spun her toward him, taking her hands into his. He squeezed her fingers, having to hold back his strength and excitement.

"You don't know how long I've been waiting for you to say those words to me."

"Surely not more than a couple of weeks?" She laughed, but the sound was brittle.

He shook the thought away. "I'm glad you said yes. Baptism classes are starting soon."

She nodded.

"And we'll get married this fall. Maybe October?"

Sadie shook her head. "I think October is probably full. Why don't we wait until December? Maybe after Christmas."

After Christmas? "That's an awful long time to wait. Why not November? Maybe the first or second? Whatever the first Tuesday is. Let's get married then."

She thought about that a second. He worried that perhaps she was looking for an excuse to tell him no. Or postpone her wedding until the end of the month.

Instead, she gave up a hard swallow, then nodded. "*Jah*. Okay then. We'll get married then."

Not quite the joyous reaction that he had anticipated. But he would take it for now. He loved Sadie Kauffman and wanted to do anything and everything to make her happy as his wife. He looked into those hazel eyes, but he couldn't find the spark that was normally there. "Are you okay?" he asked.

Her eyes fluttered closed, and she gave a small nod.

"I love you, Sadie Kauffman."

With her eyes still closed she replied, "I love you too."

It was a special occasion. It was not every day that a man got engaged, and he wanted one small kiss to commemorate. He lowered his lips toward hers, but she turned away at the last second and his kiss glanced off her cheek. He hid his disappointment. "Are you sure?"

"Am I sure what?"

"That this is what you really want?"

Sadie nodded. "Of course it is. But I think we should wait, don't you?"

There was something to be said about that first kiss being on the wedding night. A lot of Amish waited until they were married before they shared even the gentlest of touches. And as much as he wanted to kiss Sadie in that moment, he realized that this was something she wanted too.

He nodded. "Okay, then. We'll wait."

He was certainly excited that they were getting married in early November instead of after Christmas like she had suggested. But he didn't know how long he could wait to kiss his new fiancée.

Ezra pulled his four-wheeler out of the barn and checked the gas gauge. It was time to ride the fences to make sure there were no holes or problems. It was also time to look for any newborns that he didn't know about. Between the bison, bovines, and the deer, he had to keep a good watch on the babies, that was for sure.

He grabbed his pliers, some wire fencing, and a few posts and strapped those onto the cargo rack in the back. Just a few things to keep him from having to run back in the event he found a problem. All ready to go, he cranked the engine as an unfamiliar car pulled into the driveway.

It was a fancier car than he normally saw in these parts, red and shiny. Not at all like what Mennonites usually drove. His was a secondhand farm truck with more scratches than clean paint. Most everyone drove older-model sedans and economical imports. This one was a luxury car, worth more than probably all the vehicles Ezra owned put together.

Somebody must be lost, he thought.

Or not.

By that time, the car had gotten close enough he could see that a woman was driving. A woman with shoulder-length blond hair and gold earrings.

She turned off her car's engine like she intended to stay for a while, then opened the door and got out. Her white suit looked strangely out of place on a dusty Oklahoma ranch. Her big sunglasses hid half of her face from view. She took two steps toward him, then stopped as the heels on her sandals sank between the gravel rocks of the drive.

"Help you?" How had a city slicker managed to lose her way in Mennonite country Oklahoma?

"Ezra? Ezra Hein?" Her voice was clear and strong, if not a bit hesitant. As if she wasn't sure if she was in the right place or not. But whoever she was, she had found him.

He swung his leg off the back of the four-wheeler. "That's me."

"My name is Brenda. I knew your father."

Ezra felt as if he had been punched in the gut. "My father?"

She looked around, obviously uncomfortable with her surroundings. "Can we go inside and talk?"

It was on the tip of Ezra's tongue to tell her no. Whatever it was that she knew about his father and whatever she wanted with him could be said right there. But somehow he felt this was a matter that needed to be settled in the quiet of the house.

"Come on in."

She picked her way across the driveway, through the patches of grass in his yard, and up onto the front porch. "It's very different here than I expected."

"Oh?" He tried not to sound skeptical. But he really didn't want to make small talk.

"Your father told me about it."

"How is it exactly that you know my father?" Ezra asked as he held the door open for her.

She seemed grateful to be out of the wild outdoors as she stepped into their modest house. He had a feeling that her house was probably twice the size of his and she had people to help keep it clean. But he wasn't going to be ashamed of what he had, what he and his mother had worked for. They might not have a lot, but they had each other, and they had this house. As far as he was concerned, that counted for a great deal.

"Is your mother here?" He couldn't help but notice the slight hesitation before she said the word "mother."

And he had a sinking feeling that this woman knew his father very well.

He swallowed hard.

"I'll get her."

He left her in the living room perched on the edge of their sofa as if she wasn't sure if it was actually safe to sit there. Did she think they had cooties? Or maybe she was uncomfortable sitting in a strange person's living room while that person was nowhere to be seen.

He rapped lightly on his mother's door. And she wasn't in there, which meant she was sitting in the kitchen nook staring out at the road. He walked down the hall and turned the corner to find her exactly there. She looked up, her hand clutching at her throat. "Is she here?"

Ezra blinked at her. "I'm going to say yes because there's a lady here and she wants to talk to you. She says she knows Dad."

His mother swallowed hard. He had a feeling she knew something that he didn't, as if she had been waiting for this lady.

Ezra stepped back and allowed his mother to maneuver her chair down the hall and into the living room.

If the lady was surprised that his mother was disabled, it didn't show on her face. She stood as they entered the room, reaching out to shake hands.

"You must be Ellen."

His mother nodded but made no move to grasp the woman's hand. It dropped down to her side, and she perched back on the edge of the sofa once more.

"I came to tell you that Jakob is dead."

His mother buried her face in her hands. But he couldn't tell if she was crying or simply trying to get herself together.

He felt like he was going to get sick. The man who had walked out on them seven years ago was dead. There was no reconciliation. There was no time for forgiveness or explanations. He was simply gone.

"I'm sorry to have to be the one to tell you. But I thought it would be best coming from me than anyone else."

"Who are you?" Ezra asked. "His attorney or something?"

She gave a sardonic chuckle and shook her head. "I'm his widow."

To his mother's credit, she didn't point out that she was his widow as well, because according to the Mennonite law, his mother and father were not divorced and were technically still married. Instead she asked the one question that had been pinging around inside Ezra's brain the whole time. "What happened?"

Brenda gave a wobbly smile, and to Ezra's dismay her eyes filled with tears. "He hadn't been feeling well for quite some time. Nobody could figure out what was wrong. He kept going from doctor to doctor. They did all sorts of tests, but nothing. They couldn't find anything. Then one day we went to a new specialist. He ran some different test, thought he might have cancer, and did surgery." She pressed her lips together and swallowed hard as if she needed a moment before she could continue. "But it was too late. By the time they found it, it had spread too far. They sewed him back up and tried to make him as comfortable as possible until he passed."

"How long has he been gone?"

"About two months now," Brenda said.

"About two months?" Ezra managed to calm his tone to one below the screams that were building inside him. "He's been gone about two months and you're just now getting around to telling us?"

Brenda shook her head. "It's not that easy, you know. I had to get his affairs in order. He had life insurance policies and—" She shook her head again as if the motion might somehow put things back to rights. Instead she reached into her purse and pulled out several documents in an envelope. "He had time before he died, you know, to come to terms, to think about his life. He wrote each of you a letter. I have no idea what they say, but I promised him that I would bring them out here to you. Along with this." She held out two white envelopes and the brown manila envelope toward Ezra.

He stared at it a full three seconds before finally putting his feet into motion and crossing the room to take it from her. It burned his hands, and he wasn't sure he wanted it. Part of him wanted to rip it open right then and devour every word that his father had left for him, while another part of him wanted to tear it to shreds and toss it into the wind. The best thing to do for now was just hold it until he could figure out where his emotions fit in with this new message he had from his father.

"The envelope is a life insurance policy that he'd taken out for the two of you. When he and I got married, he told me that if something were to happen to him, the money was to go to you. And I promised." She stood and blinked rapidly, he supposed to keep her tears at bay. It was hard for him to realize, but it appeared that this woman, this stranger, had loved his father. Maybe even as much as his mother had. "I've done what I told him I would do. I won't bother you anymore."

She didn't bother to ask for an escort from the house. She simply turned on her heel and made her own way to the front door. It shut behind her, and a few moments later Ezra heard her car start and back out of the graveled driveway.

"Give it to me," his mother said. Her voice hid any emotion she was feeling.

Ezra handed her the envelope with her name on it in that familiar handwriting. One last message from his father. He touched the manila envelope, then shook his head. He thrust it toward his mother. "Here, take this too."

It dropped into her lap.

He turned on his heel and headed out the back door. He had to get away and he had to get away now. He needed to be alone, he needed to read this letter, and he needed to figure out something, anything as to why his father left. Why his father was now dead. Why there would never be that chance for forgiveness ever again.

"Ezra," his mother called after him. But he didn't slow his steps. He slammed out the back door and flew across the yard and into the shadowy coolness of the barn.

The smell of hay and horseflesh tinged with manure was like a balm to his nerves. But this was all too much. He climbed into the hayloft and sat down on a stack of bales, his back to the small octagonal vent. It was open and light spilled in, allowing him to better read this missive from his father.

Dear Ezra,

I've just received what is probably the most challenging news of my life. By now you know that the news is my imminent death. And I will be judged soon. Though I've asked God for forgiveness for all of my sins and transgressions, there are enough of them that I wonder if that forgiveness will be granted. Although that means my placement for eternity, there is another forgiveness that I must beg for before I leave this earth. I only wish I could do it in person.

I wish I could say a man can go through life without making mistakes, but that is not the case. Unfortunately, I have made more than my fair share of mistakes and big ones. The biggest of all was walking out and leaving you and your mother to fend for yourselves. It was never my intent to hurt you, though I know that it happened. It was never my intent to hurt your mother. But some things are harder to deal with than others, and some people have trouble dealing with their problems. Regrettably, I am one of those people. I never wanted to be a farmer. I never wanted to raise horses or cows. But I grew up Mennonite, and that was the only future I could see. Get married, farm, and milk cows. I could live that life for only so long. Every day I felt as if I was hitting my breaking point. I was unhappy and depressed.

It's not an excuse. There is no excuse for what I did. I only want you to know the reasons behind my actions, what led me to leave.

Then there was your mother's illness. What a cowardly thing. She was diagnosed with MS, and I walked out. I can't tell you how ashamed I am with myself. I know it is no consolation to you, but I pray every night for God to forgive me and to please watch over you and take care of you.

Then I met Brenda. She's a wonderful person, a wonderful woman. It was Brenda who helped me see that my depression was crippling and that it had torn my family apart. I got help and learned to live with the choices that I'd made, the mistakes that I had wrought, and the hearts that I had broken.

But those mistakes are not without consequences. As I think about my diagnosis, I wonder if it is a punishment from God, my own actions coming back to me.

I know you may not see it, but I've led a good life. I've had two good women love me. I know that you have turned out strong and steady. I've heard about your ranch, and I'm proud that you're my son. I know I never had a chance to say that to you directly, so I have to say it now. While I still can.

Please know always and forever that I love you. And if I make it, I'll be watching you from heaven cheering you on and loving you still.

God forgive me,
Jakob

Ezra crumpled up the letter as hot tears ran down his cheeks. He didn't want to forgive his father. He didn't want to know the many reasons why he left. He didn't want there to be a medical reason that caused his father to overload and leave when most men would have stayed.

His heart was in a vise, being squeezed dry of every last drop of compassion to be had. It wasn't what he wanted.

He balled the papers even tighter in his fist and raised his arm back to throw them across the barn. But he couldn't complete the motion.

He lowered his hand and straightened the papers, pressing them to smooth out the wrinkles. It was the last thing he had from his father, the last thing that told of his father's own heartbreak and heartache and walking out on the family he had once loved. And as much as it killed him to do so, he forgave his father, uttered a final prayer, and hoped that God had forgiven him as well.

Chapter Twenty-Three

"Sadie? Sadie?"

Sadie hauled herself out of her own thoughts as Melanie called her name once again. "*Jah?*" she asked.

"It's your turn. Are you going to bowl or are you going to sit there all night?"

Sadie pushed herself off the seat and headed over to the ball return. Sitting there had sounded like a fine idea. These days it was hard to do much of anything, except for wonder how Ezra was doing and if he'd had any new babies born on his ranch. She missed him something terrible. But she had done what she needed to do. She'd done what she could to save her family.

"Are you sure your arm is okay?" The second-degree burn had required quite a lot of treatment, but for the most part she could do anything she wanted. They told her it would scar and she might consider a skin graft. The Amish didn't go in for things like that. If it was fine without it, surgery would not be the answer.

She nodded and picked up the familiar blue-swirled ball with the letters "HAM" on it. Her whole life she had thought that was due to her father's love of pork;

little did she know that it was his initials—Henry Adam
Mathis. How would she have known? He had been a
Kauffman the whole time she had known him, and as
far as she was concerned, he still was.

She tossed the ball down the lane, but it was a little
too far to the right. Luckily she missed a seven/ten
split and took out the back row of pins. Not a great
score, but at least she stood a chance of picking up
the spare.

Chris sidled up next to her. "We don't have to be
here if you're tired."

"I'm fine," she said.

"Are you going to lie to me the whole time we're
married?" His quiet words made Sadie's stomach hurt.
Was that how he viewed her? Had she lied?

She truly did love Chris. She loved him as a person
and as a friend. What was romantic love when you
could have steady, strong, and true? Her best friend at
her side for the rest of her life?

That zing and tingle that the romance authors
talked about, that could fizzle away so easily. No, this
was much, much better. Not even taking into account
the fact that she had made her pledge to God, and He
had granted her request. Even that aside, this was so
much better. She had steady and true for the rest of
her life. She wouldn't be shunned, she could live with
her family, and Chris would take over his family's farm.

"But you are his second choice," some voice inside
her whispered. She pushed it down, ignored it, and
grabbed her ball from the return.

Chris stood, hands on hips, watching her.

She turned around. "I'm fine." But was she?

She closed her eyes and concentrated on the lanes,
picturing them in her head before she opened her

eyes again and hit the sweet spot dead-on. The rest of the pins came tumbling down.

"Whoo!" Hannah said from her spot as the score-keeper. "That puts us above, gentlemen. I hope you enjoy losing tonight." She gave Hannah a high five as the boys shook their heads. They'd only gone two pins ahead of the guys and anything could still happen.

It was Thursday, their usual bowling night. Tomorrow was Good Friday. Saturday was the Easter egg hunt for the buddy bunch. Or rather, Saturday night was.

Sadie was looking forward to it. She needed some normalcy back in her life. The restaurant was still being repaired. *Mamm* spent all her days there salvaging what she could of the paperwork.

Zach Calhoun had come down to help *Mamm* sort through stuff and help move it all out to the storage shed they had rented in town. Anything salvageable went there, but more often than not Sadie had a feeling things were going into the Dumpster out back.

"Sadie?" Jonah asked. "Would you like to bring Daniel out to the farm Saturday morning? We are hosting an Easter egg hunt in the cornfield."

Sadie smiled. "We would love that. I take it it's before we have our Easter egg hunt?"

Jonah nodded. "That's the plan. All the little brothers and sisters are coming over in the morning. Once they have their fun, we'll send them back to our parents and then we'll have our turn." He smiled, but it didn't reach his eyes.

Sadie remembered that he'd had Sarah Yoder out at the pond with him that day a few weeks ago. Somehow hanging out with Sarah didn't make him nearly as happy as hanging out with Lorie had.

"I'll be there," she said.

"Good." Jonah rapped his knuckles against the

Formica desk and started to walk away. He stopped and turned back. "By the way, bring a small gift for that night. We're going to put numbers on everybody's donation and then numbers inside these special eggs. If you find one of them, you get the corresponding prize."

"I'll do it."

"It's a five-dollar limit. This is about having fun."

Sadie nodded. "Will do."

"You're going with me to the Easter egg hunt Saturday night, right?" Chris asked as they chugged home on his tractor.

"Of course," Sadie said. Who else would she go to the Easter egg hunt with? They were getting married, after all. But she didn't say any of those things. As much as they crossed her mind, they were mean, and with the way she had treated Chris this winter, she could see his confusion.

"Are you ever going to tell me what happened?"

Sadie frowned. "Happened when?"

Chris shrugged but didn't take his eyes from the road. He kept on driving. "That night of the fire."

Sadie shook her head, mentally scrambling around to find an answer. "Nothing happened. I just realized that . . ."

"That what?" Chris asked.

"It's complicated," Sadie said, hoping he would drop the matter. Thankfully he didn't say anything else as they continued on to her house.

He pulled into the driveway. Sadie was reminded of all the times that she made Ezra stop at the road. Ezra had not been approved, but everyone was happy that she was marrying Chris. If only she was as happy as they were.

"You want to come in for a bit?" Sadie always asked. It was one of those things they did on a date. She asked him inside and he told her no because he had a lot of work to do on the farm the next day.

"*Jah.* I would like that."

Sadie blinked at him, then recovered. "Okay then."

Chris shut off the engine and climbed down from the cab. Sadie jumped to the ground and together they walked into the house.

It was a typical Thursday night in the Kauffman household. Cora Ann and *Mamm* were reading the Bible, their heads close together as they studied the word. Daniel had long since been put to bed.

Sadie missed those days when everyone was here. When they all sat around together and read the Bible and enjoyed each other's company. But Lorie had left and Melanie had gotten married. She was next. And she wondered how Cora Ann would feel being the last girl left in the house.

"Chris Flaud," *Mamm* said, sticking one finger into the Bible to hold her place while she rose to her feet. "I didn't expect to see you tonight." She actually smiled.

This was making everyone so happy. Sadie had to keep telling herself that, keep remembering that and everything that was at stake. This was for Daniel. And no matter what, he was worth it.

"I just wanted to say hello," Chris said. But he shifted from one foot to the other, and Sadie had a feeling there was more than hello on his mind.

"How about some pie?" Cora Ann said. She jumped to her feet and started toward the kitchen. She skidded to a halt before she got to the door and turned around with an apologetic grimace on her face. "Oops. There is no pie. How about some cake? No, wait. Daniel ate the last of the cake. I've got a couple of biscuits left."

Sadie laughed. Her sister the hostess.

Chris chuckled along with her. "I'm really not that hungry. We had pizza at the bowling alley."

"Coffee?" *Mamm* asked.

"That'd be good. Thanks." Chris smiled at each of them in turn.

Mamm sat back down and Cora Ann started into the kitchen to make coffee. Sadie led Chris to the living room, where they sat opposite each other.

"How's Johnny?" *Mamm* asked.

Sadie hated the clouds of sadness that dulled Chris's eyes. Johnny's accident had been hard on all the Flauds, none more so than Johnny, of course, but Sadie had a feeling that Chris was the one suffering the most after his brother. He had to give up his dream of going to Europe. He'd given his money to his family to help pay the medical bills, and never once had she heard him complain.

She was ashamed. She had been nothing but a grump about the changes she'd had to make, and all because she had made her promise to God. But God had saved Daniel, and she wouldn't take that back for anything. Not anything in the world. But she needed to get her attitude right. She needed to get her mind straight. She only did what she had to do, and that's all there was to it. She should be more like Chris. She shouldn't fuss and complain. She had more than most. And she needed to keep that in mind.

* * *

Chris resisted the urge to stand and help Cora Ann as she brought the tray into the living room.

She set the tray on the coffee table and smiled, quite pleased with herself as she pointed to it. "I found some cookies. They're store-bought, though. I think we bought them for Daniel's school, but never took them."

Daniel went to an *Englisch* school with different rules than the Amish. All treats had to be store-bought. Personally, Chris thought store-bought cookies were about the worst thing anyone could ever eat, but he smiled politely at Cora Ann. "Thank you."

Cora Ann gave a quick nod and left them alone in the living room. Not that they were truly alone. The table was on the other side of the large open room. Anything he said to Sadie could be easily overheard.

And he had things to say. He had watched her this last week or so. She was so sad, so miserable. He didn't think it had anything to do with the large burn on her arm or any of the resulting pain. No, this was something much deeper.

He picked up his coffee and took a sip. He could pretend to like the cookies, and the coffee was excellent as always, but Cora Ann? She would make someone a really good wife someday.

"I get the feeling there's something you want to talk to me about," Sadie said.

They had known each other too long to play games now. He supposed she knew him better than anyone else in the world. Maybe even better than his own mother.

"It can keep." He didn't want to talk about it now, not when her sister and her mother might overhear. This was serious. Big stuff. And he wanted to make sure that when they started talking about it, the time was right. She needed to be ready to talk and ready to admit that she was still in love with Ezra Hein.

He got his opportunity fifteen minutes later when her *mamm* sent Cora Ann upstairs to brush her teeth. Maddie held her place in the Bible with a crocheted bookmark, then left the Good Book on the table.

She came over and stood in front of them, looking from one of them to the other. "I've got to go to bed now. Four o'clock comes mighty early. I trust that you will see Chris out?" Maddie asked Sadie.

Sadie nodded. "Of course."

"Good." Maddie gave him one last curt nod, then headed for the stairs herself.

He waited until her footsteps had faded out of earshot before turning back to Sadie. "Can I talk to you about something?"

Sadie stopped chewing the horrible store-bought cookie and almost choked. "What do you need to talk about?"

"I think you know."

Her eyes grew wide, and she shook her head as if somehow that would erase the harm that had been done.

"I want to talk about the Mennonite."

Sadie shook her head. "I don't want to talk about him."

"Aren't you in love with him?"

Sadie shook her head. "How can I be in love with him? I haven't known him but a couple of months."

Chris had been saying those very same words to himself, but once he met Ezra Hein and saw the Mennonite and his Sadie together, everything changed forever.

"Sadie, I've known you my whole life, and I've loved

you almost as long. But why do I get the feeling that you're not telling me the truth about this?"

Sadie shrugged, but didn't meet his gaze. "I have no control over what you think, Chris." Not at all what he expected. What happened to the Sadie who wanted nothing more than to get married and have babies with him for the rest of her days in Wells Landing? She was getting her dream, but yet she didn't look very happy about it at all. He'd put his dream on hold.

That wasn't even true. He had killed his dream dead, as surely as he had chopped it into pieces.

It wasn't meant to be. He wasn't supposed to go to Europe. He was supposed to stay here and marry Sadie. So why did she look like she had received some kind of death sentence instead of a marriage proposal?

He finished up his coffee and set his cup back on the tray. He stood and stretched his legs, trying to find some reason to stay, looking for any reason to leave. Somehow the air in the Kauffman household had turned cold.

"Walk me to the door?" he asked.

Sadie nodded. Together they walked out onto the porch.

It was almost April, and it wouldn't be long until everything turned green and the fields required more attention than ever. He would be in baptism classes, trying to juggle life with a girlfriend and having an invalid for a brother. No one still knew if Johnny would ever regain full use of his arms. For now he could do a few things, lift them and such, but he had no strength and couldn't hold anything in his grasp. Someone had to feed him. Someone had to stay with him. There was always someone at Chris's house taking care of Johnny.

"I guess I'll see you Saturday at the egg hunt?"
Sadie nodded.

"Good night, then." Chris wanted to lean in and
steal a kiss. Somehow he felt like he needed to kiss
Sadie. He needed to see her feelings for him, see if
he could taste her love for him.

He swooped in quickly, using the one hand to lift
her chin as his lips sought hers. The kiss was brief,
chaste, and told him all he needed to know.

"Good night, Sadie Kauffman."

Friday afternoon Chris had just finished up his chores
when he heard the car engine.

Just in time, he thought as Luke Lambright pulled
into the driveway.

Chris jogged over to where Luke was sitting in that
shiny convertible car. Chris wasn't knowledgeable
about the names of *Englisch* cars, but this one was a
beauty. Sleek lines and shiny red paint. Even better,
the top came down. If he were to go *Englisch*, this
would be the kind of car he would want to drive.

But you're not going Englisch. *You're not even going to
Europe. You're here on this farm, and that's where you will
remain.* He stuffed that voice down. He'd made his decision, he'd made his choice, and he would see it
through. All but one thing.

"Are you ready to go?" Luke asked.

Chris nodded. "*Jah*, let me tell *Mamm* I'm leaving."

He loped up the porch steps two at a time and
shouted from the front door to his mother that he was
leaving.

She came out of the kitchen, wiping her hands on
a dish towel. Chris thought back to a time not too long
ago when he'd seen her do the same thing. But this

time her face was more pinched, more lined with worry and concern for his brother. "Be careful now, will you?" she said.

Chris nodded. "We won't be gone long. A couple hours at the most, then I'll be back. Okay?"

His mother nodded.

"After that I'll feed Johnny and read to him." He smiled reassuringly at her.

Tonight he would take care of Johnny, and his mother would have a well-deserved night off. She looked like she was dead on her feet, ready to collapse under the slightest weight of anything else.

He tripped back down the steps and let himself into the passenger side of Luke's shiny car.

"Tell me again why you need to go to Taylor Creek?"

Ezra pulled his four-wheeler around the side of the barn and parked it in the shade. In a minute he would pull it on inside, but for now it was fine where it was.

He'd gone out and rode the fences, making sure that everything on the north half of his pasture was in good shape. He had some more stock coming tomorrow. He had gotten a great deal on some bison out of Montana. But he'd had to promise that half the offspring would go back to Montana to help replenish the national park there. That was one of the most rewarding parts of his job. He provided organic, healthy meats, but he also gave back to the world these beautiful creatures that mankind had almost killed out.

From the driveway came the glint of sunshine off a windshield. Then he heard the car turn down his drive and head closer.

It wasn't Logan, for sure, he thought. The car was driving much too slow for that. He stood where he was, his eyes shielded against the sun as he waited for the car to come into view. When it did, it was not exactly what he expected. It was shiny and fancy. Nothing like he'd ever seen. At least not on his land.

He thought back to the last fancy car that pulled up his drive and the news that Brenda had brought to him about his father. All at once he wanted to run toward the car and frantically wave his arms until whoever it was got off his land. He didn't want whatever it was they came to tell him. Instead he took a deep breath, tried to settle his nerves, and waited for the car to stop.

Two men got out, one Amish, with his hat pulled down a little over his face. He looked vaguely familiar, but Ezra couldn't place him. He was too far away for him to notice much more of his appearance. The other guy was *Englisch*, with dark hair, a little long, jeans, and a T-shirt. He carried a cane in one hand and walked with a pronounced limp.

Ezra started across the yard, meeting the two visitors halfway.

"Can I help you?" All sorts of people came out for all sorts of meats and things from his ranch. But something in his gut told him this had nothing to do with business.

"Ezra Hein?"

That's when Ezra realized: The Amish man was none other than Chris Flaud, Sadie's ex-boyfriend.

Fiancé, the voice inside him corrected. She had told Ezra the last time she had seen him that she was staying Amish and marrying Chris. The razor blades that had slashed at his heart then started up again, tearing him to shreds. One day soon, he prayed that he wouldn't have to endure pain from merely thinking her name. But he had fallen hard and fast for Sadie

Kauffman, and she had only used him. Then left him in the dust.

"You're probably the last person I thought I would see here."

"Can I talk to you for a moment?" Chris asked.

Ezra wanted to tell him no, to get off his property and never come back. Chris had won, and now Sadie belonged to him. There was no sense coming to gloat. "I don't think we have anything to talk about," he said instead, quite proud of the fact that he kept his temper in check when he wanted to do anything but stand there calmly and listen to the sound of the man's voice.

"I think we do."

Chris turned to the *Englisch* man, realizing at once that he was ex-Amish. There was something about people who left the Plain faith and went to the *Englisch* world. Most people couldn't see it, but anybody who lived that kind of life could tell right away.

"Ezra Hein." He reached out a hand to shake. The man took it in his firm grasp.

"Luke Lambright."

"So?" Chris asked.

Why couldn't he tell him to leave? Ezra thought. Why couldn't he tell him to get off his property and never come back? But he couldn't. Something in him, no doubt his good raising from his mom, wouldn't let him. "Say what you came to say."

"I understand that you don't like me."

Ezra choked on a laugh. That was an understatement.

"I understand," Chris continued. "But I'm here to tell you that you have no reason to be jealous of me. Sadie still loves you."

Those razor blades started again, tearing his heart

to such small ribbons that he didn't think he could ever put it back together again. "I think you should leave now."

"Hear him out," Luke said. "He came a long way to tell you this."

Not to mention the bravery.

Ezra reluctantly nodded. The best thing was to let Chris have his say, then tell him to leave. Then Ezra could go about the process of healing once more.

"She doesn't want to marry me. I don't know why she says she does." The sadness in the man's eyes confirmed that Chris was telling the truth. His lips trembled, and he pressed them together for a moment before continuing. "I thought I should tell you that. Because I'm going marry her if you don't."

Ezra stared at him for a second. "I don't understand."

"Sadie figured out a while back that she was my second choice. I wanted to travel, but then my brother was badly injured. He'll never walk again, and I'm stuck on the farm. I promised Sadie long ago that I would marry her when I could. I'm staying in Wells Landing, and I can marry her. Then last night I realized I'm her second choice.

"She doesn't want to travel to Europe, she wants to be married. That's all she's ever wanted. I've known this since we were children. All she wants to do is be married and have children of her own. If you don't marry her, I will, because if nothing else, that's one dream I can give her."

Ezra watched the two men pile into the shiny red car to pull out of the driveway. After they left, he continued to stand there trying to assimilate what Chris had said to him.

Chris was going to marry Sadie and make her dreams come true even though he thought Sadie loved him, Ezra.

He couldn't quite wrap his mind around it. Or what he could do about it.

Sadie had flat out told him that she didn't love him. That she loved Chris and she was marrying him. Though Ezra had no idea why she would say such a thing only to have Chris turn around and say the exact opposite.

Ezra rubbed his fingers against his temples as a headache throbbed there. This was beyond confusing. It didn't help that he loved Sadie more than anything in the world. He would do anything to fix whatever it was that happened between them. But he hadn't known what there was to fix. Was Chris trying to play him for some kind of fool by telling him that Sadie really loved him?

The car had long since disappeared down the road and yet Ezra still stood in the same place, staring at nothing. He shook his head and climbed back onto the four-wheeler. He pulled it into the barn, vowing not to give this whole ordeal a second thought. It was one more way to keep his broken heart in one piece.

Chapter Twenty-Four

Sadie spent Saturday morning watching Daniel and the other children in their Amish community hunting Easter eggs in the budding cornfields on the Millers' property. Some eggs were filled with candy, some had money, and others had coupons. A free ice cream at the drugstore, a cookie from Esther's bakery, even a free child's meal with the purchase of a regular entrée at Kauffman's Family Restaurant. Of course that had been donated long before the fire, and Sadie hoped that whoever received one of those was patient enough to wait until they were completely rebuilt.

Mamm was hoping to have everything settled soon, and the insurance money would pay shortly after that. Then they had a little more cleanup before they could begin the rebuild and restoration. With any luck and God on their side, they were hoping to open again by September.

After a fun-filled morning of searching for eggs, Sadie took Daniel home for a nap and waited for Chris to pick her up for their afternoon on the Miller property.

First was the traditional picnic at Millers' Pond.

Everyone sat around and talked, wishing the water was warm enough to actually get in. They sang songs and played games, corn hole and horseshoes, and waited for it to get dark enough for their glow-in-the-dark Easter egg hunt.

They had spent part of their afternoon tying glow sticks into knots and stuffing them in plastic Easter eggs, which in itself was a fun challenge. But there were also other eggs that weren't glow-in-the-dark that would be hidden by the volunteer crew of church members. Those eggs were the ones that Jonah had told her about. They were tied to the donated prizes. The trick was finding the right Easter egg when you had no idea which one was the right one.

Finally darkness fell and the hunt was on. Chris grabbed Sadie's hand, and together they flew through the thicket of trees looking for the glow-in-the-dark Easter eggs along with the special ones. It was fun and more of a couples competition to see who found the most. Everyone was racing around, having a great time. Sadie did her best to let her guard down and not think too much about anything except the right now.

Chris had been acting a little strange all day. She caught him watching her as if she was about to grow a second head or something equally weird, and he didn't want to miss a single minute of it. She had to ask him twice why he kept looking at her like that. He smiled and turned away. She wondered if he had a surprise in store or a problem afoot.

"There's one!" She wasn't sure who hollered out, but the egg was gone in an instant.

"Sadie, you need to keep your flashlight pointed at the ground or you're never going to find one of the special eggs."

"Right." She aimed the light down and went back to her search.

"Okay," Chris started, "you find the special egg, and I'll collect the glow-in-the-dark ones. Deal?"

Sadie nodded. "Okay. Deal."

She tried to point out a few of the glow-in-the-dark eggs as they walked along, but Chris kept fussing at her to keep looking for the eggs that didn't glow.

"I found one!" She wasn't sure how she found it. It was lying on the ground in between two tree roots, a pretty little yellow egg just waiting for her.

She snatched it up and went back to where Chris stood. "Are you looking for one too?"

Chris held up an egg with a smile on his face. It was blue and didn't glow. "I've already got mine."

"Are you ready to go back?"

Around them everyone was still running around gathering up the glow-in-the-dark eggs. But as far as Sadie was concerned, the night was a success.

"If you are," Chris said.

Together they walked back to the Easter egg starting point, and had their glow-in-the-dark eggs logged. Sadie knew they wouldn't win that part of the contest. But it was more about fun than anything. "Go on over to that wagon there," the girl behind the entry table said. "They have all the prizes. Give your regular egg to them."

Sadie nodded and headed over to where she had indicated.

She handed her egg to the man at the wagon. He popped it open and took out the folded piece of paper with the number on it. Then he gave them both a nod and headed to the back of the wagon. He returned a few moments later with a small picture frame. He handed it to Sadie and took Chris's egg from him, popping it open as well to find what prize Chris had won.

Sadie looked down at the small frame she held in her hands. It was an interesting picture. Brown, orange, and tan. Or at least it looked to be that way in the darkness. She shined her flashlight on it to get a better look. And nearly gasped when she noticed it was an elephant.

The Bible verse on it read: *Remember His marvelous works that He hath done; His wonders, and the judgments of His mouth; Psalm 105:5*

Sadie stared at the picture as Chris got his prize and came to stand next to her. "What did you get?" Chris asked, for the first time truly looking at it.

Sadie shook her head. "Nothing. Just a little framed thing. What did you get?"

Chris showed her what he had gotten, a tin filled with cookies from Esther's bakery.

"Yum," she said, hoping that she sounded at least a little interested. But the picture of that elephant and the quote from the Bible that had accompanied it captured all of her attention.

"You want to trade?" Chris asked.

Sadie trailed her finger over the smooth glass, tracing the outline of the elephant underneath. "No. I'm fine."

Chris smiled at her. "I'll share."

Sadie tried to muster a grin of her own, but instead it was stiff. She hoped that the darkness would keep her secret. "I can't share back. Are you okay with that?"

"Of course," he said. "Anything for you."

The Easter egg hunt had been great fun, but Sadie was tired by the time they loaded up into Chris's trac-

tor and headed back to her house. Still, she had had
a good time though the Bible verse on the elephant
picture seemed to be a part of her every thought.
Surely it wasn't some kind of sign from God? What
were the chances that it was merely a coincidence?

She had no idea, but she was having trouble believing it regardless of her lack of facts. Of all the animals
to get, she got an elephant, and for all the Bible
verses that could have been quoted, she had to get one
about the beautiful works that God makes.

"Did you have a good time tonight?" Chris asked as
they chugged along.

Sadie nodded, trying to act as if nothing was wrong.
Yet she felt anything but normal.

She had made up her mind to marry Chris, yet
there was a part of her that wanted to run to Ezra,
wrap her arms around him, and never let him go. Still,
she had made her choice. She had made her decision.
And she had to see it through.

"*Jah.*" She felt like she needed to say more, but the
words wouldn't come.

"Good," Chris said. "I'm glad."

His words seemed almost strange, like there was
something in between them that she had yet to figure
out. But with her mind turning in circles, it was hard
for her to make out even the smallest truth.

"Would you like to come in?" she asked as he pulled
the tractor to a stop in her driveway.

"*Nay,*" he replied. "But I would like to talk to you for
a minute."

Was this it? Was this the time when he broke up with
her because he knew that she loved Ezra? What would
she do then? How would she keep her promise to God
if Chris turned her away?

She took a deep breath to steady her racing thoughts. "Okay," she said.

Chris turned off the tractor and followed her up to sit on the bench next to the front door. They stared out over the cool spring night, and Sadie let the sounds of the evening wash over her: the chirp of the birds, the horses in the barn, even a bobwhite called from somewhere along the edge of her property.

"I went to see Ezra yesterday."

Sadie turned to him, surprised. Of all the things he could have said, that was maybe the least expected.

"You did what?"

"I went to see Ezra." Chris said the words as if he was reciting the weather.

"Why would you do something like that?"

"Well," Chris started, "I felt like I had some things I needed to talk to him about."

She quirked one eyebrow as high as it would go, hoping to show her feelings on the matter. He should've never gone to talk to Ezra. And he should've never gone without her. "What kind of things?"

"You." He took her hand into his, rubbing her fingers between his. "See, I know he's in love with you."

Sadie shook her head in protest, but he cut her off. Not allowing her to speak, he continued. "And I know that you love him. Though I don't know what's keeping the two of you apart."

"Chris, I—I don't know what to say."

Chris shook his head. "There's nothing to say, Sadie Kauffman. I've known you long enough to know that you love Ezra, but for some reason you're marrying me."

She opened her mouth to say something, but no words would come. She shut it again and waited patiently for him to continue.

"You told me once that you wanted to have a family.

That was the whole of your dreams. Have a family, get married, buy a house, and live happily ever after here in Wells Landing."

Sadie nodded, still unable to speak.

"After Johnny got hurt . . . I knew I would be here in Wells Landing with you."

Sadie swallowed hard as she listened to his words. She had no idea where he was going with this conversation, and she was a little afraid to find out.

"I'll stand by my promise until the end of time. I love you. You're my best friend. But I wanted you to know that I went to Ezra and told him that if he didn't want to lose you forever, then he had to make his move."

"Why would you tell him something like that?" Sadie jumped to her feet, stalking toward the porch railing. She whirled around to face him, propping her hip against the rail behind her as she glared at him across the dim porch.

"Because it's true." He shook his head as she started to speak. "You and I both know it's true, so quit lying about it. I can live with that. I made a promise to you, and I will keep it forever. You're a good girl, Sadie Kauffman, and you deserve a good husband. But you also deserve love and the most happiness you can get. I believe that love and happiness is going to come from Ezra Hein."

"What makes you think he wants to marry me?"

"I don't. And I don't know what happened to you at the fire. After that you started acting all crazy, pushing some people away and holding others closer. I don't know what's in your head. But I do know this. I know that you love him. And I'm pretty sure that he loves you. As much as I will do anything in the world for you, you deserve a chance at that as well."

"Wait." She shook her head. "I don't understand.

Are you going to marry me or not?" Her patience was wearing thin, her heart pounding in her throat.

"Of course I am. I wanted him to know, in case he wanted a chance with you."

Sadie shook her head. "He doesn't want a chance with me." If he had, he would've never let her tell him the things she had that afternoon. How she didn't love him, how she loved only Chris. Ezra didn't love her. Not enough.

Not that it mattered.

"I made a deal with God," Sadie said.

Chris stood, took one of her hands into his, and pulled her back to the bench. "You made a what?"

Sadie swallowed hard, trying to find the words. "The night of the fire. I made a deal with God. I told Him that if He would help me find Daniel in that building, then I would do what I was supposed to do. I wouldn't go against everybody's wishes. I would stay here, I would marry you, and I would be a good Amish girl."

"You don't think you're a good Amish girl?"

Sadie pleated her fingers in the skirt of her black dress. Her sisters and *Mamm* had already gone back to wearing their colors. But somehow Sadie didn't feel right putting on those bright colors when she felt such a sadness in her heart.

"You're one of the best Amish girls I know. You're kind and loving. You would do anything for your friends and family."

Sadie couldn't meet his gaze. She stared down at her fingers all wound up in the black fabric.

"I don't know if anyone's ever told you this before, but you don't make deals with God."

Sadie desperately wanted to meet his gaze, see if his words were sincere, but she couldn't bring herself to. What if he was saying that to make her feel better? What would she do then?

"But I did," she whispered. "I asked Him to do something for me, and He did. I told Him that if He helped me, then I would do something for Him in return."

"Marry me?"

"Not that exactly, but I suppose it was part of the package."

"Sadie, I would marry you tomorrow if the church would let me. Even knowing what I know now. I would love you and cherish you for the rest of your life. But you deserve the most happiness in the world. And I think that's a happiness that you won't ever find with me. I think the only person in the world who can give you that is Ezra Hein."

Thankfully everyone was in bed when Sadie let herself into the house. Since Lorie and Melanie had moved out, she and Cora Ann had their own rooms, though Sadie would have given just about anything to have Lorie in that bedroom beside her. She sure could use her sister's wisdom and advice about now.

Sadie let herself in her room and turned on the propane-powered lamp, then prepared for bed. She undressed and put on her nightshirt, the one that Ezra had bought her at the zoo. A small smile tugged at the corners of her mouth as she thought about that day. It had been such a wonderful time. She hadn't known then that things could turn so bad. Then she hadn't known the fear of losing Daniel.

She removed her prayer *kapp* and set it on her dresser, then took the pins from her hair. She sat cross-legged on the bed and began to brush through the tangles, thinking about everything that Chris had said.

She should be mad at him. So angry that she could hardly see straight. But she wasn't. It just proved what she already knew. Chris had told Ezra that she loved him, and if he truly cared for her he would have come to see her before now.

She shook her head at the confusion of it all. She could hear Lorie say that was the most ridiculous thing she had ever heard. Sadie herself had told Ezra Hein that she didn't love him, and he had believed her. So why would she think that he would now believe Chris?

But still those thoughts rattled around in her head as she tried to forget them.

She loosely braided her hair to keep it out of her face for the night. She knew Amish girls who slept with their hair completely unbound. But she tossed and turned in her sleep too much to leave her long tresses free.

She took out the little picture that she had won at the Easter egg hunt tonight and examined it once again.

How could Chris say that people couldn't make a deal with God? Hadn't she done that very thing? She had asked Him to help her save Daniel, and He had. She had been asking Him for signs for weeks to let her know that she was headed in the right direction, that what she was doing with Ezra wasn't all bad, wasn't against Him or the Bible. Instead she had gotten a fire and the fear that her brother could have died there.

She ran a finger over that elephant pressed beneath the glass and read the verse over once more.

Remember His marvelous works that He hath done; His wonders, and the judgments of His mouth; Psalm 105:5

God had performed a miracle in helping her save

Daniel. She would always remember, but was this a sign? How else could she explain that out of all the gifts, she received the one that held so much meaning for her and Ezra?

And the scripture! One more reminder that God performed miracles every day. He didn't have to be bargained with in order to answer prayers. Was He trying to tell her that He wasn't holding her to the promises she'd made to Him in her hour of need?

The little picture frame had a stand on the back, so she propped it up on her nightstand and slid beneath the covers. She turned out the light and laid there in the darkness, her mind swirling as if it were the middle of the day.

Was this a sign or coincidence? Why was she so sure she had seen signs and this one wasn't?

She loved Chris with all her heart. He had been her best friend for years, a companion and the one man she knew she could always depend on. He would make her a fine husband, a loving father to their children, but she also knew that as much as he cared for her, she was always his second choice. He wanted to leave Wells Landing. He wanted to travel. If he married her, there was no hope of that dream ever coming to pass. As of right now, one day he might be able to leave. He might have the opportunity to see some of this world that he dreamed about.

She couldn't be responsible for holding him back.

It also occurred to her that as much as she was his second choice, he was hers.

She loved Chris, yet she loved Ezra twice that much. With Ezra her feelings were different, deeper. With Ezra she had found the romance she had always dreamed about. She hadn't known it existed until him. It was the one thing she had dreamed about in life, the one thing she'd never thought she would find, and now she was going to give it all up.

She turned over in her bed and looked back at the little picture frame sitting on the nightstand next to her. God performed miracles every day. Babies were born and people fell in love. Why was she so convinced that he had not performed one of those miracles for her?

Chapter Twenty-Five

Sadie barely slept a wink all night. When she did, she dreamt of elephants and miracles and occasionally a fire that she could walk through without getting burned.

Her arm was still a long way from being completely healed. But it would always be a reminder to her of the miracle God had given her that night, the ability to find Daniel in a burning building and somehow get the both of them out alive. He had done that because she had prayed to Him. She loved him, and God was good. Not because she had promised to stay in Wells Landing and marry Chris Flaud.

In fact, her sleepless night made it even more apparent that she and Chris wanted different things from life, and neither one of them should settle for second.

The next morning, she pulled her favorite blue dress from the closet and shook it out. The last time she had worn it she had gone with Ezra to the zoo.

She had broken so many rules for him, and so many more she had been unwilling to bend. But she knew, as she donned that dress and put her apron on over the top, there was a compromise somewhere. It was up to them to find it.

She wound her hair into a bob and pinned her prayer *kapp* in place. Then she brushed her teeth and skipped down the stairs, looking forward to the day more than she had in a long time.

Mamm and Cora Ann were already in the kitchen when she came downstairs.

"My, you're looking chipper today," Cora Ann said.

Mamm studied her with those knowing blue eyes.

"Did you have a good date with Chris last night?" Cora Ann asked, her voice filled with teasing.

"You could say that."

All she wanted to do was go see Ezra, find out how he felt about her, not let him take her words, her lies, for the truth. She had to tell him that she loved him and then pray that God would help them find a way. After all, He worked miracles every day. Surely He could work one for them.

"Can you go get Daniel ready?"

"Ready?" Her confusion must've shown on her face.

Mamm frowned. "It's Easter Sunday, and we have church."

She had forgotten. How could she have forgotten? Immediately she felt ashamed, but managed to hold those feelings inside as she nodded. "*Jah*. Of course." She ran back up the stairs to take care of Daniel, wondering when she would have an opportunity to talk to Ezra.

* * *

Easter Sunday. Ezra had always loved Easter. But today he had so much on his mind he could barely enjoy the sermon.

Why had Chris Flaud come to his house to tell him that Sadie was in love with him? She had expressly told Ezra that she didn't love him and that she was marrying Chris.

Of course Chris had verified that bit of information, telling Ezra that he would marry Sadie and give her the dreams she had always had in her heart. Dreams of having a family and living in Wells Landing. But was Chris telling the truth when he said that Sadie was in love with him and if he didn't do something about it, Chris was going to marry her?

There was only one way to find out.

After church he helped his mom over to the truck, listening as the others around him talked about going home and their Easter egg celebrations that were about to take place. It'd been years since the Heins had anything truly special for Easter dinner. Ranching never stopped, and his mother wasn't in good enough health that she could prepare a big meal by herself. Sometimes they found an *Englisch* restaurant and ate a nice meal out. But Ezra always felt a little guilty that whoever served them was having to spend Easter away from their family in order to allow him to celebrate. The thought didn't sit well with him.

"Ellen?"

Ezra got his mom settled in the seat, shut the door behind her, turning to see who had summoned.

Billy Peters was headed in their direction.

Ezra and Billy had done business in the past. Billy had come by to get meat and other things. But this time he only had eyes for Ezra's mother.

"Hi, Billy," Ellen said.

Ezra nodded in the man's direction as he reached out a hand to shake.

"I was wondering," Billy started, looking from each one of them to the other, "I was wondering if you would like to come and have Easter supper with us."

Ezra was about to say no, when Billy continued. "I mean, it's at my brother's house with his family, but I thought maybe . . ." He all but kicked the gravel beneath his feet. That was when Ezra knew. Billy Peters was interested in his mother.

Ezra blinked a couple of times to get the world back in focus. He wasn't sure how he felt about his mom having a suitor. But that was his protective streak kicking up. His mother needed this. She needed to start over. Billy had been a widower for several years. And since his mother was newly widowed, then they had a lot more in common than they had before.

But more than anything his mother needed to get out of the house, and this looked to be the opportunity that Ezra had been praying for.

"Well, I appreciate that, Billy," Ezra said. "I can't make it, though. I've got too much to do on the ranch. But perhaps my mother could come?"

He thought Billy was going to collapse in the sidewalk in a puddle of gratefulness. "That would be great. That'd be fine. Is that okay with you, Ellen?"

His mother looked from him to Billy and then back again. Ezra gave her a small nod and a little wink to tell her it was okay. It was time to start over. She needed that. More than anything, she *deserved* it.

"I-I guess. If you're sure that's okay, Ezra."

Ezra nodded. "It's okay." He had a few chores to do and then maybe he would head over to Billy's place a little later and check in, pick up his mom.

He opened the door for her, and between the two of them, he and Billy got her out of the truck. Ezra lifted her wheelchair out from the back and set it up for her.

She sat down gratefully and shot Billy a trembling smile. She told Ezra bye, and Billy pushed her away. Ezra watched them go, a little hopeful, a little sad. This was a new beginning for them both.

Everything was done. Well, as much as everything could ever be done on the ranch. All the animals had been fed, the horses brushed down, the fences were all okay, hay was down, the books were caught up, and it was only four thirty. This should have been the time when he ran over to Billy Peters's to check on his mother, but he couldn't stop thinking about Sadie. Or rather, the words that Chris Flaud had told him. How Sadie loved him. How her pride or something had kept her from admitting that love and instead had her saying that she was going to marry Chris.

Ezra had been so hurt and betrayed that he hadn't questioned her at the time. But he deserved an answer. He deserved to know why Sadie had pushed him away. Why she had picked Chris over him. It might not change anything in the world, but it was one thing he needed. He needed to know why she felt they could never be together.

Was it because he wouldn't join the Amish church? Fine. He would join the Amish church. He would figure something out. That's what people in love did. They didn't run. So did that mean she wasn't in love? That she ran straight to Chris to get away from him?

Ezra shook his head, but the thoughts kept coming one after another, each more confusing than the next.

There was only one way he could find out the truth. Only one way he could learn what was in Sadie's heart.

It was past five by the time they got back to their house. Easter Sunday church was always a little longer. There were decisions to be made about the upcoming season, the sermon to be held, lessons to be remembered, foot washing and communion. Sadie somehow managed during it all to push aside her feelings for Ezra and concentrate on the matter at hand. Somehow she knew that was what God wanted from her.

Maybe this was her sign. Maybe this was a test. To show her faith, to show her love for God and her fellow man before she and Ezra made their compromise.

Daniel had fallen asleep on the way home, and Sadie offered to bring him into the house. She loved the warm, soft weight of his body as she carried him up the stairs to his room. He stirred as she went to lay him on the bed.

"Sadie?"

"I'm here."

"Promise me you'll always be?" Daniel asked.

"Always. I'll always be here for you." Even as she said the words she wondered if she could uphold that promise, but she wasn't about to tell him that she couldn't be there for him. Because somehow she would find a way.

She removed his shoes and pulled the covers up over him, planting a quick kiss on his head before she started back down the stairs.

Mamm and Cora Ann were in the kitchen when she got back to the first floor. They were getting together an evening snack, leftovers from the day before, cheese, crackers, and pickles. They usually ate so much after church that a small snack was all they needed on Sunday nights. That would hold them over until breakfast the next day.

"Is he still asleep?" *Mamm* asked.

Sadie nodded. "I think so. He stirred, but I think he'll sleep for another hour or so."

"We better not let him sleep that long. Maybe give him another half an hour, then wake him up. Otherwise he might not sleep at all tonight."

"*Mamm?* A word?" Sadie asked.

Her *mamm* looked at her, then turned to her sister. "Cora Ann, why don't you go on upstairs and put on a different apron?"

Cora Ann looked as if she was about to protest, then decided not to. She gave them each a quick nod, then hurried out of the kitchen.

Sadie waited until her footsteps had faded to next to nothing before turning back to her mother. "I know it's Sunday. But I need to take the buggy out."

"It's more than Sunday. It's Easter."

"I understand that." Sadie nodded. "But this is important. Really important."

"This doesn't have anything to do with that Mennonite boy, does it?" her mother asked.

Sadie sucked in a deep breath, trying to calm her nerves. "This has everything to do with that Mennonite boy."

Mamm gestured toward the table, giving Sadie a nod. They both sat down.

"Do you love him?" *Mamm* asked.

"*Jah.* I do. More than anything."

"Does he love you?" *Mamm* asked.

"*Jah.* I believe he does," Sadie said.

Mamm closed her eyes for a moment. Long enough

that Sadie thought she might be deep in prayer. Then she opened them again and leveled that serious blue gaze on Sadie. "I can't tell you how hard it was to lose Lorie. I felt like part of my heart had been cut out when she went to live with Zach Calhoun. But it taught me a few things. Love is powerful. And it's hard to understand. *He that loveth not knoweth not God; for God is love.*"

"First John chapter 4, verse eight," Sadie said.

Maddie nodded. "I have to believe that if you love him and he loves you, that it's from God. And I don't know what the answer is, Sadie. I want you to be Amish. I want you to stay here so I won't have to shun you." She held up a hand as Sadie started to protest. She fell silent to let her mother continue. "Bishop Ebersol is a fair man. I don't believe that he wants anything but the best for his people. And if the best is for you to marry Ezra Hein and become a Mennonite—" She closed her eyes as if garnering strength. "Then that is what you should do. We'll work out the rest from there. Somehow it'll all be okay."

Tears welled in Sadie's eyes. "Oh, *Mamm.*" She came around the table and knelt in front of her mother, wrapping her arms around her. She laid her head on *Mamm*'s chest, listening to the thump of her heart beneath her ear. "I love you so much. And I would do nothing to disappoint you."

Mamm kissed the top of her head and set her away. "I know that."

Together they stood, and *Mamm* wrapped Sadie in a warm hug. "Now—" She wiped the tears from Sadie's cheeks with the pads of her thumbs. "Go tell your Mennonite how you feel."

Sadie squeezed her mother a little tighter, then all but ran to the door. She would hitch up the buggy and . . . How was she ever going to get to Taylor Creek in a buggy?

Who had a car and would drive her all the way to Taylor Creek on Easter Sunday?

No, she wasn't going to let this stop her. It was a minor setback. She loved Ezra. And she thought that he still loved her. At least he did before she stomped all over his feelings. With any luck and God on her side, he would love her still. She had to get to him. She had to tell him the truth. And she would find a way. Even if she had to drive into Wells Landing, borrow one of the bikes from Esther Fitch, and pedal her way to Taylor Creek.

She grabbed the bridle and placed it on her mare's head. Then she led her out into the bright spring sunshine. It was a crazy plan. But it was the only one that she had. Maybe by the time she got into Wells Landing, something else would occur to her. But she needed to be in motion. She needed to have things set to do. She had to do something or else she felt like she might lose her mind.

She heard the engine before she saw it, that blue truck turn down her driveway. Her heart stuttered in her chest. Her mouth went dry, and she almost fell to her knees at the sight. *Ezra!*

She stood stock-still and waited for him to come closer. He parked the truck and cut the engine, then got out. His eyes immediately sought her. And she stayed as still as she could, afraid that he might be some weird mirage, and he would disappear if she made the slightest movement.

He cleared his throat, then started toward her.

Her heart beat faster. What was he doing here? She could only hope. But she was afraid to allow herself the dream that he had come for the two of them.

He stopped in front of her, that familiar smell that was only Ezra surrounding him, that clean smell, the detergent, aftershave, and outdoors. "Are you going somewhere?" he asked.

Sadie nodded. Unable to find the words at first. "*Jah* . . . I mean, *jah*."

"Do you need a ride?"

Were they really talking about this? Sadie shook her head. "I was coming to see you."

"Yeah?"

Sadie nodded again. "I didn't mean any of it. All that stuff I said to you." She shook her head. "I didn't mean any of it. I was just so afraid."

"Then why?"

Sadie took a deep breath. She wanted to reach out, touch him, but she kept her hands wrapped firmly around the mare's bridle. "That night. That night of the fire." She shook her head. "I had to go back and get Daniel. When we left the restaurant, he wasn't with us."

Ezra inhaled sharply, but didn't comment.

She closed her eyes, then opened them again, the pictures of that night in her mind too vivid. "I was so scared. I was so afraid that I wouldn't be able to find them, and the fire was getting worse. I prayed and I prayed, I just wanted to find him. So I told God some things . . ." She shook her head.

"You told God what?" Ezra asked.

"I told God that if He would help me find Daniel and get him out of that building, I would stay in Wells Landing. I would be the good Amish girl, and I would marry Chris and I wouldn't go against the church."

"I'm glad Daniel's okay," Ezra said. "But we don't make bargains with God."

"I know that now," Sadie said. "But I was so grateful to have him safe . . . I don't know. It was so hard. I love you so much, but I don't know what we'll do. Do you think I could turn Mennonite? I didn't think my family would accept me. I didn't know how God would feel. But that never stopped me from loving you."

Finally Ezra moved. He grabbed her hands into his, the leather straps of the horse's bridle tangling in his fingers as well. "We can do whatever you want. If you want to be Amish, then we'll be Amish. If you want to be Mennonite, then that is what we will do. I don't ever want to lose you again."

Sadie's eyes filled with tears as she disentangled her fingers from the bridle and wrapped her arms around Ezra's neck. She buried her face in the crook of his shoulder and held on to him as if her life depended on it.

His arms came up around her and held her close.

She pulled away from him, and he used the back of one hand to wipe her tears from her cheeks.

"Why are you here?" she asked. She had become so caught up in her own emotions and her own guilt that she hadn't even thought to ask him why he had come out on Easter Sunday afternoon to see her.

"I came for you."

"You mean that? And what you said about the church?"

Ezra nodded. "I don't know how to live Amish, but if that's what you want, that's what we'll do, Sadie. It doesn't matter what church we belong to, not as long as we have God and each other."

Epilogue

"Are you ready?" Lorie asked.

Sadie looked up and smiled, biting back the tears that threatened. This was supposed to be a happy day, not one for tears, even if they were tears of joy.

Lorie bustled over to her, fussing as she came. "Don't cry. You'll mess up your dress if the tears get on it."

Sadie looked down at her white satin wedding dress. It was so different than what she would've worn had she had an Amish wedding, but she and Ezra had decided that they would live Mennonite. She would move to the ranch with him and his mother. They would work the land and animals together, and she would learn to drive. Then she could go to Wells Landing any time she wanted and visit with her family. It was the perfect solution, but they needed to take the time and make the decision together before it all became clear.

"You look beautiful, sister," Sadie said. Unlike Amish weddings, the bridal party wore different colors than the bride. Sadie had chosen a bright shade of green to celebrate hers and Ezra's joining. It was the green of spring buds, of new beginnings, and new chances. So fitting to use such a color today.

Lorie propped her hands on her hips and turned this way and that as if imitating an *Englisch* model. Today she was dressed more Mennonite than *Englisch*, but Sadie wouldn't have cared it she had come in jeans and a T-shirt. She was just happy to have her sister with her on this special day.

"It's time." Melanie poked her head in the door, the bouquet of flowers in her hand beckoning to Sadie.

Today was the day. They had waited until late May to get married, though neither one of them really wanted to wait that long. It'd taken a little while for them to get the dresses sewn and the minster convinced that they were going to be the greatest couple ever.

Sadie enjoyed the Mennonite church. It was different to have church in a building, with one minister who spoke English and only talked for an hour every Sunday. But she was adjusting.

The main things were always the same: She loved Ezra and they loved God. After all, wasn't that what really mattered?

Sadie took another deep breath to calm her nerves. She shouldn't be so nervous. She was marrying the love of her life. The one man God had made for her.

Melanie handed off her bouquet and together they got in the line. Flower girls first, one of whom was Elam Riehl's little sister, Joanne. Behind them stood the bridesmaids, Melanie and Lorie, and then the bride herself.

Music played from the sanctuary as the others started to file out of the back room. Sadie smiled even though she was alone, knowing that this was exactly where she was supposed to be.

She walked to the door and nudged it open, then

stepped out into the church. Her hands trembled, and the flowers shook. She paused there, allowing the gazes of their guests to wash over her.

It might have been the oddest congregation for a wedding they had ever seen in these parts, but she looked at each of those faces and was glad they were there.

Zach Calhoun sat next to Luke Lambright and his girlfriend, Sissy. Behind them sat Esther and Abe Fitch and next to them sat Hollis and his wife, Caroline, Emma, and baby Holly along with Andrew himself. Elam and Emily Riehl were there, as well as James and Joy.

Sadie lost count as she walked up the aisle of all the Mennonite friends she'd met. Even the people who had not welcomed her at first realized that she loved Ezra and made him happy. Somehow that love wiped the slate clean.

The love in the chapel was tangible. She could feel it, like the arms of her mother wrapped around her, comforting. She wished her dad had been there to see this, though she knew he was watching from above.

Her mother smiled and reached out a hand as Sadie grew even with her church pew.

Sadie squeezed her fingers and then moved to take her place next to Ezra at the altar.

"Friends and family, we have gathered here today to join these two people in holy matrimony."

More by Bestselling Author
Hannah Howell

__Highland Angel	978-1-4201-0864-4	$6.99US/$8.99CAN
__If He's Sinful	978-1-4201-0461-5	$6.99US/$8.99CAN
__Wild Conquest	978-1-4201-0464-6	$6.99US/$8.99CAN
__If He's Wicked	978-1-4201-0460-8	$6.99US/$8.49CAN
__My Lady Captor	978-0-8217-7430-4	$6.99US/$8.49CAN
__Highland Sinner	978-0-8217-8001-5	$6.99US/$8.49CAN
__Highland Captive	978-0-8217-8003-9	$6.99US/$8.49CAN
__Nature of the Beast	978-1-4201-0435-6	$6.99US/$8.49CAN
__Highland Fire	978-0-8217-7429-8	$6.99US/$8.49CAN
__Silver Flame	978-1-4201-0107-2	$6.99US/$8.49CAN
__Highland Wolf	978-0-8217-8000-8	$6.99US/$9.99CAN
__Highland Wedding	978-0-8217-8002-2	$4.99US/$6.99CAN
__Highland Destiny	978-1-4201-0259-8	$4.99US/$6.99CAN
__Only for You	978-0-8217-8151-7	$6.99US/$8.99CAN
__Highland Promise	978-1-4201-0261-1	$4.99US/$6.99CAN
__Highland Vow	978-1-4201-0260-4	$4.99US/$6.99CAN
__Highland Savage	978-0-8217-7999-6	$6.99US/$9.99CAN
__Beauty and the Beast	978-0-8217-8004-6	$4.99US/$6.99CAN
__Unconquered	978-0-8217-8088-6	$4.99US/$6.99CAN
__Highland Barbarian	978-0-8217-7998-9	$6.99US/$9.99CAN
__Highland Conqueror	978-0-8217-8148-7	$6.99US/$9.99CAN
__Conqueror's Kiss	978-0-8217-8005-3	$4.99US/$6.99CAN
__A Stockingful of Joy	978-1-4201-0018-1	$4.99US/$6.99CAN
__Highland Bride	978-0-8217-7995-8	$4.99US/$6.99CAN
__Highland Lover	978-0-8217-7759-6	$6.99US/$9.99CAN

Available Wherever Books Are Sold!

Check out our website at
http://www.kensingtonbooks.com